PRAISE FOR
Adopting Secrets

"In *Adopting Secrets*, Jessica Noelle viscerally explores the themes of pain, guilt, love, and ultimately hope. Her prose deftly mirrors the evolution of Kat, a stoic young woman who has locked herself in a state of emotional exile to avoid the pain of a very difficult memory. But you can't outrun your past. As people and circumstances help her pry open the door to this self-constructed prison, Noelle reminds us that sometimes the most powerful way to cope with guilt and shame is to be brave enough to share it. Sunlight trumps the dark. *Adopting Secrets* is an elegant, compelling testament to the healing power of trust and vulnerability."

—Alfredo Botello, Award-Winning Author of *180 Days*

"*Adopting Secrets* spans the inner depths of pain and escapism at the hands of abuse. Regret, self-understanding, and, ultimately, the power of love and connection that make it all worthwhile are felt profoundly through this mind-bending novel that leaves you wanting more. Jessica Noelle has given us a fantastic story. Please read it and feel deeply."

—Dianne C. Braley, Author of *The Silence and the Sound*, Winner of the NYC 2022 Big Book Award

"The twists and turns in this book made it absolutely impossible to foresee the ending. Jessica Noelle wrote such lovable characters that dealt with such real-life trauma. She really put her characters and us readers through the wringer. We were hooked from paragraph 2, but our jaws literally DROPPED when we hit chapter 8, and from that point on we stayed on the edge of our seats. In future books, we would love to see the story [going] more in depth [on] Alice and Lily's relationship along with their meeting for the first time. This book was truly bingeable, and we hope to read more from Jessica Noelle."

—*Tipsy Book Reads* Podcast

"A heartfelt exploration of the unbreakable bond between two sisters, forged in love and tragedy, and the secrets that survive the grave."

—Rachel Stone, Author of *The Blue Iris*

"A sister's bond transcends even in death. *Adopting Secrets* takes you on a ride that keeps you guessing at each twist and turn that won't let you put it down."

—Michelle Wishner, Author of *Ever the Same*

"*Adopting Secrets* is a powerful expression of sibling love and more with a plot twist that makes it impossible to put down! I highly recommend this book to anyone wanting to be swept away and captivated by the expression of love, travel, and trauma. Made me question what I would do. I could not stop thinking about this story long after turning the last page. A book club must!"

> —Tami Babij and Lisa Blakely, Authors of *If You Knew, Would You Say I Do?*

"A compelling debut novel that will leave readers wanting more! Uncovering Kat's past teaches us about the dual nature of vulnerability and strength and the triumph of the human spirit. *Adopting Secrets* is a twisty ride filled with surprises."

> —Kathleen Reid, Award-Winning Author of *Secrets in the Palazzo*

Adopting Secrets
by Jessica Noelle
© Copyright 2024 Jessica Noelle

ISBN 979-8-88824-219-3

All rights reserved. No part of this publication may be reproduced,
stored in a retrieval system, or transmitted in any form or by any means—
electronic, mechanical, photocopy, recording, or any other—
except for brief quotations in printed reviews,
without the prior written permission of the author.

This is a work of fiction.
All the characters in this book are fictitious,
and any resemblance to actual persons, living or dead,
is purely coincidental. The names, incidents, dialogue,
and opinions expressed are products
of the author's imagination and
are not to be construed as real

Published by
◤köehlerbooks™

3705 Shore Drive
Virginia Beach, VA 23455
800-435-4811

Adopting Secrets

JESSICA NOELLE

VIRGINIA BEACH
CAPE CHARLES

This book is dedicated to you, Mom.
It's my first pancake,
but I am your first pancake in theory,
and I think we both turned out pretty great.

PROLOGUE

{ 2012 }

Both Alice and Katie Clemonte were floating face down in the pool, their identical features ever the same, even in their unconscious suspension. It had always been impossible to tell them apart. Both were blonde and young and beautiful with green eyes that looked like kiwis spotted with black flecks.

There was a serene sort of beauty in how disturbing it all was. Drowning can be an enigmatic way to die, and to look back on the memory of these two sisters, limp and lifeless in the chlorinated teal water, was nothing short of morbid.

Katie had one distinguishing feature. Placed neatly on the back of her shoulder was a black and white thin-lined tattoo of a lily. The recent tattoo had been an easy way to distinguish them.

However, assessing the back of them, it was clear that both sisters now shared the matching permanent marking, removing any ease of identification. Each tattoo looked inflamed as if freshly done.

Their tight blonde curls were floating, catching the colors of the Malibu summer sunset, their skin still pink and sun-kissed with life.

What once was a crowded pool of rambunctious underage drinkers was now empty of all other beings. A few free-floating bottles bobbed around them; random pairs of sunglasses left behind in the fray. The water undulated in a rhythm left behind by the stampede of teenagers that had escaped. After the panic, everyone had stilled. They just stopped and stared.

Both girls looked weightless, and their fellow classmates observed the slack in their bodies.

Calm and panic were symbiotic companions. The cacophony of screams and cries of terror had echoed throughout the entire estate, and yet the expression shared between Alice and Katie was that of complete peace.

The party was over.

CHAPTER 1

Kat

{ 2022 }

"Hey KAT! A round of shots over here girl!"

The bar is rambunctious tonight with partying revelers, and the nightlife is vibrant. It always is. However, this Friday night is a little livelier.

I'm pouring drinks for a couple of men in suits when I see a group of wild girls enter. They must have noticed my ID tag because they call me by name, and I most definitely do not know them on a first-name basis. Their energy is excitable and in desperate need of tequila.

It is clearly a bachelorette party. Each girl is wearing all the defining garments. I find it tacky at best. It is most obvious in the girl who called out to me; a striking, tall blonde in a stark white dress and a poofy tulle veil pinned haphazardly in her loosely curled hair. No curl survives this type of humidity unless they are natural. Of course, I can't forget the sash that says *Future Mrs.* so and so. Of course her garment doesn't actually say so and so. I just don't care to look closely enough to see what her future surname will be.

Changing your name in marriage is an archaic tradition that serves no purpose, creating unnecessary complications, such as piles of paperwork and going back to your maiden name after divorce. The whole ritual of bachelor/bachelorette parties is obnoxious.

"Um hello?" an unenthused voice drawls.

I had completely zoned out. It isn't until the bride's annoyed call for attention snaps me from my daydream that I jump back into bartender mode. Rightfully so, she is super irritated that I haven't acknowledged her first call for shots, but her monotone Valley girl voice garners no respect from me.

I quickly and skillfully pour six shots of tequila and serve them to the party wearing *Bride Tribe* garb in support of their friend's upcoming nuptials. They look ridiculous.

I've never understood the reasoning behind forcing bridesmaids to wear such unattractive clothes. Why wouldn't you want everyone dressed in his or her best? You would think that in 2022 we would have evolved beyond such petty behavior. But I am not a bride, and that chapter of my life may never come. Maybe I will never understand.

The bride and her tribe are now satisfied, though not even one slid me a tip. I probably don't deserve one. Moving away from the counter, they match each other's energies with their over-exaggerated buzz and shrill *"Wahoo's!"* Clearly, the tequila's impact has already begun to take effect.

The bar is especially crowded tonight so I know that I must keep my hands moving for fear of falling behind. Every table is taken, and the noise is deafening. I attempt to utilize the ensuing chaos around me to silence my own intrusive thoughts. Frankly, it isn't working well.

Earth to Kat! Where is your head tonight?

Amber snaps her fingers and touches my shoulder to scoot past me and serve someone a beer she just poured. I should have been the one to attend to this customer but had spaced out instead.

Amber pulls a better beer anyway, whereas my true talent shines when making margaritas. My salt rim is always the perfect thickness. Amber, however, pours the perfect amount of head on a cold stein. It's incredible. She makes it look like art, which of course it is. Bartending takes a creative and patient mind.

"Girl, you are not on your game tonight," Amber says, stating the obvious.

"I'm sorry, I'm just . . . distracted." It's not a lie, but it is the vaguest version of a truthful answer I can possibly give.

I am finally used to people calling me Kat after ten years of adopting the nickname. I didn't want to be called Katie any longer. There were several legit reasons why I adopted the nickname, but Kat still feels new.

The moment I revived after drowning and my sister didn't, I vowed I would carry on in the best way that I possibly could. That entire night is kind of hazy, but I can recall a few details that propelled me forward. I still need my sister, but she's gone.

What does it matter anymore what I called myself? It's like I died too that night. One of us lived and that was the *only* detail that altered what my future would hold.

Pull yourself together. Jeez!

I can't seem to snap out of my funk, and this is not the night to think about the past. My frenzied behavior must be paused.

I had offered to take the late shift knowing full well the tips alone would be more than my hourly wage. Especially at the start of a summer weekend. To be truthful, I like the hours. I like to work. I have made my job my entire personality. Type A workaholic here. I like the chaos that weekends at the bar can bring. The louder it is around me, the quieter it is in my mind. Or I can at least usually ignore it easier.

One thing I have learned in this industry is that it's true what Ted Mosby says in the show *How I Met Your Mother*, "nothing good happens after 2 a.m." Not only is this true. This is gospel.

With this kind of crowd, I am fully anticipating having to call the cops to break up some sort of testosterone induced bar fight. I have a sixth sense about the guys at table eight. I can just tell something will go down between them and I am usually correct when it comes to my predictions. Some might call me an empath or say that I can read people's energies. Others might call it a trauma response as a side effect from my past. I am always on edge. Spiritual or inherited, both could very well be true. Whatever the reason behind my superpower is inconsequential. All I know is that the patrons at table eight are giving off a vibe that is keeping me empathetically alert and on my toes.

The clock just chimed midnight and I have been eyeballing my watch repeatedly, anxiously awaiting closing time for the first time in a long while. Normally, I use my job as an escape from the voices in my head and the gnawing quiet of my apartment, but tonight my mind is scrambling, and I am very much interested in sleeping off this weird mood.

My face and body language, however, convey something completely different. As only the best servers do. All my personal problems remain unknown to anyone who crosses my path. I am a professional mask wearer. For all they know I am having the greatest day of my life, like nothing is more fulfilling than my ability to serve a top-shelf gin and tonic.

I have been a very successful bartender. All these years of pretending I am okay and utilizing the slenderness the good Lord gave me has prepared me to be great in this role. I have always been a bit more on the gangly side of thin, but over the years have learned to manipulate certain parts of me to look more curvaceous. I don't take honing that skill for granted. I didn't have a lot of girlfriends growing up to teach me the ways of unattainable beauty, but as an adult it doesn't hurt to use the male gaze to my advantage. I make amazing tips and can act as a therapist for other people's issues rather than confront my own. Maybe I could have been an actress, only I hate the spotlight.

At times, I can be animated and vivacious, a trait my sister would be proud to see, even though I am completely faking it. She would have noticed that, too.

Fake it until you make it. Isn't that what people tell you to do?

Even what I wear has a part in my facade. Again, I play to my strengths and decided to wear my black flare pants that hug and lift my butt into the ideal apple shape. Spandex has an amazing knack for defying gravity and placing all the good parts back high and tight. I also made sure that the lace shirt hanging over one shoulder shows just enough cleavage. That usually means the guy staring will leave a bigger tip because he couldn't help himself. There have been a few wandering eyes already this evening and the pockets on my waist apron are very satisfied with *guilt* tips.

Having additional money is a relief right now since rent on my apartment was just raised and that extra $250 a month. It is starting to make things tight. I know I could always find a cheaper complex to live in, but one of the only things I truly love in this world is my view, so I cannot part ways with it just yet.

I could care less about the size of my home. Six hundred square feet may seem cramped to the average family.

I don't mind feeling confined and alone. In fact, I prefer it. I gain a sense of control over my life knowing it's just me to care for.

I don't even have pets to come home to, not even a low-maintenance animal like a fish or a cat. Not that I'm not an animal person per se, I just prefer complete solitude. I thought about getting a cat once, but five minutes at the shelter had me sneezing uncontrollably. Not even sure which creature caused the swelling in my face, but I made a judgment call to simply avoid them all. Pretty sure it was the cats though.

The view alone is why I chose the apartment in the first place. The balcony overlooks the Atlantic Ocean in all its supreme majesty. I feel so small against its power, and I can hide in its wake. The sound of the waves hitting the sand, and the shifting tides wash away the silence. I like being alone, but never quiet. The quiet and I are not choice companions.

One might think that I would be afraid of water since I almost drowned, but it's quite the opposite. I have found solace and healing in the waves knowing that I didn't succumb to suffocation. I was given a chance at life, but I also know that I can reverse my fate and hand my life over to the water at any moment. To die the same way my twin did seems most fitting, the way I should have died as well. It's been ten years, and I haven't given in yet, but it's comforting to know I could.

Ever since that night, water and I have had a strange, but committed relationship. I can hear my sister calling to me in the waves and can imagine her suspended and effortlessly weightless as a lanky seventeen-year-old. I was there at her birth, and I was there at her death.

It haunts me constantly, but it also makes me feel closer

to her, and I try to ignore all the questions I have regarding that night. All the ones that she can no longer answer. I lost all hope a long time ago about ever receiving clarity. Our twin *telepathy* or bond or whatever, doesn't do me any good either. That moment in our history blocked our connection, and I think she wanted it that way.

No one has been able to get close to me ever since. Don't get me wrong, there have been a few men who have come in and out of my life in the last decade. I have not been exercising celibacy by any means, but I have too many walls to consider any of them seriously relational. I know this about myself, and it hasn't bothered me yet. I am not able to be in a relationship. I can hardly invest emotionally in myself let alone invest in anything romantic and committal. Plus, no one seems interested enough in my life to break down my walls anyway. It is what it is, and I am okay with it. I am the one who usually closes that door when the rare someone dares to get too close. Loudly and in their faces I might add. I am not anyone's idea of a good girlfriend.

This doesn't mean that I don't admire attractive people. Most of the people in here tonight are men in suits with the top buttons undone and their ties mysteriously gone, slumped in booths to decompress from the long day at the office. I find many of them very attractive, though I only flirt if I know it will make me an extra twenty percent on an already overpriced cocktail.

The bar, Salud, is often privy to serving a lot of men getting off a draining day's work. I wouldn't classify us as a dive bar. Not by a long shot. We are one of the nicest establishments that serve libations, if I do say so myself.

There are lots of highbrow business offices nearby and we serve the best top-shelf liquors, even among all the neon party signs. Something strong enough for forgetting the grind of the nine-to-five. Pretty much everyone who walks in is clean-cut and ready for a good time.

"Can you focus, please?" Amber says it like I am in trouble, but I know her well enough to know she isn't irked at me.

Amber reminds me a lot of my sister, and I guess that is why I feel so comfortable around her. Although, she couldn't be more different than her in appearance. We would never get mistaken for twins—not even close relatives.

It's interesting how someone's energy can match when their appearances are opposite. Amber's bouncy black hair and perfectly tan skin scream that she lives spiritedly under the Miami sun and carries herself with a Latina flair that would make anyone want to absorb the amazing culture that surrounds us. She made me fall in love with Miami. The way she presents herself makes me jealous. I have always been jealous of people who naturally exude confidence, which is probably why I gravitate to her as a friend.

She doesn't ask about my past much, which I appreciate about her. Our conversations are never forced or uncomfortable. She keeps me in the present mostly, and I adore her for that.

I remain guarded around everyone. She, however, is an open book. I didn't even ask, and I know all about her family—the good, the bad, and the mundane.

I know about her brothers and how the youngest one was just arrested for robbing a Publix. I know how her niece was just awarded best in show for her art piece she made in her fifth-grade class. I know her sister shamed the entire family and was shunned because she had an affair with the owner of the bodega down the street, ruining her marriage by cheating and getting pregnant. And I know that her *abuela* is the matriarch of the household, much like many multigenerational households.

"Too much." Amber would always say. Too much of what I don't really know, but something was definitely too much for her.

Amber's life decision to support herself as a bartender was not what her abuela had in mind for her precious granddaughter. She only ever wished for her grandchildren to marry well and have lots of little Puerto Rican babies running around, all under *her* roof.

Amber is too taken with life to slow down for kids anytime soon. She has been asked out by many a drunken patron but seems to never notice or care. Some have even proposed on the spot. One even had a ring, but that was a different story. The guy had just proposed to his girlfriend, she said no, and Amber was the first woman who made him feel something other than sad, which is also known as, she allowed him to get drunk. She's stunning though, and no one could blame them for trying.

I have no clue if she is currently seeing anyone, which means she probably isn't. I haven't inquired about her dating life in a while, but since she is a walking tell-all and gossip, I think she would be gushing over dreamy Prince Charming if she had such a man in her life.

Amber seems overly intrigued by my distracted mind tonight, but we are too busy to chat about it like I know she wants to. So, I put on my best smile, pull my shoulders back, and get back to business. My haunting thoughts about life and my dead twin can and will undoubtedly continue later.

Now that I have regained some focus, I can actually hear what's going on around me. My ears perk at the song playing on the jukebox. Bruno Mars's *Treasure* is melodically playing, and the guy who put it on is still standing over the jukebox. He's kind of hunched over and seems to be humming along while his fingers tap to the drumbeat. I have always found rhythm expressed in finger taps *really sexy*, and is the first thing I notice about him.

He doesn't look like the other suits in here. Instead, he is wearing a nice pair of dark jeans and a slim fitting navy polo, business casual attire. His dark hair is tousled a bit, and it looks like he needs a haircut. His heavy stubble suggests that he is a little undone tonight and hasn't found the time to shave yet. I am curious if he is too busy to shave or simply not as hygienic as the other businessmen who come in with their work uniforms still on.

There is a lot about him that has me curious. I am hypnotized by how intently he stares at the music selections. I wonder if he picked this song for a particular reason. It's not exactly a new top charter, even though most of Bruno Mars's stuff never goes out of style, especially in Miami. Bruno Mars is an icon, but I haven't been privy to his jams in a while.

As if the night didn't seem odd enough, this song takes me back to the bottles and the bustle of the McCoy party that night.

Like I needed another reminder. Everything seems like it will trigger me tonight. I hate days like this where I can find a little bit of that night in almost anything. Even a perfect stranger can set me off.

I am trying to shake the ghostly sensation of reliving it all and look down to fidget with my pens and the dollar bills sticking out of my apron. When I look up, the mystery man is sitting with the group of guys at table eight.

Oh great. I knew there was going to be something about table eight.

"Table eight has requested another round; can you cover that?" Amber asks me as she rapidly mixes a pitcher of margaritas for a group scrunched up against the countertop, impatiently waiting on her. Her hands are very clearly full, so how can I deny her? Plus, it's not like it is a favor. It is my job, and she is the manager on duty.

I cannot believe how many people are here tonight.

I knew it would be a lot at the start of the weekend, but this is extra intense. I should check to see if it is a full moon. People always come out and get weird during a full moon. I think the tide changes and people can feel the shift. Plus, the additional light outside is like having permission—or at least an excuse—to stay out late and do stupid things.

Table eight is the worst kind of table on this night, or any busy night to be honest.

I felt from the moment they walked in that trouble was ruminating. It's a group of four guys, most of whom are dressed in jeans, a hoodie or some kind of casual jogger. Very out of sorts for our clientele. Only one has the traditional businessman off-work look with his button-down unbuttoned to almost his naval. I have learned to judge people by what they deem appropriate to wear in public.

Do you look at yourself before stepping outside? It is crucial to own a full-body mirror. I try not to show my judgments on my face.

A few are obviously single, but button-down looks like a disgruntled married man who is ready to hit on anything that walks by, loudly and without shame. There's a tan line where his wedding ring recently rested.

Maybe divorced? Who knows?

Alcohol can do wonderful things, but it can also lower all inhibitions, making even the nicest of men reveal their inner turmoil in a brutish manner. This particular frat party is already on the verge of being cut off, but I take their order anyway.

"What can I get you gentlemen?"

Gentlemen is putting it nicely, but I have no right to express my judgment openly.

"Another round sexy, and turn really slowly when you go back." He might be wearing a suit, but that does not make him classy. I do notice the ring on the table when he so eloquently slurs in my direction.

So, he took it off.

"Are we all having the same thing, or can I get you guys something different?"

"A pitcher of beer will be just fine." I feel a hand touch my forearm as the guy closest to me in the booth whispers. It's like he knows his friends are about to embarrass the hell out of him and he wants me to leave as quickly as possible.

It's the guy who was at the jukebox I can't help but stare at. I flinch at his touch, and I can tell my sudden jerk reaction sets him on edge. He looks very apologetic and also painfully sober. He must be the poor sop who was assigned as designated driver. At least this group is smart enough to think ahead and be responsible. Sure enough, I look down at his drink and he is slowly nursing a simple soda water with lime.

What's so disheartening about a group like this is they all are attractive men. Three of them look like they workout daily. Even the one who seems to prefer beer as a food group is still not the worst looking guy to walk in here. They probably all have wives and are just blowing off a little steam after work, but I think about that kind of marriage, and it honestly makes me grateful to be alone rather than in a relationship I feel I need to escape from on occasion.

My space is mine, as is my time. I don't need to let loose or seek liberation from anyone. Some might call that kind of existence lonely, but I honestly can't say that being married to someone I feel a need to retreat from would make me feel any less alone.

The guy who touched my arm recoils his fingers from my forearm quickly so that I can write down the one order of beer for all. Like I'd honestly need a pad to remember, but I feel the need to use my hands for something.

"Can you also bring us a side of fries for the table and a burger for me? I haven't had a chance to eat yet."

"Sorry, the kitchen closes at eleven," I say, speaking solely to him because everyone else is too busy trying to keep their heads up to notice I'm even still here. "But maybe you should take off soon and get some food in your friends."

His downward nod tells me he agrees and wouldn't mind calling an early end to their evening. I haven't seen him smile once and the circles under his eyes look deep and painful. He is obviously not having a good time.

"Ah I see, well thanks anyway." He hands me his card. "You can charge it all here."

I couldn't help looking at the name on the card, *Trevor Daniels*. I don't know how these guys were drinking without a card on a tab, but it's been so busy I am not surprised we accidentally let it slide.

"Should I get that other round then or are you guys closing out?"

"Bring the drinks sweetheart!" I was directing my comment to Trevor, but his buddy felt the need to be obnoxious. Even from on the opposite side of the booth he continues shouting at me gleefully.

It is interesting to note that each one of them has a different reaction to the copious amounts of booze they have ingested. The guy shouting at me is what we call a *happy drunk*. They are always fun to watch, but so far, the prehistoric nicknames, like *sexy* and *sweetheart*, are starting to rub me the wrong way. If one of them pulls out a "Hey there, baby doll," I might lose whatever chill I have left.

I quickly spin on my heels in what turns out to be the wrong direction because I feel a hand, with an awfully firm grip, wrap tightly around my lifted butt. I was definitely going for more of a, "you can look, but you can't touch" sort of tease when I chose this outfit.

I am flabbergasted. In the last three years of working at Salud I have never been groped. Most men here are too business-minded to ever let loose enough to treat me like a hooker.

Fight or flight? Fight or Flight or what's that other one. . .oh yeah freeze.

I stop in my tracks, not wanting to make a scene and hoping that I can just walk it off, but Mr. Grabby Hands stands up and blocks my path, placing his mouth directly on mine. He grabs my butt again as he slides his tongue into my mouth, pausing on my teeth briefly before I feel his body pull away forcefully. The aroma of beer fills my mouth and swells my senses.

Move . . . Move . . .

Amber is already stomping in my direction and Trevor is up, holding his friend back trying to calm him down while apologizing to me with a piercing stare of intricate hazel eyes.

The nauseating taste of alcohol now swirls between my tongue and my lips, and I try not to swallow. I want to find the words to guard myself, but I am still just frozen in place while Amber shouts expletives on my behalf. Her protectiveness is another trait she shares with my sister.

Trevor is balancing his friend from toppling over, using his torso as a brace. I assume he is his friend. They don't look very friendly right now. Trevor looks furious and flushed with embarrassment. I am furious too, but also still just frozen like a deer in headlights.

Next thing I know, Amber whisks me to the backroom, but we both spin on our heels when we hear a loud crash. I look back to see Trevor falling to the floor. He was punched and took the glasses on the table down with him. The person he was just buying drinks for hit him square in the mouth. I don't get it. My first thought is *how incredibly rude*. My second thought is *I hope he is okay*.

I find it hard not to run to his aid when I see his lip begin to bleed and the cuts to his hands from the shards of glass on the floor. Not sure where my empathy for this stranger is coming from. I admit I am usually more selfish. I have every reason to be more concerned with myself than Trevor, who has given me weird flutters all evening. It feels like more of a connection than a crush. Like our souls have met in the past or perhaps he just reminds me of someone.

"Get out. C'mon, out. Before I call the cops!" Amber berates as she plops me in a seat and stomps back over to the raucous. Despite her petite stature, she can be quite intimidating when provoked. She leaves me in a booth next to the doorway to the backroom so she can end the scene. I just sit and watch this all play out.

"Do you need medical attention?" she asks Trevor bluntly as he fumbles himself back up to a standing position. She is professional and courteous, exuding decorum even in the midst of a tussle. I am glad she asked so I don't make a fool of myself by inquiring if he is indeed okay.

"No," he answers.

I didn't realize just how tall he is. If I had to guess, I'd say he stands at about six foot three. The perpetrator on the other hand is significantly shorter. Not sure how he reached Trevor's lip. He was probably reaching for his nose.

I stand and inch myself out of the booth and into the doorway trying to get closer. I am about to tell Amber to make Trevor stay for first aid care, but she is back tending to me, and Trevor is gone with the goonies before I muster enough strength to grasp the reality of what happened.

The door chimes as they leave, and I am grateful that Trevor is at least sober and can safely drive. Although, if he was hit hard enough, he might be dizzy and maybe he shouldn't be the one to get behind the wheel.

I hope they all stop for food, I think.

My concern for Trevor's wellbeing and the others isn't like me at all. I am usually not interested in other people. I am concerned about me, myself, and I, and that's about it.

He captured me by how he looked at the jukebox and how subtly he touched my arm when he ordered. A tingle crawled up my forearm. I don't know why, but it felt funny. Different.

I look down at my watch to see it's one-thirty.

"Are you okay?" Amber is now completely devoted to tending to me even though the crowd is now done watching the drama and is back to demanding drinks at the bar.

"I'm fine," I mutter hoping she believes me because it's about as convincing as I can get.

Yes, I feel violated, but I've had worse things happen to me before. More so than any stupid intoxicated kiss could induce. That drunken slob was another trigger in a night that seems filled with unwanted reminders of my past.

The brazen effects of alcohol I have seen time and time again. Having worked in a bar for so many years coupled with a traumatic childhood, I became privy to its damage at a very early age.

However, my first time ever drunk was the night I almost drowned. I too became stupid and reckless. I pity the guy who assaulted me more than I am angered by it. I saw the wedding ring. I saw him slip it back on after Trevor fell to the floor. I feel bad for his wife. Whoever she is.

I try not to let myself feel too shaken up by it and just move on. It's better that way. Silence the shame.

"Do you want to press charges? I got his info from the guy he punched just in case."

"NO!" I shout.

Amber can tell there is something more behind my outburst, but like the good friend she is, she doesn't ask any more questions. How do I tell her I want to stay as far out of trouble as I possibly can? I could just tell her I thought the friend was hot.

All my excuses sound so stupid. Except the truth.

"You should get back out there," I say with a smile, toning down my voice and trying to prove to her that I am really okay. "All is well, truly. I will be right behind you."

She has no idea how good of a liar I can be.

The hustle out on the floor ramps back up, and I can tell in her stance and stare at me that Amber is still deeply concerned, but we both know she must get back on the floor. She is bouncing her head back and forth from me to the bar. We have a few others on staff tonight, but not enough to justify both of us being off duty.

Part of me wishes that I could divulge my entire past with someone, but the demons I carry are too dark, so I bottle it all up. It's the same song and dance that I am used to by now.

My past is unforgivable. I am not about to ruin the one friendship I have by unloading all my dirty secrets onto someone so innocent and kind. I don't exaggerate when I say Amber is literally my sole friend. She keeps the true loneliness away. I don't want to run her off.

She takes one more deep breath and heads back out on the floor, which is good because we are very close to closing and things need to be done so we can wrap it up. Hazardous nights like this one always result in a lot more broken glasses and a lot of sticky floor spots to mop before the first shift in the morning.

The kitchen crew usually gets in around ten for an eleven o'clock open and they are immensely perturbed if they have cleanup to do in addition to food prep. No one likes their shoes sticking to the floor or accidentally having glass crunch under you. I've done a morning shift. I get it. It's really annoying.

I take only a few more minutes to compose myself. More for show so no one thinks I am completely numb to what just happened. I am numb though. I can't feel things like this anymore. They can't hurt me.

I can hear Amber after the last call, ushering the last several people out the door before she locks up. I grab the mop and bucket and start filling it with suds. As that fills, I remove my apron and set it in with my purse and other belongings in my locker. I am emptying out and counting my tips for the night while I wait for the tub to fill. That's when I noticed his name staring back at me in hard plastic. Buried in my pocket I still have Trevor Daniel's credit card.

CHAPTER 2

Trevor

{ 2022 }

I DON'T WANT to go out tonight at all. I am exhausted. I have happily pulled into my condominium's parking structure when my monthly notification of "guys night" dings the minute I put my dinky little Toyota in park. I must set notifications on my phone, or I can't remember anything.

I really should get another car and be less busy so I can maybe remember things. It's not that I can't afford a new car. I could theoretically walk onto a lot and drive away with any vehicle I wished. It's just that I have not been in the mood to go car shopping. The hours at the office have been intense this week, and all I want to do tonight is order Twin Dragons Chinese food for dinner while being totally lazy for the first time in what feels like forever.

I secretly hope that the guys will call and cancel, but they aren't about to postpone the one night a month we all get to let loose a little. As I am typing a well thought out, methodical, and decent enough excuse, my text chime goes off. *One . . . two*

... *three*. All three of my so-called friends are texting to make sure I am still coming because this month is my turn to be the designated driver, and I am already running late. There isn't an excuse good enough to bail on them.

It has been a long Friday to begin with. Between a few crises emails I took care of at work that demanded my immediate response, and the weekly shopping and errands that need to be run in order for the following workweek to run smoothly, I am straight up burned-out. And as DD, I can't drink anything straight up to help me out.

I know we said that we would maintain our friendships outside of law school, and we agreed the best way to do that would be to have an outstanding drinking date once a month, no exceptions. It doesn't matter that I simply am not in the mood. Doesn't matter how good of an argument I concoct. I am committed.

I exhale all the hopes for solitude and much deserved laziness and then put my car in reverse and head to our usual spot—Salud.

I was about to text everyone that I needed to stop for food first, but then figured I would be able to grab a burger or something when I got there. Of course I should have taken into account the lateness of the hour and the likelihood of the kitchen having already closed. We don't usually frequent the bar this late, but I am not the only one who has had a busy week.

The restaurant part of the bar is one of the best in the city and serves some of the most authentic Mexican food on the East Coast. Along with a host of American bar eats, the ethnic dishes are truly outstanding. And, I am *HALT*—hungry, angry, lonely, tired. Or at least most of them.

When I get busy, I forget to eat. I've had a pit in my stomach since that first unopened email at six this morning. That's the kind of day it has been.

Sure enough, I am the last to arrive. My law school buds all took an Uber, knowing I'll chauffeur them home when the night ends. Brady is already slurring and twiddling his wedding ring as if absorbed in a great angel v. devil shoulder debate. That is, before he removes it and sets it on the table in front of him. Something isn't right.

I think some days he gets jealous that I am still single and can theoretically hook up with anyone I feel like. I might try, if I can get in a better mood. I do love watching Brady turn green with jealousy as I talk up some pretty little thing right in front of him. It does give me sick satisfaction. However, Brady is married to the most incredible girl and should have no reason to look anywhere else.

Single guys should be jealous of him. He literally could not do better than Bianca. Tonight, it all feels different though, like he intends to stray from her.

I do share a level of concern for him. Bianca doesn't deserve the way Brady appears to crave the single life. They were madly in love and married while in college. The world could not tear those two apart, but that was five years ago. Both are type A, dominating career driven people. You don't go to law school to be a slack. The student loans alone don't allow for a blasé approach. You go to law school to be successful. Period.

It's why all of us hung out back then. We all had matching career aspirations. However, the frat boy persona feels ancient now that we're in our early thirties. I am far too old for a beer bong.

The place is hopping tonight, and the guys snagged us a booth in the corner. I did not want to stand at the counter. I feel as though at any moment I could topple over from exhaustion and possibly low blood sugar. Adding alcohol will only make my desire to sleep more profound, so I am fortunate to have an excuse not to drink tonight. Even though I plan on pouring myself a scotch and soda in the comfort of my own home where I can comfortably pass out.

I need a minute before heading to the table. My friends seem to be the highest contributors to the noise booming inside the establishment. I make my way over to the jukebox first and play around with the buttons for a minute. I can't seem to decide what I want to listen to. Nothing feels like it is lively enough to turn my mood around.

It takes me a minute, and I look up briefly, hoping the guys aren't sensing my weirdness for not joining them. They have no idea why I'm taking my time and seem not to care as they are well into a comically loud conversation that seems to keep them all engaged.

Before my eyes lock back on what track to choose, I pause briefly and get hung up on the bartender. She seems to be in as weird of a mood as me and has a dazed look as she pours a group of bridesmaids some shots. Probably tequila. Bridal parties this close to Cancun always shoot tequila.

She is not the type of girl who usually grabs my attention, which is no disrespect to her because she is stunning. Her outfit looks very intentional, but that is true of most female bartenders. Her hair is like an untamed mane, and she looks really sad. Most girls I lean toward are vapid and giddy with blowouts that they put on daddy's Amex. What can I say? My job is hard and the girls I look for are easy. This girl doesn't look easy.

I've never really stopped to think about how women in the bartending industry could be construed as a kind of prostitute. I guess that's kind of harsh. It's a lot tamer without the selling of sex, but they do often dress to gain objectifying attention and serve a liquid poison that makes even the most upstanding of gentlemen morph into utter fools.

Note to self. Don't audibly call a female bartender a prostitute. Might end up with a drink in my face.

I had completely forgotten what I was doing because I was too busy staring. She looks somber. She also looks like she hasn't touched a brush in a year, and I can't tell if it's because her blonde curls are tight around her head, or if it is just how she has a few long strands in the front haphazardly pinned back out of her face. Because of that though, I can see all of her face. Her big green eyes are vibrant and stand out from across the room, and her cheeks are flush from the insatiable demand for cocktails from the increasingly boisterous crowd.

I'm even getting a little bit red in the face.

Am I blushing? I don't blush. The heat running up to my cheeks is completely foreign to me. *Has a girl I simply gazed upon made me blush?*

I choose to blame it on the Florida summer heat and the fact that there are literally a hundred people packed in here beyond the capacity of the building.

I quit my schoolboy daze and resume picking a song. The guys are now glancing over with that "piss or get off the pot,'" kind of look. They notice my lollygagging.

Bruno Mars's album *Unorthodox Jukebox* flips into view, and I choose that one. That moment feels very unorthodox at the jukebox, ironically. Plus, I know Brady's wedding song is on that album, and hopefully that makes him squirm a little. It is kismet, but it also may escalate the issue.

The song *Treasure* plays first, and I use the uplifting melody to improve my mood. It is a night out with the guys, and I often look forward to it. I really do enjoy their company most of the time, even when they are plastered and obnoxious, but maybe I only feel a little hesitant tonight because today has been harder than usual. I don't know. I would like to think I am not that self-involved.

As soon as I sit down at the table, the mood changes. I don't know if the guys can even sober up enough to notice how uncomfortable I am sitting in the booth, but they do quiet down for a minute.

"Welcome to the party. Jeez it took you long enough." Brady is obviously grumpy about my lack of punctuality. I don't dignify him with a response. Instead, I flag down the waitress. I feel quite silly for not getting up and ordering at the bar so I can converse with the curly haired sad blonde.

The waitress I manage to grab the attention of seems like the queen bee of the hive and I can tell she notices me because she nods as she very skillfully balances a bunch of empty cocktail glasses on three trays. The shattered glass in the room tonight is not contributed to by her lack of waitressing skills. I notice her go back behind the bar and nudge another employee to come and take our order. There is a line of people cascading at the counter so I can't quite see who she is talking to.

My heart skips a beat when I notice a tuft of blond catch the neon light and turn the corner.

My heart skipped a beat, yuck. Who am I?

Man, I might as well have been drinking with how ridiculous I am in front of this woman that I have merely laid eyes on for a few minutes.

Her presence at the table startles Brady while the other guys are simply chilling and ready for another round. Not sure how many rounds I missed, but this is not the second or even the third. Brady acts like he hasn't seen a woman in years. I know that look in his eyes. Like he's hungry. He's unpredictable at best, although I've never seen him get aggressive.

I don't know what comes over me, but I pull her away from his intoxicated "charms." I lightly touch her forearm and quietly give our order. I am surprised she even hears me over the noise. The guys order me a soda water, but I am still so incredibly hungry from the day that a carbonated drink isn't going to cut it.

I sink about ten inches when she tells me the kitchen is closed. All I think about is food, so when she suggests that maybe I sober my friends up with a little food elsewhere, it really doesn't sound like a bad idea. She obviously wants us out of her hair. I hand her my card to close out the drink tab and I notice her lingering over my name before sliding my card into her apron. Maybe she's as mystified by me as I am by her, but my stomach is too empty to dwell on it. I think of all the places open past midnight that are close by. There are only a million in this part of town and my craving for Chinese food intensifies. Then Brady goes off the rails, grabbing her in the rear.

Are you kidding me?

I cannot believe it! I mean, I had *thought* about doing the same thing about sixty times since walking in and laying eyes on her. Hell, so had every other man in the room, but he actually got sloppy enough to do it.

If he had suffered some sort of stroke, his actions might have been forgivable, but how do I forgive him for this?

An urge to protect her kicks in when I fail to keep Brady back and he shoves his beer-soaked tongue down her throat. Poor thing is just frozen. He's an idiot for taking that as a want for more. He knows better.

Steam pours from my eyeballs. I don't want to be in the same vicinity as him, let alone be considered his friend. But I calmly pull him off her as the brigade of bartenders and servers, including Queen Bee, swarm over.

How I stay calm, I don't know. The second I place hands on Brady he swings at me. I am significantly taller, but he still manages to hit me square in the mouth.

The metallic taste of blood settles in a pool under my tongue. I must have bitten it when I fell back. This was not my idea of getting something in my stomach, and I'm queasy from all of it and dizzy from hitting the floor. Where is all my core strength? My personal trainer would be ashamed.

The staff asks if I need medical attention to which I reply *no*, though not very confidently. Glass is stuck in my hands and a few shards in my legs. I want to be left with some semblance of pride, my gosh, but let's note that getting kicked out of this establishment has never been more justified than right now.

I don't bother looking behind me to see if Brady is following me out the door. Jason and Connor haphazardly help him walk out, which some other drunken fools may take as a sign of a good time.

I have never been more embarrassed or angry—not sure which emotion surpasses the other—in my entire life. Brady had no right to do what he just did. He acted like a drunken bastard idiot. I have always considered him my brother in many ways, but not tonight.

My lip is still swelling, and I can feel my pulse in my face as all the blood rushes to the injured spot. Tonight, he became a person I do not know. Blood is still seeping into a paper napkin I grabbed on the way out. I didn't dare ask for ice, and no one offered me any.

He's such a dick. I should have hit him back, but the moron was far beyond his usual intoxication, volatile, and I didn't want to start a brawl in the bar. The night was embarrassing enough without a fight to escalate it.

I cannot believe I am about to agree to drive him home. I should leave him on the sidewalk. Maybe I can watch Bianca lay into him when I drop him off. Out of the four of us, Brady is the only one married, and let me tell you he is not making a strong case for the rest of us to do the same.

"Get in the car dickhead," I yell, not sure entirely which dickhead friend I am referring to. For Jason and Connor, it's simply a night of overdrinking; they didn't take it to the lengths that Brady had. But I am seething with rage and hunger, and it is directed toward the first person it reaches. HALT. Now I am the second of the four.

Jason and Connor shove Brady into the front seat because if they attempt the backseat, he will end up sprawled out and I won't be able to fit the rest of them in my tiny Prius.

This decision does not thrill me. I don't want to be breathing the same air as him right now. I don't wish to even see him in my peripherals. My only goal is to get him home like the decent person I am pretending to be and get some food in my body as soon as possible.

"Hey man, is your lip okay?" Jason says. He seems to have sobered up a little. Maybe he's not as drunk as I thought. If so, I am pissed he didn't step in to help me.

"It stings like hell," I nod in the rearview mirror, "but it won't damage my good looks."

Connor snickers, trying not to laugh at what a complete Gumby I was to have fallen from Brady's slack punch in the mouth. I am blaming low blood sugar and the element of surprise.

Fortunately for me, Brady doesn't live too far away. In fact, none of us live very far from each other.

The bar is directly in the middle for most of us and that was a key factor in why we picked it as our usual spot. It's barely ten minutes before we pull up to Brady's home. Jason technically lives closer, but I need to get away from Brady, and Jason doesn't make a peep otherwise. He knows.

I see a light upstairs but the desire to rat him out to his wife dissipates when I see how pathetic he looks passed out in the passenger seat. I think about punching him in the lip to rouse him awake, but I am too fatigued to be petty. Jason and Connor help me get him inside and on the couch.

"Pathetic," I grumble before we leave. Jason and I make sure he is on his side, while Connor uses the bathroom. Convenient timing. I know that Bianca will be down any minute to make sure he has a bucket by his side and some water and Advil before she heads back upstairs for bed. I am sure she is annoyed. Who would want to take care of this kind of behavior at what seems like an increasing rate. We all keep our mouths shut about it.

Bianca used to hang with us. We were integrated as one unit, but this last year or so has been different. None of us know the intimacies of their marriage, but something has happened recently that they aren't open to us about.

I've dropped off Jason and Connor and am finally alone at 3 a.m. in my car. There is total silence, but my mind is reeling. I can't help but wonder what Brady got to experience.

How did she feel pressed up against his body? How did she taste? Does the subtle smell of jasmine get stronger the closer you get to her? Are you able to breathe that all in before your lips meet? Was she soft? I imagine she was pretty rigid considering the immediacy of it all. . .

I cannot dislodge that perverse nugget of curiosity from my head. It does, however, get me to stop for that Chinese food I want. It isn't Twin Dragon, but the twenty-four-hour place isn't so bad either. I want garbage greasy food anyway, something starchy and filling to settle my constantly churning stomach. It's more like breakfast, but I have every intention of sleeping in long and hard tomorrow.

The massive apology text will come from Brady at some point when the hangover recedes, but my phone will be off. No emails, no apology texts from bummed out and no longer buzzed bros, just salty Chinese food, scotch and sleep for the majority of the weekend.

I pull into the parking lot and begin to fumble for my wallet. I grab my keys and phone, but when I start to reach for my card I realize. . .

Dang! I left it with her.

CHAPTER 3

Kat
{ 2022 }

AS I WALK into my tiny apartment, nothing is any different than when I left it earlier. I still have a few dirty dishes in the sink and my couch blanket is still strewn across the sofa enticing me to finish that episode of *Grey's Anatomy* that I didn't finish before my shift began. Yet something about it all feels very different. I feel different. I don't know if violated is the right word. I don't feel good. I know that much. I am stressed into a state of submission, which feels all too familiar.

It has been a long while since I have been kissed. It feels like a different lifetime since my last true, earth shattering, weak in the knees, I want to grow old with you and have your babies NOW kind of kiss. This kiss tonight was not that, but regardless, it has been a long time. Not even a bad kiss has crossed my path in recent years. The kiss breaking my drought was horrible and non-consensual.

The last time I had sex was about two years ago, and that was a brief mistake that wasn't made a second time.

I'm pitiful.

Many other phrases of self-deprecating negative talk bounce away aimlessly in my head.

The first thing I do is run to the shower. I'd like to wash away the memory of it all. I would like to feel clean. I brush my teeth to remove the foul taste of beer. I don't personally enjoy beer but mixed with someone else's saliva it's nauseating. I inevitably did have to swallow and was instantly queasy. It's not like I leave a toothbrush at work. However, I do grab mine now and let the mint swish back and forth in my mouth before I hop in the shower.

Should I cry with my clothes on in the shower like in that James Bond movie? She had a good reason to cry and scrub her skin off. She had witnessed murder. I simply had a very unwanted intimate moment with a drunken guy in a bar.

I've seen a tragic death before. I didn't run to the shower then either.

Such intrusive thoughts are working overtime tonight. Even though I just brushed my teeth, now feeling minty fresh, I pour a glass of red wine and hop in the shower. I down the first glass, bypassing the odd flavor, hoping it will drown out my anxious mind and then shower quickly, and yes, I strip first.

It was probably a little too quick of a shower considering I also had an entire shift of spills, sticky stuff, and fry grease in every crevice of my body. I shed a couple of tears for sure, but then moved on. It's not the first time and it won't be the last that someone's advances are unwanted.

The kiss was slowly leaving the forefront of my mind and I had a million other things to clean up mentally, but if ten years hadn't silenced those tormentors, I am not sure one single shower would either. I don't recall pixie dust falling out of my shower head and all my thoughts altering to happy ones.

I pour myself my second glass of red when I hear a knock on my door. I haven't turned on the TV, so I know it's not coming from some show. I am still in my towel when I hear a knock yet again.

I am not a fan of company. I want the noise to be noisy neighbors, but at this hour I know they are sound asleep. I tiptoe over to the peephole and see that it is Amber. I should have known it would be her, she lives on the floor above me (she is one of the noisy neighbors) and her motherly instincts would of course be checking up on me no matter the lateness of the hour.

"Hey. What are you doing here? It's three, and we have that party we are working at tomorrow evening."

I completely forgot about the party until I said it just now. Luckily, it's a sunset yacht party and doesn't start until the evening, so I can at least sleep in.

"Can I come in? I came to check on you, but I see you're totally fine," Amber says as she nods to my glass of wine, and the fact that I answered the door in a towel.

"I knew it was you and you have seen me in a towel before."

"Correction, I have seen you naked before. The towel is a step up." Amber laughs as she waits for me to step aside and let her in. Always protecting my boundaries.

I am comfortable around Amber after so many years of being friends. I am not self-conscious. And she probably has seen me naked, though for the life of me I cannot recall when. I move aside and let her pass. It's nice to be out of the hallway. No one is going to pop out at this hour of the morning, but I admit I was a little exposed.

Amber is already in her pajamas, showered and dressed for

comfort. There is very little I could be wearing that I would feel embarrassed about in her presence. We are comfortable around each other in anything. Apparently even if I was completely naked, and a towel covers more than some of my bartending outfits. Bottom line is she has seen plenty of my skin.

"Let me go get dressed," I say, leaving Amber in my kitchen. She wastes no time and pulls out another wine glass and pours herself some of the Cabernet that is still in the bottle on the countertop. There is about half a bottle left, so it is a big pour.

I emerge from my bedroom in a baggy Doobie Brothers tee and some bleach-stained black sweatpants still holding my full glass of wine. Amber gives me a little top off anyway and with that the bottle is empty. Now we both have glasses that are almost full to the brim. We wouldn't be caught dead pouring like this at work.

"You just can't help but pour drinks for people, can you?" I snicker as we make our way over to the couch. "I am fine really, but I don't mind the company if you want to stay and finish this episode of *Grey's* with me."

Amber is the one who got me watching these soap operas. She calls them American *telenovelas*. We started *Grey's Anatomy* about three months ago.

"I can't believe you are only on season three. You realize there are like nineteen, don't you?"

"These episodes are over forty-five minutes long! I have to work, sleep and eat! I have a life. What do you expect from me? You could give me less hours at the bar." I smile. "But please don't give me less hours at the bar."

We both laugh and cover ourselves with the fluffy blanket I left on the couch from earlier. It resides there permanently, anyway. There are many nights I never make it to my bed after a long shift, and this blanket is softer than anything I have on my actual bed.

"You eat and sleep right here in front of the TV. You should at least be on season seven by now."

This feels just like one of our regular *girls night in*, one of many that Amber and I have had in our apartments. It helps to be neighbors, co-workers and friends. It works out well for both of us. Our friendship is more than a matter of convenience though.

"I think finishing one season each month is not that bad of a flow. I will finish them all in nineteen months at this pace."

Amber doesn't look convinced, only pretending to be annoyed. She really could care less how far I am in her favorite television series. She is just trying to distract me from myself and I have to say it is working.

Not much else is said as we sip our wine and watch Meredith and McDreamy make out yet again in one of the many *secluded* rooms of the hospital. Someone always walks in on them, and I can't imagine real hospitals have that many rooms ripe for lovemaking.

I thought the tropical weather in Miami made people horny, but according to Shonda Rhimes, Seattle is the most sexually titillating city in America. It could also be because everyone on that program looks like they came straight out of Greek mythology, or perhaps Seattle is so cold that having lots of sex is the only way to keep warm.

I amuse myself when I am tired.

Hospitals in real life induce panic attacks for me, but something about the show seems so unrealistic, my brain doesn't associate the two. I haven't told Amber that I have had to skip a few episodes though because they were too much for me to watch.

Both our wine glasses are sitting empty in front of us on the coffee table when the episode ends. Amber's eyelids are barely open, and I too am ready for my pillow. Red wine and early morning hours equate a lot of drowsiness. We should have been asleep in bed hours ago.

"Are you sleeping here?" I ask as I get up to put our glasses in the sink.

"No," she mumbles, not even opening her eyes before she stands. "I need to get a good sleep before the day truly begins. I'll stop by here around four-thirty tomorrow evening, and we can drive to the marina together. Sound good?"

"Yeah, sounds great," I tell her as I open the door for her. "See you tomorrow."

I make sure she is stumbling in the right direction and that she makes it to the elevator before closing my door. Her presence sure has a knack for making the voices in my head shut up, and I love her for that. I am hoping the two and a half glasses of wine, plus the fact that it is now 4 a.m., will help me sleep soundly.

I yet again don't make it to my bed, and I settle for my couch and my blanket. I forget to brush my teeth again after the red wine and don't bother to worry about any stains, which I am sure I will regret when I wake. Sure enough, I am right and the voices in my mind are at bay, at least for now.

I don't wake up until two in the afternoon, only a few hours before Amber said she would come get me. There is a large yacht party tonight and a few of us girls from Salud have been hired to bartend and serve appetizers on this sunset cruise for a well-known law firm here in Miami. I believe a lot of young men work in this firm, pretty fresh out of college, so they planned a less stuffy office party and swung for a more youthful soiree. Less cigars in a gentlemen's club and more *Miami Vice* with margaritas, I guess. At least the uniform isn't a bikini or some lame frilly flamingo leotard with a ton of feathers.

I debate not even showering because I just did only a few hours ago, but I still feel grimy from last night. Probably because I didn't brush my teeth after the wine, and I can feel the fuzz as I rub my tongue over the grooves of my teeth.

I slink out of bed, and instead of some much-needed grooming, I head straight for the coffee maker I got at a rummage sale last month. I'm cheap, and I like things that are a little battered and used. Makes me feel like I am not alone in this world. I have created my own *island of misfits*.

This specific coffee maker sputters a little out of the top when the water goes through the filter and makes a few of the coffee grounds volcano out momentarily, but I don't mind; it was only five dollars, and it does the trick.

Is it good coffee? I don't know if I have a refined enough palette to judge. I get a good jolt when I drink it. That's all that matters to me.

I've never cared too much for sweetener and frilly coffee things like caramel and oat milk cookie creamer, so a quick swig of the black magic, and I can already feel my nerve endings in my fingers and toes start to come alive. I refill my cup and take it to the back patio and sip on my second cup of the day in the afternoon humidity.

The apartment itself is painfully tiny, but this patio and

view alone makes it worth whatever rent increase comes my way, as long as I can stay afloat with my job. Working a lot doesn't seem to burn me out, and I am a pretty good saver. I have honed my survival skills over the past decade with a fine-toothed comb. I only have to worry about me, myself and I. The fewer people I get close to, the fewer people I have to lie to.

The ocean is calm this afternoon, or *morning* if you are operating on my time schedule. I love watching the waves froth and crash. Florida has some of the best beaches. This one is particularly busy on a Saturday afternoon. Lucky for me, my apartment complex has private beach access. I don't utilize it as much as I should, but I occasionally take a beach stroll to feel the water on my toes.

I usually prefer the morning because the entire world feels calm and the only people outside are early bird joggers or those who crawl out of bed just in time to watch the sky change colors. I feel incredibly blessed to be able to consume this atmosphere wholly and with so much ease. Just a slide of the glass doors and I have all the best of Miami at my fingertips. It's more spiritual than environmental.

I can see the neon signs of the nightlife and the majesty of the landscape all at once depending on the time of day.

It is very similar to where I grew up in SoCal, but a different kind of laid back. It's also way closer to the Caribbean, which is a huge bonus even though I have never actually been. Makes me feel like I could go any time I wanted to, though. I long for a Captain Jack Sparrow to dock in the marina in his sinking dinghy and whisk me away on an island adventure. In another life I would have been a pirate. I have the right personality for it. I am a little calloused to the world and only wish to care about myself. Plus, what girl would say no to a little sparkle and hidden treasure?

Miami has a lot of culture. Bright colors and kind people who are loud and engaging. Miami seemed like a place my sister would have wanted to go to one day. We knew nowhere, except California. When I was seventeen, I fled to the opposite coastline, which is what I imagine we might have done together some day.

With that thought, my peaceful morning has turned sour. I finish my coffee and allow my skin to soak up some of the extra moisture in the air before heading back inside. The air feels salty and heavy as I take a deep breath and my hair has never felt better. Yes, I have very tight curls and an awful lot of them, and the humidity here really tends to frizz them up, but I love it. I love how much volume the salt gives it and I rarely ever feel the need to bicker with Mother Nature about my curls.

I walk back inside and close the door. My apartment suddenly feels like the Arctic tundra with the AC unit blasting. I undress to get in the shower, and I set my empty coffee cup on my bedside table.

Oh shoot, I forgot about his credit card.

Trevor Daniels name is staring back at me, and I pick up his card and twiddle it between my fingers a bit.

What is it about him that has me fixated? I am not looking for a relationship, although I don't think I have ever actively sought out a companion in the past. The few I have had always sort of just happened.

I can't deny that there is something in the minuscule interaction we had that draws me to him. It isn't his choice of friends.

What on earth do I do with this?

That was a stupid thought because I know the answer. I

need to return it to the bar and hold it in the safe for when he inevitably returns for it. I am not going into the bar because of the yacht party, and I am kind of hoping he returns for it today so that he thinks it's just lost and can cancel it and get a new one. I don't know if I want to see him, but I'm sure he will frequent Salud again, but maybe I'll be off or too busy to notice him. I hadn't noticed him until last night, and I doubt that was his first time in.

I am wasting so much of my time staring at this silly piece of plastic like it chose me somehow, and I need to get my butt in gear before Amber shows up. She doesn't take kindly to a lack of punctuality in anyone and hates when I am running behind, which I always am. Being on time is more of her strength, which I think is why she opted to drive us to the marina tonight. If I showed up late for some reason it would look poor on her and the company she manages.

The shower is steaming, just as I like it, and I don't step out until every inch of my skin is red from the heat. It is divine.

I have barely begun to put on my embossed polo and mini tennis skirt when Amber knocks.

"My hair is wet, just hang on one second." I say as I fling open the door. I don't even wait to see if she comes in or not because I run straight back to the bathroom to blow-dry my hair and finish my makeup.

"You're fifteen minutes early anyway so you can't be mad at me for not being ready. OH, AND YOU LOOK CUTE." I shout from the bathroom while Amber is still in the doorway. A compliment always softens her toward my tardiness.

Amber knows her presence alone lights a fire under me, which is why she showed up early. We are both out the door and headed for the marina right on time.

CHAPTER 4

Kat

{ 2022 }

"Phew, we made it just in time," Amber sighs as we arrive.

We are early, but for Amber sure, that's right on time.

For someone who is so laid back, she has an immense amount of anxiety about being in the right place at the right time.

Several staff members from a host of catering companies carry crates and trays of seafood and goodies on board one of the largest yachts I have ever seen up close and personal. Amber and I were hired as freelancers to tend bar, so we don't recognize anyone else.

Commercial cruise ships pass by all the time, but for something that is someone's personal property, I am surprised by its stature.

I am not immune to gratuitous wealth. I grew up around so much of it in Malibu. My home was considered somewhat upscale, but every once and a while I think about how much someone must have sold their soul to afford such extravagance as this yacht.

Amber can see that I am gawking and uses her palm to close my jaw while laughing a little at my expense. I bite my tongue. Luckily this specific catering company is providing everything we need to do our job correctly. I honestly don't know why they chose to staff us, but I guess they needed a few extra servers.

Amber and I are always willing to put in hours on the weekend. That may have been why they sought us out. It can be quite difficult to find people to work on a Saturday afternoon. My days off never align with the typical weekend. In fact, I think my next day off is Thursday.

I am happy to be here, though. On the water is my favorite place to be. I don't care if it's for work or play.

We step aboard in our matching uniforms and seek out the host of this shindig before all the guests start to pile on and we set off.

The hostess is a petite brunette force of nature dressed in a white matching suit set and calling all the shots. She's very professional and very fashionable, and a lawyer to boot. She carries herself like she has her life together, and I envy that.

"Hi, I'm Bianca," she says confidently, pointing us to our station. If being a lawyer doesn't work out for her, she would make an excellent news anchor. Her voice is commanding and rumbles in a perfect alto.

Amber and I get to business and try not to linger in the awe of our surroundings. The bar is centered in the middle of the yacht. Everything is decorated to aesthetic perfection. We try not to show by our expressions that we are both super giddy to be here. We want to be professional and make a good impression so hopefully we get hired again.

People are now shuffling on board. There are well over fifty guests when the engines start to rev, the propellers begin to spin, and we are setting off into the Atlantic Ocean. Each guest, now safely aboard, looks more put together than the last. The men look sharp and the women all look very resort cocktail, dripping in Gucci and their millionaire statuses.

When Amber told me she had booked us a yacht party, I thought there would be a lot more bikinis, and men in tiny swim trunks, who probably shouldn't be. But there isn't a single bathing suit in sight. Amber reminds me that this is a law firm employee appreciation party. Of course, no one wears skimpy swimwear at an office party. Once again, I am serving mostly businessmen ready to cut loose for the night.

"Coconut shrimp and mango chutney?"

The food is decadent. I sneak a shrimp or two. I am making my rounds with trays offering appetizers to a man who is keeping his head low and looks like he might be seasick. His sandy hair tossing in the wind may not be the only thing tossing in a minute.

"Um . . . no thank you," he says. When he looks up, I take about five large steps back.

No, no, no, it's him from last night. Oh gosh the beer kisser. No, no, no. How in the actual hell? He's a lawyer?

I dash off with such haste that a few fried shrimps have fallen on the deck. I do not want to stick around for a half-hearted apology, blatant forgetfulness, or worse . . . round two.

"*AMBER* . . . Amber!" I am very loudly whispering. The hum of people talking and their lack of interest in waitstaff is protection enough.

"*HE* is here."

"Who is here?" Amber asks stoically.

I point over to where my attacker from last night is standing, only now he isn't alone hanging over the edge queasy. Instead, he has his arms wrapped around our petite little host, Bianca. When he gives her a peck on the lips, I feel a chill running down my spine. *That is definitely not how he kissed me last night . . . holy crap, I kissed the host's husband last night.* Or rather he kissed me, but based on her body language and kind demeanor, I am guessing she is ignorant about last night's debacle.

"What are the chances? Are you okay? Do you need a minute? I can take your tray if you need to go breathe in the back of the boat for a bit. I can't believe it. I mean what are the odds? This all cannot be a coincidence. Do you think she knows? Well, obviously, she doesn't, or we would probably be out of a job right now. Not because of anything you did. Dang, I wish we had seen him sooner and we could have left. I would have made a huge scene with you and walked out with a bottle of the most expensive hooch. One for each of us . . ."

Amber is nervously rambling. She does this when she is riled up; I call it her "spicy attitude." Usually it's adorable, but right now I am overwhelmed.

I don't feel threatened, especially knowing his wife is here and he will most likely be on his best behavior. Even without an audience he should behave, but people like him are hard to read. Between having his wife around and this being a business event, he would be clinically insane to make a scene on a boat we can't leave.

I need to escape Amber's rattling to calm myself.

"You know, I think I will take a few minutes to myself," I

say as I pass her my tray and head to the back of the boat to watch the water break from the sides of the ship.

We are getting close to sunset, which is my favorite time of day. Everything glows. It's called golden hour for a reason. It makes everyone look flawless and the earth feels touched by Midas himself.

I lean over the edge of the railing just a little and welcome the spray of the sea onto my flushed face. Each prickle of water grounding me and making me feel at ease.

"You found my secret hiding spot," I hear a voice say from behind me. I thought I was alone and jump. This voice assumes I am approachable, which I am most certainly not. I turn abruptly in his direction.

Trevor Daniels is standing before me in all his tall dark and handsome glory.

Can this night get any weirder?

The golden sun reflects in his hazel irises and his skin is so sun-kissed it almost looks like browned butter. He's wearing a more casual fit—a button-down short sleeve with pineapples on it and navy pants that look like they were custom tailored. His clothes seem to match his laid-back attitude, and the sweetness of the piña colada he has in his hand.

"I'm sorry. I thought I was alone," I say as I turn around. "I can go. I was just taking a little break."

I spin on my heels, and he does that thing again that he did last night that had my brain go all fuzzy like static on the radio. He gently grabs my forearm, like he isn't going to stop me from leaving, but also really wants me to stay put.

There is no aggression, just a commanding presence that my body wants to respond to.

"I must apologize for last night. I cannot believe what

happened, and I am sincerely sorry."

Look at that. I got an apology . . . only this wasn't half-hearted, and it wasn't from the offender.

"You didn't do anything to be sorry for. I probably should be thanking you for helping me," I mumble in honest discomfort.

At this point I am looking at the small cut on his lip, and it looks like it could still be swollen.

"How's your lip?" I ask as I obviously stare. I have clearly noticed what his lips look like, and I don't know that I should be continuing this conversation with someone who makes me feel so uneasy. The last time I felt this way around someone, a lot of trouble followed, and I don't have it in me to deal with trouble.

"Nothing that a little ice, ibuprofen, and time can't heal. My pride is hurt more than anything else. It's a little unprofessional to have a lawyer look like he gets in bar fights over the weekend."

"So, you're a lawyer, too?" I ask and feel rather stupid because we are on a boat full of lawyers. *Duh!* He observes my embarrassment and giggles. "What I mean is what kind of law do you practice?" I cough as a cover.

"Criminal law," he says as I slowly retreat from his body, which makes my desire to draw closer to him insatiable.

"Let me buy you a drink," he says after a pause. "It's the least I can do to make up for my friend being such an ass."

I want to say yes to his proposal so badly that for a momentary lapse in time I forget that I am on the clock.

"I can't, I'm working." Thank goodness I have a legit excuse.

"I'm sure that's not a problem. I know the boss and she won't mind. C'mon, the first drink is on me." Trevor laughs, and I catch the joke. It's an open bar.

"Oh, I think she will, considering she is married to the man

I kissed last night."

His eyes looked shocked by my candor. He then blurts out a rather loud belly laugh that almost makes me laugh, too. I obviously didn't get the joke, but his laughter is contagious. His charisma is enigmatic, unlike anyone I have ever interacted with.

"C'mon, my drink needs refreshing, and one drink with me won't hurt. I'll make sure Brady is nowhere around us and if it makes you feel better. We can avoid Bianca as well."

Now I finally have a name to the face, and I have no excuses nor willpower to just flat out deny him.

He takes my forearm again and leads me to the bar in the middle of the boat where he orders himself a Macallan 12 and soda (*I guess one piña colada is enough*) and then turns to ask me what I'll be drinking.

"Margarita on the rocks with a salt rim, please." Luckily some guy from another company is bartending and not Amber, otherwise I'd be completely humiliated.

"So, tell me a little about you. Where are you from?" Trevor asks as he sits on a bar stool bolted to the floor.

Wow, we are diving in with questions so simple, and yet I haven't told anyone where I am from and I wasn't about to break that trend with someone I just met, no matter how much I want to seep into all his secrets and learn every inch of his mind and body.

"Oh gosh," he stumbles mid-swallow. "I don't even know your name. Let's start there."

I am so grateful for the change in question without me having to be awkward or lie.

"Kat."

I've gone by Kat rather than Katie for the longest time. Being called Katie and hearing that name follow me everywhere is far too haunting. And remembering the past and the situations it put me in as such a young adult remains heartbreaking. Kat gives me a sense of being a whole new me.

"Do you have a last name," he asks with the corners of his mouth creeping into a small smile. A smolder, one could even call it. He is flirting and I know it, so I decide there is little harm flirting back.

"Three more drinks and you can get a last name out of me."

I get a cursory chortle and a smile out of that comment.

"Okay, so you intend to sit with me for a few more rounds then?"

"Oh no, I never said that those drinks would be tonight. I gotta get back to work and probably should be sober enough not to drop the shrimp cocktail on Bianca's white pantsuit."

The flirting is effortless, and I feel witty and charming. It's right then that I see Amber.

Her stare is hard to decipher. Is it a question of why I am drinking while I'm supposed to be working? Is it shock that I am interacting with the guy from last night? Or is it an encouragement to keep sipping with the hottie and tell her all about it later? I decide I'm going to let her come over and clear it up, which she does without hesitation.

"My boss is actually on her way over to us, so I really should be going," I say right as Amber reaches us. Calling Amber "my boss" has always felt too formal, but Trevor needs to know there is a difference in rank between us when she arrives and she's not just my best friend.

I also want Amber to know that I am aware of her presence and her potential judgments, even though she has always acted like an equal toward me.

Pretty sure Trevor picks up on my fidgeting and turns to direct his attention right at Amber. His mannerisms completely dissolve any potential animosity. I'm beginning to think he does this a lot, and that he is good at it.

"Hey, I'm sorry. I dragged her away for a drink. I figured it was the least I could do after what went down last night."

Trevor is covering for me like he assumes Amber is going to be mad. They very clearly both recognize one another. To be fair to him, the only emotion he has ever seen on Amber was rage after she threw him and his drunken friends out of the bar last night.

"She *does* deserve a drink. In fact, I think we all do. A sex on the beach please," Amber said, ordering herself a cocktail.

Way to casually mention sex Amber. I have been trying to keep that image out of my mind since laying eyes on Trevor.

It has been a really long time for me; I imagine Trevor cannot say the same. Every time he touches my forearm my skin feels like it is a hundred degrees. He makes me feverish. He looks like a Jonas Brother, and women swoon as they pass. Plus, he's been nothing but kind to me in the brief time we have known each other. What a crazy coincidence that he is here tonight. Too bad I don't believe in coincidence. Fate, perhaps.

Amber is a third of the way through her cocktail when Bianca starts in our direction.

"Can you please wait to hit on the help until after I am done paying them?"

Bianca is sarcastic to Trevor, like she is simply being playful and teasing rather than frustrated that the hired help is drinking on the job.

"Brady, babe, come over here. Come have a drink with us and Trevor's new friends." Bianca is waving over Brady who nervously orders a her glass of pinot noir. Brave of her while wearing an all-white outfit to be drinking red on a boat, but it stains her lips the perfect shade of blood red, which only adds to her intimidation.

She cuts Brady off before he has a chance to order a drink for himself. "Brady had a bit too much to drink last night and is abstaining this evening, right babe." Brady is by her side now and she wraps her delicate arms around his middle and hangs onto him ever so lovingly despite the resentment in her tone.

"Okay Trevor, introduce us," she says as she points to me.

"Oh, Brady *knows* who these two are," Trevor says in a mocking tone that hints to Bianca that she is the only one out of the loop.

Brady shoots Trevor a look of rage. The poor guy is still hungover for crying out loud, and I am worried about what might happen if Trevor doesn't button his swollen bottom lip up. I wonder if Bianca knows that her husband was the one who put that there. My guess is no.

Before another brawl ensues and someone gets tossed overboard, I chime in to soften the subject, informing Bianca that we are bartenders from Salud. I can see the muscles in Brady's face begin to relax. But I am protecting myself, not him.

I don't feel the need to come clean to his wife on a boat where the only escape is the deep sea waters of the Atlantic. I think Trevor gets the hint and backs off his friend as well. Bianca seems to let the weirdness go. "It's a party! Everybody should enjoy themselves," she says in yet another subject change. She's not stupid, just busy.

After one long sip of her wine and a touch of awkward silence, Bianca sets down her glass and remarks, "Sorry to leave you all, lots to tend to." She pulls Brady along. I'm starting to sense Bianca likes control. She seems like the most amazing person to be around, but sometimes I get the feeling men feel emasculated by such powerful women, and Bianca is nothing short of a force of nature.

"Oh shoot, that reminds me, do you have my credit card by any chance?" Trevor asks as soon as Bianca and Brady are out of earshot.

"Not on me. I didn't know you would be here." I say a little too defensively.

"Of course not. I mean do you know where it is?" Trevor never looks like he feels uncomfortable, but I feel rather foolish more often than I would like.

"I found it in my apron last night when I got home," I said, "I'd be happy to bring it to the bar tomorrow and you can swing by whenever."

"Or you can just swing by her apartment tonight. We live in the same building and can give you a ride." Amber must be feeling the effects of that cocktail, and I nudged her in disbelief at how forward she was to invite a strange man over to my home. Even if it was just to get his personal credit card.

"That would be amazing, actually. My week is really busy and if I could get that back tonight, I'd really appreciate it."

"Sure," I say very weakly. "We can head over as soon as Amber and I are done cleaning up." And with that I am pulling Amber by the arm as she inhales the last of her drink through a straw. My margarita was left untouched.

※ ※ ※

Amber and I finish cleaning up and everyone has long left the yacht, including Bianca, who was buzzed off her wine, and Brady, who looked sadder sober than when drunk, but maybe that was just the hangover. I try not to judge people and their marriages off one interaction no matter how indisputable that interaction was.

I don't see Trevor, and I am secretly hoping he got bored and left already. However, there he is standing on the side of the yacht, his navy pants in stark contrast to the white boat. Darkness has blanketed the ocean by now, but his silhouette in the moonlight seems to dance along the side of the yacht as the waves kiss it in the marina. I'm hypnotized.

"You ready?" Amber shouts in his direction. His tormented trance breaks and he strides in our direction.

The car ride was full of conversation. I decide to sit in the back because I know that Amber will be way more talkative than I am at this time of night. She looks at me like I am an idiot, but I don't really care; I have never been good at holding a conversation while driving, and I wasn't about to put Trevor in the backseat like some cheap chauffeur.

They seem to really get to know each other, and I grow curious that maybe Amber has a blossoming crush on Trevor and isn't just trying to be my wing woman. But no. Amber quickly ducks out with a "goodnight, nice to meet you Trevor," and scurries off to her apartment a floor above me with a wink. She probably is running to her balcony to see if she can hear us. I know she worries about my love life and enjoys playing matchmaker, but it's not like I see her with a man headed back to her apartment. Well, not often at least.

I am so uneasy when it comes to being alone with this man. Especially in my home. My only sanctuary. I am very particular about who I allow into my comfort zone. Any man would make me retreat into my shell, but this one in particular gives me goosebumps.

"Can I get you anything? A glass of water? A glass of wine?" I swallow hard while we are still in the doorway. My mouth feels dry. I have no idea what is appropriate. I probably should just go get him his credit card, let him call a car and head out, never to be seen again. But I don't want him to leave. My heart and my head are not on the same page.

I get the feeling that he is coming on to me. My heart wins and I decided to steer into it. What's one night of trouble anyway?

He accepts my offer for a glass of water, and I lead him out onto the back balcony. I can't help but notice him looking around my apartment, and I become self-conscious by the small bit of mess I left behind. It's obvious that his job provides financial security. He probably has a much bigger home, and I hope he isn't judging, just observing.

We are both looking out toward the ocean when he takes my elbow in his hand and pulls me just a little closer. He must do this little dance a lot; his execution is smooth. I, however, am so novice, and it shows dramatically. He sends tingles to my toes and everywhere else. I am ashamed to admit it. I feel as though I turn into the floppy consistency of oobleck when I am around him, even though he is a stranger, one with a lot of confidence and skill around women.

"I see why you like it here," he says, "what an incredible view."

"I'm obsessed with it." I say and he slowly turns me to face him.

If he says he's obsessed with the view too (referring to my face) I will either laugh or faint.

"Let me go get your credit card," I interrupt before he has a chance to use such a cheesy line on me.

Once again, I am turning away from this man when I so badly want to be turning to him. I run awkwardly to my night table and pick up his card and rush back to him still staring at the ocean, seemingly unbothered. I envy his peace.

"Here you go."

I can barely get the words out when he pulls me into him and kisses my mouth so intently that I squeak a little when our lips meet. I feel like he jumped about twenty conversational steps to get here, but here we are. I can feel the swell of his bottom lip as it moves across mine. If the kiss stings, he doesn't let even a wince show on his face. This is a surprise kiss that I actually enjoy. He tastes a little like scotch and smells a little like citrus, and when he gently presses his tongue past my teeth, I can taste it even more. He tastes like how a sunset looks, if that is even possible.

I don't think I've ever had a first kiss that hypnotizes like this one. Our mouths are moving in perfect rhythm and synchronize with the crashing of the waves on the shore. The peace he had a moment just before spills over me, like I am able to siphon it off of him.

This might be my favorite first kiss, ever.

His hands slide to the small of my back and are supporting me up to his mouth. I feel the bandages on his hands as they graze my skin.

I don't want to think about why they are there. Not now.

He is significantly taller than me, but the way he is carrying me up to him feels effortless. I feel weightless in his arms.

All the discomfort I felt a few minutes ago vanishes. There is only one other time that I felt this comfortable with discomfort before. I pull back a little at the thoughts of my past. Of the one who enters my mind.

Why is it that I can never escape my past even in my own thoughts?

The peace wasn't long lived. When Trevor leans back into me, I try to clear my mind. His lips are very useful in helping me forget anything and everything around me, so I choose to lose myself in his touch. We're lip-locked like a couple of middle-school kids making out.

He must be getting tired of leaning over because he moves me swiftly to the patio loveseat I have on my balcony. I've always loved this chair.

Is that why they call it a loveseat?

I want to climb up on him and crawl all over him at the same time. I slide my legs over him so that I straddle his lap without our lips ever parting. I must still have sea legs because it feels like our hips are rocking with the waves. He slides his hands up the backside of my shirt and strokes the bumps of my spine. His hands are mitts that find their way through my collar and into my hair.

I am suddenly very aware that I am on my balcony and that Amber is probably making popcorn and listening in right above us. Not to mention the other neighbors who could pop onto their balconies at any moment. The hour is late, but being spied on is still plausible. The night gives us a false sense of security, though Miami is never fully dark. I don't allow him to remove my shirt for that reason, even though I desperately desire his hands touching every inch of my skin. It's torture when his fingers get hung up on any fabric barriers.

His kiss deepens, and I can feel his perfectly fitting navy pant fabric tighten under my thigh. I can feel all of him under my tennis skirt.

"It's exactly how I thought it would be." he says, partly breaking the seal of our lips with his musing.

"What is?" I ask, pausing the kiss.

He pulls away just enough to allow his lips to move over mine to form the words.

"Tasting you."

CHAPTER 5

Trevor
{ 2022 }

I LEAVE THE YACHT PARTY before even thinking about how illogical it is to accept a ride when my car is waiting for me back at the marina. I don't want to turn down Amber's invitation. They probably assume that I took an Uber to the event. I probably should have, but now I will be taking an Uber back. I want to spend as much time as I can with this girl. I don't know her, but I know I want to kiss her by the end of the night. Oh my gosh, how I want to kiss her.

I don't plan on kissing her, but I know if the moment presents itself, I will take it without hesitation. I've had the desire to kiss her since I saw her staring off into space behind the bar last night. I cannot believe I've been jealous of Brady. He was sloppy and unforgivable. I hate myself for wishing I was him, but he got to touch her. Standing now on her balcony is the perfect moment for me to try. I kiss her. I am relieved when that jealousy leaves me. She kisses me back. It is a gift Brady didn't receive.

After our conversation on the yacht and being invited back to her place, I figure it won't be too out of left field if I attempt a kiss, despite the reality that we are still strangers. Weirder things have occurred. I've kissed many strangers before, but Kat doesn't feel like a stranger.

Her mouth is intoxicating and the movement of her body on mine is too pleasurable to pace. When reaching my hands around her hips and under her skirt she pulls away and claims to have an early morning. I've heard that enough before from others to understand its true meaning—*We are not having sex tonight.*

Releasing myself from our braided bodies feels near impossible, but I'm not too let down. I feel honored to have been close enough to touch her, and definitely did not anticipate anything else. Her body makes it hard to stop though. No man in my position would want to.

I gather my credit card so as not to forget it again. I can't say I'm not tempted though, as it would give me an excuse to see her yet again. I linger in the doorway for a moment and gently kiss her forehead, which feels more intimate than what we did on the balcony. I feel her wince when I step back. I leave, and she seems to still be in a good mood. If she's upset by the intimacy, she doesn't show it. However, this girl is a mystery wrapped up in tight blonde curls. Not sure if she'll show candor in her emotions with me still in the room. I don't know if I'll ever breach her walls, but she makes me want to try.

I stand outside awkwardly reaching for my phone to call an Uber. I see that she is back out on her patio. I don't think she notices me just yet. I watch her, intently hoping to see a smile or a small glint of anything affirming in her eyes. Instead, she seems sad, like she is losing some deep internal battle. The only glint in her eyes is from tears daring to flood. She's too strong to let tears take her down.

Maybe I did upset her?

The turmoil in her eyes makes me want to hug her and hold her so close that my weight extinguishes her sadness. I mostly just wish I knew why she's so sad, and I have to hope that my actions are not to blame. I can't shake the nagging feeling that I contributed.

The ding of my phone notifying me that my driver is only a few minutes away, alerts Kat to my presence. Whatever tears that had fallen are quickly wiped away. The echo in the courtyard carries to everyone's balconies, the engineering of which I find intrusive.

Even in the night's glow her eyes are brilliant. I feel a chill as she looks down at me, but instantly warm as she smiles and waves before heading inside.

I hope she doesn't feel embarrassed like I am by what just happened. Despite it all, I want to do it again. She invited me into her home, so she is at least comfortable with the fact that I now know where she lives, and she even told me that she was in no hurry to give up that view.

Wouldn't that be just great if I ran a woman out of her home and her favorite place just because she was embarrassed to have kissed me? That would definitely be a first for me. Maybe I am giving myself too much credit. I have kissed several women I never wish to kiss again, and it has never run me out of my home. They all eventually just take the hint.

I've only ever been captivated—body and soul—by someone once before. I guess we call that falling in love. It was an intense relationship that ended a few years ago. I could see myself marrying her, but when she moved back to her home in Australia things got way more than a little complicated. "Geographically undesirable" is the term she used. Long distance is like a deadly virus. Between the time difference and the constant video chats, it just wasn't enough to sustain us. Even the seasons don't match up. I couldn't get on board with Christmas in the summer either. Sand instead of snow . . . weird.

I don't think I have felt this way since then, or maybe even ever, which is baffling to me considering how short of a time I have known Kat and just how little about herself she has shared with me.

I guess I told her my name and what I do for a living, which is exactly all that she knows about me. And all I know about her. I'd like to imagine she is feeling the same way and that she can't believe she has feelings for someone she knows so little about. Against all glaring evidence, I have chosen to remain hopeful until proven otherwise. I'm not an idiot who is going to come on too strong and tell her I love her tomorrow. However, I also can't be the guy who never calls her again.

Oh shoot, I never got her phone number.

"You Trevor?" The Uber driver asks as he pulls into the courtyard. I am the only one here, so *duh*.

I slide into the backseat of the sedan and start heading back to the marina for my car. Lucky for me, the driver doesn't seem to be in too chatty of a mood. I couldn't focus on a conversation right now. I am too busy calculating out a plan on how to get in touch with Kat without being a complete stalker. Miami isn't as big as it may seem, and we arrive much faster than we would have with day traffic.

To my surprise, Brady is leaning against my car.

"I figured you had to come back to your car at some point,"

he says. "Could have been tomorrow though, and I would have been out here in the cold all night." His passive-aggressive remark is so dramatic. It is never really cold in Miami, and how was I supposed to know he was even here?

His neck must be so tired from hanging all day. "I was starting to worry that it wasn't going to be tonight, and I was going to have to sleep on the pavement."

Sure, he was worried that he wouldn't be able to get comfortable. Not that his best friend never came back for his car and could potentially be missing. I don't expect anything less. Brady has always had a narcissistic knack for only looking out for himself.

He is in a weird mood. Not quite confrontational, but not quite apologetic either. Typical. Brady is never one to admit he is wrong or be the first to apologize. I make excuses for him a lot, but not tonight.

"What are you doing here?" I ask. "Shouldn't you be home with Bianca right now. It's late man . . . go home."

He looks up and talks fast. "Yes, I should be home with Bianca, but do you know why I am not?" *No doubt now, he is absolutely confrontational.* "Hmmm? Oh gee, it couldn't be because my best friend alluded tonight that I knew that bartender chick, and while Bianca played dumb to your hints, she pried me after the party, and I was forced to spill my guts. You knew that she would pick up on your lack of subtlety, but she was too polite to inquire during a public event. I just got scolded like a child and was told not to come home tonight. She's pissed, man, and she didn't have to be. There was no reason she should have known. You didn't have to say anything, and I would be in a warm bed next to my wife right now. But instead, I am here next to boats, the smell of fish, this stupid car, and you. *I blame you!* This is all your fault."

"You cannot be serious!"

Not one ounce of me has any patience for him. Does he want me to feel bad for him or help him? His body language suggests he is ready to punch me again. Extreme candor is the only way I will get through to him. I'm not playing his silly games.

"Funny, I don't remember being so drunk that I non-consensually groped and then shoved my tongue down a strange girl's throat last night. Oh wait, no, that was you, and I have the fat lip to prove it. What do you mean you blame me man. . . c'mon! Yeah, I said something to Bianca, but then I shut my mouth.

"You married a smart woman, but that's just it . . . *you* MARRIED her. You were an idiot last night. She should have kicked you out. You screwed up. She'll take you back though, she's a good woman and you are lucky to have her, but none of what has happened in the last twenty-four hours is in any way my fault. I was expecting an apology more. You had no cause to hit me, and yet I was still the bigger person and drove you home, but it is somehow all my fault. What the hell has been going on with you lately? You forget we are all close. You're like my brother. I care about you, but you need to know my loyalties don't lie with just you. You know Bianca means a lot to me too."

There is a moment of pause before I blurt out what comes next. The true question. Just not the nicest way to phrase it. "Why are you acting like such a prick lately?"

I feel a tinge of remorse, and Brady breaks down crying. I have never seen this man cry. He's built like an NFL player, and usually stoic to boot. The only thing Brady emotes is anger and annoyance. Seeing him soften and break down is alarming, but it erases my frustration, and I don't feel the need to shout at him anymore. I feel terrible that whatever's going on in Brady's life has gotten to this point, and he never felt he could share with me.

His muscular shoulders begin to shake. I just want to get us out of the marina now. His vulnerability makes me feel exposed. Even in the seclusion of the empty parking lot.

"Get in." I sigh as I unlock the car door with a click.

Brady obeys, wiping his eyes with his sleeve. "You can stay with me until Bianca forgives you, but you have to tell me what is going on."

We ride in silence for a while and I take his silence as he gathers his thoughts. He knows he has no choice but to be honest. I also don't want him to start crying again, so I change the subject. I'll get him to explain soon enough. I direct the subject toward me and the only subject I've had on the brain tonight.

"I kissed Kat." I wait for his shocked response, but all I get is a confused, "Who?"

"Kat," I say again. "The bartender YOU kissed last night." I laugh and Brady shows a look of disbelief.

"Nah. No way . . . but really? Like when?"

For being a lawyer, he sometimes lacks articulation.

Now that the adrenaline has worn off, I can feel the ache in my fat lip again after kissing Kat and yelling at Brady stretched it open again.

"Can I ask you a weird question?"

He nods.

"What did she taste like to you?" I mumble, almost hoping he doesn't hear me.

"What the hell?"

"I told you it was a weird question." We both laugh.

Brady takes a moment before answering. Like he is trying

to remember or trying to process my odd request.

"Beer dude, she tasted like beer. I think she drinks on the job." I laugh out loud. He has no idea what she tasted like, which in some way makes me feel like she is mine. All I can say back is, "I am pretty sure that was all you." And we drop the subject to ride home in an unspoken apologetic peace.

CHAPTER 6

Kat

{ 2022 }

I AM BACK at Salud for my shift before I see Amber again, and part of me is dying to tell her all the details. Not that she won't ask first thing when she walks through the doors later.

I detest working at this time of day. No one is here. There is nothing to do. We have an excellent kitchen but from the hours of two to four it is a ghost town. That is until the happy hour crowd comes to get a drink after a long day of corporate slavery.

I chose being a bartender because I like being the person serving someone's vice, a reprieve from their struggles. I know it sounds crass or that maybe there would have been more money for me in dealing drugs, but this is legal and every person on the planet has a vice. Remember the phrase, "Don't shoot the messenger?"

I am cleaning the counter when Amber comes blasting in like a rocket. Her Latina flair in full force as she breezes up to me and begins speaking Spanish so fast I can't keep up. I have lived in Miami for a decade so I can at least understand most of it, but I am far from fluent. My brain cannot translate quickly enough to keep up with those whose first language is Spanish. Amber seems to forget this sometimes, until she notices that familiar look of confusion on my face.

"Oh sorry, I am just so excited I forgot what language I was speaking. Dish it out. I need details girl! Give me all the *detalles jugosos*."

Now that bit of Spanish I understand. "There are no juicy details," I tell her, but I am blushing and don't make eye contact, so she knows I am lying. I can lie convincingly about a lot of things, but this man makes me turn a shade of red that lobsters would be jealous of. Plus, I want to talk to Amber about it all. So, I am not trying to lie to her, just play coy to build suspense.

"We kissed a little, that's all." I admit because I am so stinking giddy about it still.

Amber's squeal is so piercing that only certain types of dogs can hear her. Then she teases me endlessly and asks when I am going to see "Boat Boy" again.

Boat Boy is a clever nickname, and I prefer that over "bad bar night boy," so I laugh at her cleverness.

"I don't think I will see him again," I admit.

"Why the hell not. I have not seen you this excited about someone in a while." Amber's face screams that she doesn't believe me, and she won't allow me to be so stupid. "No, I take that back. I have not seen you like this ever. You are absolutely smitten. Give me one good reason why you won't see him again. There can't be a good one. Come on. I dare you to come up with one."

"I never gave him my number." It's the only reason that feels legit and truthful.

Amber cackles in disbelief. "You are so stupid."

"Wow, gee thanks friend." I know she says so endearingly. It's like calling your best friend a bitch, which she also does on occasion.

"You know what I mean." She always feels bad when she calls me names. It's kind of comical. She won't stop, but she always feels sorry after.

"That doesn't mean he won't get in touch with you somehow. He knows where you live, where you work. The ball is in his court, and I bet he will," she says as she nudges me in the back and comes behind the bar to clock in for work.

I just smile and nod her off. All the while I am thinking that he really doesn't seem like the guy to pursue. I gave him the perfect out. He doesn't need to call. Not only did I not ask him, but I never gave him the option. The few moments I have spent with Trevor assured me that he isn't a boyfriend kind of guy. He is far too charismatic to enjoy being committed to one woman, and I feel like he owns that. What other reason could there be for him to be single?

Why do people think I am single? Wow, that is a scary thought.

We haven't had a soul walk into the bar for the last twenty minutes, so when the bell dings that someone has just entered, I am eager and responsive. Secretly I hope it's Trevor who walked through the door, but I would never admit it. Not even to myself.

The patron is someone delivering a rather large and rather colorful, tropical floral arrangement.

"Hi, are you Kat?" the young delivery kid asks. He looks like he couldn't be more than fifteen years old. I am the only one on the floor since Amber ran in the back.

I look at him stunned when he hands me the vase and blocks my view of everything else around me with its sheer size. Before I am even able to confirm my identity and set them down, the kid is gone, and I am left to figure out where to put this elaborate bouquet. He didn't even wait for a tip.

I rush to the breakroom and completely ignore Amber and her gaping mouth. I have to give credit to Trevor; he at least found a gesture that left Amber speechless. There is no one on the floor, so I take my time and open the notecard slowly. I also don't want to seem too eager in front of Amber; she will never let me live this down as it is. She is practically dancing around me in anticipation.

The note reads:

Hey Kat,

I really enjoyed our time together last night. I am not sure what your favorite flower is, so I just picked all the ones that make me think of you. There are orange blossoms because we live in the greatest state of Florida. There are birds of paradise because you make me feel like being with you is paradise. There are orchids because they are stunning and simple and beautiful, but also a little complicated at the same time. I chose begonias because their blooms look like hearts, and mine hasn't stopped rapidly beating out of my chest since we met. Jasmine, because you faintly smell of it and it was one of the first things I noticed. Lastly, I chose two different types of fluffy yellow flowers that I do not know the names of. I picked them solely because it reminds me of your crazy curly hair that hypnotizes me and smells like flowers anyway.

I don't know much about you Kat, but I intend to stick around and find out so that the next time I buy you flowers, I will know exactly which ones you like best. I

> can't do that though if we never see each other again, so please text me your number so I can take you on a proper date. Somewhere that's not at a bar or on a boat. My number is (786) 289-6742. Hope to hear from you soon,
>
> Trevor Daniels. (p.s. I know this is cheesy)

Well, that was way more than I anticipated in a note. He is obviously very good at this sort of thing and the smile on my face just will not quit.

"Who would have pegged Boat Boy to be such a romantic?" I guess Amber was reading over my shoulder. "I dare you to stop smiling right now," Amber gushes as she walks to the other side of the breakroom. She looks just as thrilled for me as I feel, but it is also terrifying. There is someone out there who wants to get to know me on a personal level. He wants to know my favorite flower and take me on a date and spend time with me. I haven't let anyone get that close in a very long time. All my trysts have been superficial, more physical than anything else, and once over, there's no reason to continue anything. Trevor and I have already breached that physical barrier a bit. My trust issues are deep at play here and I need to keep my emotions in check, or I feel like this man could easily ruin my life.

Regardless of my hesitations, Amber is already reaching into my purse for my phone and typing in his number.

"Text him . . . now. Or I will for you." I grab the phone out of her hand and obey. I kind of feel like she is my guardian angel, a protector who is looking out for my love life.

Kat: Ranunculus

"Okay I hit send," I say as I show Amber the text.

"What the hell does that mean! He is going to think you are crazy."

"He will get it, eventually," I say hopefully. I may be forcing an inside joke before there is one, and there is a good chance he does think I am a little nuts. Amber doesn't look convinced, but regardless, I put my phone back in my purse and head onto the floor.

"My love life is going to have to wait. We have work to do."

CHAPTER 7

Kat

{ 2022 }

I WAS HOPING Trevor would come in tonight, but it is Monday, and I am sure being a high-profile criminal lawyer keeps him very busy throughout the day and well into the evening. Salud isn't too busy on weekdays or Mondays, either. I think about sending him some dinner, but I don't know which law firm he is associated with. There were several different firms represented at the yacht party. I would like to reciprocate the kind gesture of bringing me flowers, but dinner might be a few steps ahead of whatever this is turning into.

Just like I assumed, the night was slow. The first thing I do when I clock out is check my phone to see if Trevor has texted back. I have two notifications, both from him. I head to my car and sit in the parking lot before I start to text him back. A cursory wave was all I gestured toward Amber. I didn't even say goodbye to her, but I figure she will be knocking on my apartment door tonight, anyway. The glow from my phone illuminates my face against the darkness in my car. An exposure

I'm certain details my true anticipation no matter my facade.

> **Trevor:** I am a lawyer and had no idea what this word meant that a random number texted me. So, I looked it up and it's a freaking flower.

His first text makes me giggle. I am so glad he has the foresight to use Google.

> **Trevor:** Also, I am assuming this is Kat and you are at work right now and that the flowers got to you. Otherwise, this entire text makes zero sense. Text me when you are off of work.

My fingers are typing so fast that autocorrect works overtime to make sense of my blather.

> **Me:** Yes lol, the ranunculus is my favorite flower, and ironically it was mixed in with all the others. It was one of the yellow ones you said reminded you of my hair, which I don't know if I should take offense to or not. Lol
>
> **Trevor:** Absolutely not! It's your favorite flower and it reminds me of you. I find your hair enigmatic and tantalizing.
>
> **Me:** Wow, "enigmatic and tantalizing." More like tangle-izing. Fancy vocabulary points. I am talking to a lawyer. lol.
>
> **Trevor**: Are you making fun of me?
>
> **Me:** Absolutely I am ha-ha.

Trevor: So, when can I take you out? I hate to ask you out over a text, but we were a little preoccupied last night and I want to get a date on the books before you might chicken out.

Me: You're making me blush, but you can't see it so I don't know why I texted it to you. I just tattled on myself. I don't work on Thursday this week.

Trevor: I work late on Thursday. How do you feel about a late date?

Me: How late are we talking here? Like 10 p.m. or like 3 a.m.? I can do late nights, but I have a rule that nothing good happens past 2 a.m.

Trevor: Isn't that the rule from "How I Met Your Mother?"

Me: Yes lol, but it is a good general rule of thumb anyway. I am impressed you knew the reference. It bodes well for you that we like the same shows.

Trevor: Haha very true. I can be off work at ten. I'll pick you up? I know where you live anyhow. lol

Me: I will be ready at ten. I am not that good at being punctual.

Trevor: Let's call it 9:45 then. Only because I want to spend every available minute with you and not waste a second.

Me: Amber would be impressed by your tactics. She does the same thing lol G2G, headed home. Talk soon. Oh, this is Kat by the way.

Trevor: I know.

I am brimming from ear to ear when I approach the hallway of my apartment. I am already chomping at the bit to text him more, but I feel I should let him text me next. So many stupid rules when it comes to dating.

Oh my gosh, am I dating?

The thought of doing something normal in my day-to-day life and something other than work surprises me in how good it feels. I feel warm, and not because of the humidity outside, but more of an internal fire.

My cheeks feel chronically flushed and my face will be sore tomorrow from smiling. I am looking forward to Amber stopping by like I know she will. Maybe she can help me reign in my emotions a bit or, maybe, give me permission to dive in. I don't know why I seek her validation so much. She acts like she's my sister sometimes, and I miss that more than I care to admit.

I crave the normalcy of it all and am positively floating when I see yet another bouquet of flowers at the base of my door. The height and weight of the bouquet I'm carrying almost topples me down the staircase.

Two bouquets in one day, who is this guy?

I have to open my door and step over the other bouquet to set the first batch in the kitchen before retrieving the second.

This arrangement is much simpler. It is a dozen lilies wrapped in paper and no vase. They are much less intricate and much more to my taste. Except I'll have to tell Boat Boy that the lily is my least favorite flower despite having one tattooed on my shoulder.

I am still standing in the hallway when I read the card poking out of the top. There is no name, only this small inscription:

After all this time, I finally found you Alice.

CHAPTER 8

Alice

{ 2012 }

I WOKE UP in the hospital.

I woke up. I woke up. Why did I wake up?

I wasn't supposed to wake up. I was supposed to understand what the spiritual beyond was like right about now. Heaven (I think I believe in) was supposed to be my eternal resting place. I was supposed to be there with Katie.

Katie . . . what happened to Katie?

The beeping of the monitors around me is the only noise, and the needle sticking out of me for vital fluids is sore in my left arm, but that is it. I'm alone.

Has everyone just stepped out for a coffee break? Where are Todd and Cheryl?

My eyelids are so heavy. How long has it been, and, most importantly, where is Katie? If I didn't die, maybe she didn't either.

The quiet doesn't last long as my monitors notify nurses that I have stirred. Sure enough, Todd and Cheryl come tearing into the room. Cheryl falls at my bedside in sobs. *Tears of relief or tears of grief*, I guess.

"What happened to. . .?" I roughly stuttered.

My throat feels like sandpaper and the words scratch as I try to talk, an effect from inhaling chlorine into my lungs, I assume. I guess the panic in the pool meant that I swallowed quite a bit of water, and my chest aches, and my throat feels coarse like I have eaten something sharp. I remember having several bottles of expensive champagne in place of food, but the dizziness I feel is not from the lingering effects of the alcohol. I conclude maybe it's been enough time for me to sober up.

Maybe they pumped my stomach.

I feel like I woke up in another dimension, just not the dimension of death I had resigned myself to alongside Katie. *I failed.* Nothing is clear, and no one is considerate enough to fill in the puzzle pieces until Cheryl wails into my bedside, "Alice is dead!"

Alice is dead, what? Aren't I Alice? Why are they telling me I am dead? Am I dead?

No one has acknowledged me in the room yet, so I consider the possibility that I could be a ghost, that is until Cheryl brushes the top of my shoulder and I realize she is stroking my tiny lily tattoo. Perhaps they're unaware that Katie and I have (had) the same permanent marking.

My eyes swell with tears and I'm unable to omit any sound.

Oh Katie. Katie is dead.

I hear the words rumble around in my head. They bounce around, contributing to the splitting headache throbbing my temples, but I am very careful not to say anything out loud.

This is all my fault. Why didn't I die?

I am about to try to ask some questions when Matthew enters.

His stature seems smaller, as he is hunched over. His eyes are shining crimson from crying. If he bled tears I wouldn't be surprised.

He notices my confused expression, as if disoriented. He plants a soft and timid kiss against my dry lips. My mind is spinning.

He must have kissed me because he thinks I am Katie? He kissed me though; he must have sensed a difference.

When he pulls away, I can see his mouth curled, holding back beckoning sobs. He must now know it's me and not Katie, otherwise relief would be the overwhelming emotion coming through. No one seems to notice as a nurse slinks in to inform us the other daughter can be seen now.

Not sure who made the original mistake, but everyone thinks that I am Katie. Todd and Cheryl leave the room with merely a quick glance back to Matt and me. It is time for them to say goodbye to their daughter who didn't survive.

"You know it's me. . . right?" I feel bad for asking him. I look at Matt who is barely holding it together.

"I am so sorry Alice. I didn't mean to kiss you, I'm sorry, I am so sorry." His voice is several octaves higher than his normal eighteen-year-old baritone, and I wonder if he is apologizing to me or apologizing to Katie because he cannot seem to look me directly in the eyes.

"It's alright," I whisper. "Do you know what happened?"

"You don't remember?" he asks concerned, and like we only have a matter of minutes alone to discuss it all. I do remember. I remember it all, but I want to siphon out what he knows.

"I remember drowning alongside her."

"You did, but the paramedics revived you before you got in the ambulance." Matt seems perplexed, like I should know this.

I don't recall anyone or anything after the water hit my airway.

"I have a favor to ask."

I have always loved how Matt looks like he would deliver the world to someone he cares for. Katie was on the receiving end of this look, the most out of anybody. "Quickly, before they all come back, everyone assumes I am Katie, and I would like to keep it that way for now. So, if anyone asks you who I am I want you to respond that I am indeed Katie."

I am saying it like I can't comprehend the concept, but I spell it out for both of us like we are children in preschool.

At this point, I can hardly even get the words out because we are both weeping. Matt sniffles and tries to shake it off, but I just crumple. He doesn't seem to like showing so much emotion, but I cannot keep myself together even a little bit.

I was sitting up and now I am cradling my knees trying not to fall off the bed. My sister, my twin, my best friend, is dead. I can't let it be that Katie died. This can't be true. Everything will be easier if I let Alice die and assume Katie's life. I will adopt all her secrets and bury mine in the grave with her.

We had switched places once before and hated it, but this is the only way I feel I can move forward. At least for now. Being Katie makes me feel like I have regained a small measure of control.

Matt is holding me tight with his head nestled on my shoulder where my still new and still sore tattoo is. There is a reason it's not advised to go swimming right after you get a tattoo. My shoulder is hot with the beginnings of an infection, and sore from the needle piercing my skin only a short time ago.

Matt and I have always been friends. He is like the brother I never had, so this sort of affection, his comfort, is more desirable than any comfort I could receive from Todd and Cheryl.

"There is something else." Matt says as he pulls away from me just enough to hand me a letter written clearly in Katie's handwriting.

"She wrote me a letter," he says. "I figure you should read it too. Don't tell a soul this exists, alright? I want to keep some part of Katie's and my relationship sacred."

I can tell he is hesitant to share with me, but I am grateful for his generosity. I'm curious what Katie's final thoughts to her soulmate were.

"Why would you share it with me then and not keep this all to yourself?"

"I figure she would have shared it with you anyway. Plus, some of it doesn't make sense to me, and maybe you can clue me in."

I don't immediately open the letter and neither of us releases from an embrace for quite a few silent minutes.

"I guess I have a new girlfriend now." Matt's comment is mildly inappropriate, but we both laugh even though it makes me feel sick to find anything humorous right now.

The laughing passes as quickly as it came, and Matt's head hangs low again.

"I am glad you didn't die." His voice is so sincere.

That makes one of us.

Matt takes a deep breath and places his head back in my hair, his cheek to my temple. I wonder if he is trying to breathe in a little bit of Katie, and I hate to disappoint him knowing that we don't smell the same. I've always smelled of flowers, whereas Katie always smelled of sweets, like vanilla or cotton candy.

It is the third intimate moment we have shared in the last few minutes, and I feel oddly comfortable with him so close to me. Even his kiss felt familiar, like a close friend more than anything.

It wasn't romantic. The only thing that is making me feel uneasy about him right now is how comfortable I feel in his arms.

The moment doesn't last long when Todd and Cheryl return and have a look on their faces of fury, and a bit of embarrassment. They must have seen the tattoo on Katie and are now questioning who is who. We aren't their biological children, which is the only excuse I give them for rarely being able to tell us apart.

When Katie returned from her half a year long trip to Europe with a tattoo, most parents would have been horrified. Todd and Cheryl, on the other hand, were relieved to have some sort of obvious distinguisher between us, finally.

They don't outright ask me if I am Katie though, the embrace that Matt is giving me as well as the kiss from earlier provides confirmation enough that I am indeed Katie. He doesn't even need to say anything.

He isn't actually having to lie for me. . . yet.

Matt moves his letter under the hospital blanket and looks me in the eyes, which spells out everything we had just talked about without saying a word.

"They want to keep you overnight for observation. You took in a lot of water, and mentally they want to make sure you aren't a potential harm to yourself." Cheryl huffs between sobs. That is the first time anyone has mentioned the possibility of this whole thing not being an accident.

Todd has said nothing this entire time. The rumors that will inevitably circulate after an event like this will embarrass him, but I am sure he only cares about his reputation when in public. He holds Cheryl up as she buries herself into him. But there is no affection in his embrace. He almost looks bored.

I have always disliked being around Todd, but Cheryl has been tolerable. She mostly hides out in her bedroom and isn't around much to interact with. Neither one of them is around much.

They didn't have any kids of their own, and it makes me wonder if the *dad gene* just wasn't part of Todd's DNA. Cheryl isn't the most maternal, either. That is partly why we call them Todd and Cheryl. "Mom and Dad" just never felt normal to any of us.

"We are going to go now," Todd utters, "and we will be back tomorrow." A seemingly harmless phrase, but when uttered by Todd feels more like a threat than a neutral statement. Like it will derail his life to come back to visit his daughter in the hospital and he wants me to know just how much of an inconvenience it is. Matt also removes himself from my side and begins to follow as my adoptive parents leave.

"I'll be back too, um, tomorrow," Matt touches my hand as he slides away from me. It feels tingly as he glides his fingertips so lovingly on the surface of my skin.

I'm sure the warmth I feel around Matt is because I've never experienced these sensations, and not because I am in any way encouraging it. I know he is trying not to give away the fact that I am not the girlfriend he has been with for the last two years, and the longer he is here, the more likely he is to show his true emotions of grief and anguish.

A nurse enters and starts fiddling with my IV.

"May I go see my sister? Can I go see Kat . . . umm, Alice?" *Gosh I've already almost flubbed that. This is going to be hard.*

Between getting drunk and almost dying I surely missed a few details. *Details . . . that's right. And what is in this letter that was confusing to Matt? Why does he think I will have the answers?*

I feel for Matt's letter under the sheets. I don't want the nurse telling Todd and Cheryl that I have it. Not that she would, but Matt made it clear that I need to be very cautious in not letting anyone know that we have it.

The nurse is kind, and her hands are warm as she helps me go see my sister. I recognize, though, that it isn't the same warmth that Matt's hands had when they touched me. His touch was electric while hers is healing.

"You may want a minute to prepare yourself."

The nurse seems kind, but I don't think any amount of time can prepare you for seeing your twin sister dead and cold. It's like looking into the future of what death will look like for you. I walk in slowly for good measure, but when I see her I can't bear to look. My stomach turns. I might throw up, and I rush back in the hall where the nurse catches me just in time before I collapse.

Alice is dead.

❀ ❀ ❀

I wake up again back in my hospital room and the world is silent. I've never felt more awake in my life. I'm aware of everything now. The reality of it all is sinking in so deeply that I can hardly breathe through the pain of it all.

I am alone once again, and I roll over Katie's letter creating a subtle crunching. I tear into it without hesitation and digest every word.

CHAPTER 9

Katie

{ 2012 }

Hey Matty,

I know this is completely morbid and super lame and all very "P.S. I Love You," but I don't know how to express how sorry I am that I couldn't be more upfront with you in life. I am not as strong as you are no matter how many times you think otherwise.

First of all, I love you so much. Between the love I have for you and the love I have for Alice, I almost didn't go through with it, but hopefully one day you will see it had to be done.

I also want to thank you. You were one of the only bright spots in my life, and you made those moments worth living. I will love you until I take my last breath but know for certain I am at peace now. There is a great beyond. I am sure of it (you should be sure too) and I hope that one day you can see why I so desperately needed peace and just couldn't obtain it in this realm of reality.

Please don't let this ruin your life. Be vibrant and do

things, and don't dwell on the past. I was never good at being upfront in person. I am much better at spilling my secrets in writing. It's much easier and I can get all the details right.

Don't fixate on me forever. Let our love fuel your next. Find someone who makes you happy. Find a girl who reminds you of us. Make sure she takes care of you. I would have ruined your life. I just couldn't be that selfish.

Okay, so let's get to it.

I wanted to run! Run away with you and Alice, and I mean I wanted to run far, far away. I wanted to pack up my stuff and leave everything behind. I just wanted to get lost. To tell no one where I was going and start over.

Believe me, there was nothing but pain for me if I stayed. I soon realized that even in running away I would never be free. I could never escape the demons that haunted me. They followed me endlessly and lingered in my room. I could never find rest.

My only relief was when I was around you. I don't know where you are when you are reading this, but I am sorry I couldn't be good enough for you. Seventeen is far too young to venture out on your own, but I have already experienced things most adults haven't. I knew death was the only escape.

Thank you for loving me even when I wasn't worthy. I never meant to push you away. I just couldn't be loved anymore. Not even by you. You deserve so much better. I have my reasons and I have my secrets I know won't die with me. I beg you to keep loving others as well as you do.

I wish I could leave you with some sort of hope for anything really. My only hope to give is to remind you that you have a great big future ahead of you. I was not the biggest part of that future. I want you to fulfill all your goals and most of all I want you to move on from me. Don't think of me when you are older and married with beautiful babies.

There is a part of us that will live on even when I am gone, I know. However, don't cherish it like a tale of some tragic romance. Move on. I can carry the love you had for me, as well as my love for you, wherever I end up after this life is over.

There were many moments when I was in Europe that made me stop and think of you. I missed you every single day. I remember looking out at the view while I was on the train as it zipped by me in a flash.

That is all I should be to you. I was simply a view that passed by you in the blink of an eye. You were my entire life, but I am only going to be a chapter in yours.

Some lives are short, Matt, and some drag on and on. It was just my time and I claimed it.

Speak to as few people as possible about me. I don't want my suicide to be a topic of conversation that follows you. I just want you to know that I am so proud of you. There is nothing you can't do. I am watching you from heaven. Who knows, maybe I can be your guardian angel. I love you. I am always with you. Leave our love in the past though. That is where it belongs. I give you permission to forget me.

Love, Katie

CHAPTER 10

Alice
{ 2012 }

My breath feels shallow as I finish the words my sister so beautifully placed on paper. I know why Matt didn't want this note to get into anyone else's hands. Not only is it a beautiful tribute to their love, but it's also evidence that what happened at the McCoy's was not entirely an accident.

Death didn't claim me the way it claimed Katie. It should have, but it didn't. Running wouldn't have done Katie any good. I always just assumed we would live out our childhood days with Todd and Cheryl, and the minute we could, we would get a place of our own.

Guess she felt she couldn't stick around another year for us to make that happen. I understand better than anyone how our secrets can end us.

Not sure running away would have done us any good. Katie's secrets became mine the minute she decided her life should end.

My eyelids burn from exhaustion and the tears that still

preside on my face. I don't even know what time it is, but staff personnel on the floor feel few and far between, so I am assuming the hour is late.

I want so desperately to re-read Katie's words and to feel her presence, but I don't want to risk falling asleep with the letter in hand. Matt wanted to keep her thoughts private and I cannot betray him. I would like this whole thing to seem like an accident. It's yet another secret to add to my pile.

I neatly slide her words safely under my pillow. I close my eyes and pretend this nightmare I am living is something I can wake up from. Before I dream, I remember a line in her letter, "*I have my secrets I know won't die with me.*"

I knew a lot about Katie's life and the tragedies she carried, but that line makes me wonder.

Did I know all of Katie's secrets, and which ones did she fear might be exposed?

CHAPTER 11

Alice
{ 2012 }

I WAS DISCHARGED the next morning, and aside from sore lungs and the panic episode I had seeing my dead sister's body, I was declared in overall good health. I learned that EMTs did indeed pump my stomach, so I am also kind of nauseated from that and still don't feel like eating. It feels like the alcohol burned my insides, leaving me emotionally and physically raw.

I keep thinking I am going to wake up from this nightmare, but with each passing moment it becomes more and more evident that this is my new reality.

Cheryl picks me up, and to my surprise Matt is with her. I thought he might leave all of this behind him and move on, which is exactly what Katie asked him to do in her letter.

Cheryl looks more put together than she has in years. Her mousey hair is pulled into a tight bun, and she isn't wearing sweatpants for the first time in months. Maybe she finally washed the crust off of them. Instead, she breezes into the room wearing linen pants and a beachy knit sweater. She still looks like she could nap comfortably without changing her outfit, but it is an elevated comfort that makes her look really put together and tidy.

I find it odd that the death of her daughter has elicited such an uplifting response from her. Most people would use it as an excuse to be lazy and unkempt. Todd probably coaxed her so they could maintain a certain status in the community.

Regardless, I find her mourning strange, and must remind myself that she still thinks that Alice died, and that I'm Katie.

It's an interesting world perspective when you can watch those who are closest to you in life mourn your death in front of your very eyes. James M. Barry wrote, "to die will be an awfully big adventure." I am one of the few who is permitted to watch that phenomenon play out while still breathing.

Matt, tagging along for my discharge, also perplexes me. I know I asked him to keep the lie going, but I didn't think he would want to be around as much as he has been. He hesitated when he said he would come back. I assumed he was just being kind. All I want is to be alone.

"How are you feeling?" Cheryl asks while whizzing around the room, opening curtains and gathering my belongings. "I brought you some clothes from home."

Thank goodness I don't have to put back on that bikini. The light pouring in is blinding. I am trying not to be offended by her attentiveness because I haven't seen Cheryl this alert in years. Her "migraines" have made her a lazy hermit.

Why didn't all this initiate one of her debilitating headaches?

That is an excuse I would buy at least. I think she can tell I am a little taken aback because she comes over and sits on the bed and hugs me. It's awkward and our torsos remain far apart.

I can feel the crinkle in the hospital gown as she holds me. The pile of Katie's clothes sits on the edge of the bed, and I am grateful to her for bringing them. I didn't want to leave here in my damp swimsuit. Another reminder that this is my new reality and not just some influence induced nightmare.

"We are going to be okay," she says, sounding more like she is convincing herself than comforting me.

Hugging her feels warm though, and I don't want to let go. I can't remember the last time I was hugged by my mom. Cheryl hasn't been the most involved parent, especially throughout the early teen years.

"I've already signed all the discharge papers and we can head home any time now."

Right then I hear a knock on the door of my room and a middle-aged gentleman in a blue police uniform leans on the doorframe with casual authority.

"Sorry to interrupt," he says in a voice that sounds like bacon sizzling on a stovetop pan. "I am Officer Cobalt. I'd like to take a few minutes and ask you a few questions regarding the incidents of last night."

His gaze is fixed on me.

Before waiting for my response, he enters the room and reads off a few questions from what looks like an official report.

"Do you know what happened?"

"In your own words, what were the events of last night?"

"Did Alice have a known drinking problem?"

"Was she a troubled youth?"

"Was she suicidal to your knowledge?"

"Did your sister ever consume illegal substances?"

"Do you know if anyone would have any motive behind wanting to harm you or your sister?" *This one is doozy.*

I don't answer a single one. I feel like an absolute idiot for stuttering and sitting there with my mouth agape. Cheryl asks if we need a lawyer present and that her husband is an attorney and is just outside if we need some legal representation.

She lies. He isn't just outside. Todd is in his office downtown. She knows how this game is played and is relaxed and direct toward the officer.

"Never let your fear make you look guilty," she would always say.

He assures us that this is just standard procedure in a case like this.

"The inquiry is necessary based on the events involving minors. Mostly, we want to rule out a homicide. My team and I will be doing some follow up interrogations, but for now there is no reason to be alarmed. Right now, all the evidence we have points toward an accident."

I keep my mouth shut.

I am kind of surprised they aren't expecting suicide, but because I almost drowned alongside my sister and was heavily intoxicated, suicide doesn't seem as likely.

I am more nauseous now than five minutes ago. The feeling of guilt is creeping up inside of my chest. It feels like a heavy wet blanket was just placed over me and I am starting to suffocate. I remember the nurse educating me that my symptoms were a clear indication of a panic attack. It is all very new to me, but at least it has a name.

The officer can tell that I am starting to hyperventilate, and that it's all becoming too much too quickly. He quietly excuses himself with a nod. I'm relieved when he's gone and hope I never see him again. There is too much he could uncover that has nothing to do with what happened in the McCoy family's stupidly large pool.

Matt, who has been standing in a corner, is now immediately at my side, rubbing my back in a circular motion coupled with a low calming shushing sound. His lull is like a flow of water, incredibly comforting to be around.

Matt is hurting too, yet he is more concerned with my emotional wellbeing. I am impressed by his dedication to Katie. I've been around him enough to know that he does for others more than he does for himself.

"Take a deep breath." His words are thick in my ear, and being this close to him is making me forget why I was panicking in the first place. I become more fixated about acting appropriately around him because drinking in his softness has me whirling.

I could always play into it all and just say that I was trying to sell my lie, that I am the true Katie and as such act like his girlfriend, but that just feels wrong. I listen to his voice roll over me, making my chest rise and fall dramatically as I inhale and exhale so deeply. I can feel his hand pressing into me while I breathe in and his touch soften as I breathe out.

When I am finally calm, I dress into Katie's clothes. Matt kisses my temple, helps me into a wheelchair I must ride in to be properly discharged.

I am such an impostor.

These stupid wheels on the wheelchair squeak as I am being pushed to the hospital's front entrance. Matt has taken over seeing me out and Cheryl is walking behind us. Matt leans over and quietly asks, "Do you know what you are doing?"

"No, absolutely not." I whisper back. "I started to fall asleep before I read the letter. So, I hid it."

The lies just keep stacking up. I don't like to lie to Matt. He deserves better.

We are both acting suspicious, but Cheryl is none the wiser. Why would she be?

I am not sure how I am going to pull off being Katie for longer than a few days like we had done in the past for fun. It was always humorous to see how long it would take for people to tell us apart. Despite our hijinks, we never swapped boyfriends or dates or anything intimate, and now I am supposed to be all cuddly and in love with Matt, who I have viewed as more of a brother and good boyfriend to my sister. I am going to slip up. I just know it.

Matt can sense my breathing start to labor again and places his hand on my shoulder.

Is he forever going to be my safety every time I start to panic? He may need to be around a lot more than I want if that's the case.

Cheryl twitches around us cautiously, like I might break, and sets off to get the car.

"I think I am going to ask to sleep over for a couple of nights. That is until you have a plan on how you want to move forward," Matt says when Cheryl is out of earshot. "That way, you aren't overwhelmed, you know. Staying in Katie's room is going to be hard, and I can help you take an inventory of her stuff, make a plan, etc."

Matt is my only confidant right now. Katie shared a lot of our secrets with him. I don't know how many, and I should probably keep him close to find out what all he knows. If Katie is right that some of her secrets won't die with her, I now must ensure they at least remain dormant forever.

"I don't even know where my car is. We took it to the party and obviously didn't drive it home."

"I know the answer to that." Matt doesn't sound too confident. The pink in his skin pales just a bit. Maybe he's the one now having a panic attack, which doesn't make me think he has good news about the car.

"Todd went to get the car at the McCoy's and the police are doing a search of it for their investigation. I don't know when they are conducting their search."

He poses that last thought like it was a question. Like it isn't imminent. All of Katie's things and mine are about to be rifled through. I feel like I am going to be sick when Cheryl pulls up to the curb and they both help me into the car.

I buckle into the front seat and blast the air conditioning on my face in hopes that it stifles the nausea. This California heat wave is intense, and my gnawing stomach pains are making the world feel swirly. I don't want to talk to Cheryl, who is driving for the first time in months. I want her to pay attention to the road. I am not convinced she even remembers how to drive.

Maybe I'll die in a car crash.

The intrusive thoughts are vicious but comforting. *I can still die and join Katie.* I am waiting for one of her super headaches to kick in and for her to become the Cheryl I know, the person I don't expect anything from.

I can just picture her pulling over and asking Matt or even me to drive instead, but she doesn't. Her face looks a little fallen now, which gives me some peace of mind that she is a little sorrowful in my death. We may have been adopted, but Todd and Cheryl have been our parental figures since Katie and I were eighteen months old. They are all we have ever known.

I don't believe you have to give birth to your children in order to love them as if you had. Todd and Cheryl, however, didn't express that sort of parental love for us.

It's not like they *never* cared. Cheryl left her career as a nurse to stay at home with us. She changed us, fed us, and took care of us daily. It wasn't until about a few years ago that she seemed to stop caring. Maybe because we were reaching our older teen years and didn't need as much from her, but something else seemed to change. She didn't ever consider or entertain the idea of going back to the career she loved. I think that pissed off Todd a bit, even though his income as an attorney provides us a comfortable living. I'm guessing that he took her unwillingness to work as an admission of laziness.

"Mrs. Clemonte? "Matt breaks the silence. He has always been so respectful with the "Mr. and Mrs.," a byproduct of growing up with a dad in the military.

"May I stay over a few nights? Just to help Katie acclimate." He is so polite. Matt doesn't even stutter when he calls me Katie.

I can trust you.

All Cheryl says is, "hmmm." I like how she pretends to think about it, when Matt has spent the night on several occasions before and even slept in Katie's bed. It's comical to watch her try so hard to be a good mother.

Cheryl must want to put more boundaries in place since one of her daughters drowned drunk at a party full of high school students. I imagine she feels like a failed mother for that one. The last thing she needs is her surviving daughter to get pregnant or to be the subject of gossip. If so, that would feel really disingenuous.

"Sure, that's fine Matt, but make sure your mother knows

and is also okay with it."

I am excited. Why am I excited?

Because Matt is the only other person on earth who understands parts of what really happened and who I really am. It's not a complete lie. He is my only ally and nothing more. I am grieving and that is why my emotions seem to be heightened and exaggerated.

Matt is texting in the backseat, and I can't take the silence anymore or I might burst into tears in the car where I can't run and hide or leave.

I'm trapped in between someone who comforts me and someone who makes me anxious.

The instability is torture. I don't want to cry in front of Cheryl. This new version of her bothers me, and I don't know how she would interpret my tears or how she would attempt to comfort me while she is driving. I liked the hug in the hospital, but I'm not sure how well I would respond to any more touching in such a short period of time.

※ ※ ※

We are finally pulling into the driveway after what feels like a three-hour drive and Matt jumps out of the backseat to help me out. I am moving a little quicker than I should. I feel dizzy when I stand, and Matt has to brace me briefly. The black almost takes me, but I soon recover from the intensity of my low blood sugar headrush. Ringing still thrums in my ears.

I wonder if he works out other than playing on the soccer team. His legs feel strong, which is obvious for what he does, but so do his arms, and I am impressed he can hold me so effortlessly.

Katie and I have always been slender creatures, but there is something about how he holds me that makes me feel like if he let me go I would simply float away. Maybe that can be my means of escaping it all. I will simply float to the other end of the earth.

When my head feels steady again, I start for the Prius, which is now quietly parked in the driveway. I am hoping it's open, but Todd never leaves anything unlocked. I want to grab as much as I can before anyone else can rifle through my stuff.

"I am going to go inside and make us all lunch," Cheryl shouts from the front of the house.

"Okay, sounds fine," I lie.

Cheryl usually doesn't cook. Katie would do the cooking, and for lunch I would usually just throw together a sandwich, or microwave a cheese quesadilla for myself. Fingers crossed that whatever Cheryl concocts is edible.

I am definitely still not hungry and probably won't be until I get my stuff together, but I know something to eat would make my head and stomach settle just a little bit. I have to find one thing in particular.

Sure enough, the car is locked, but Matt is one step ahead of me and has already run inside for the keys. It's like he can read my mind. It's cute but also unnerving. Life was so simple just twenty-four hours ago. Not great, just simpler.

I hear the click of the door unlock before Matt gets to me and I throw the door open and slide in. I am being far too anxious not to arouse suspicion, but I know Matt is there and would cause some sort of distraction if someone were to intrude.

There isn't much in the car aside from some Chapstick and several of our favorite CDs we burned over the last few years.

I know it is in here somewhere. . .

I start tearing apart the compartments and moving seats.

"Did you find all you need?" Matt is once again over my shoulder, hovering over me as I am leaning into the passenger seat. I can feel the heat of him radiate onto the skin of my back.

"I am looking for my toiletry bag."

I am pretty sure I left it in the glove box, but it's stuck on something, and it won't budge.

"Can you help me pry this open?"

I am still fatigued from the hospital. Another reason is why I should probably eat something.

Matt pulls the glove box open, and a pile of letters falls out. They are all bundled together and wrapped with one of Katie's favorite hair ties.

If the handwriting wasn't a dead giveaway, the hair tie absolutely shows who the author of these letters is. Behind the letters is my toiletry bag. which I quickly hide under my arm while my eyes stay fixated on the letters.

"What are these?" I ask Matt like he is supposed to clue me in somehow. All they say on the outside is *Dear Alice*.

CHAPTER 12

Katie
{ 2012 }

Dear Alice,

Remember when we were little, like maybe four or five, and we kept sneaking candy from the Christmas dish in the living room and we would hurriedly sneak back to our room to eat it? It was when we were living in that smaller home before Todd got his big promotion and then decided to show off his wealth. It was a better time. We thought we were so clever and couldn't get caught. That was until we were asked to show our tongues at dinner, and they were bright red. We were caught red-handed, or rather red-tongued. I'm sure Cheryl caught on sooner because the bowl on the kitchen counter was almost empty by the time we were finished, and she had just restocked the candy for the annual Christmas party that weekend.

I don't think I had ever laughed so hard with you in our entire lives. We walked around shouting "RED TONGUES," over and over again until I think even Todd laughed at our mischievous behavior.

Do you remember how sweet they were? The candy that is. I am pretty sure it was made from solid calcified sugar and nothing else except maybe corn syrup to boot. Who invented such a delicious poison? And how come as kids we could eat so much sugar and rarely break the barrier to feeling sick, but the older we got the less we could consume without some massive repercussions like a stomachache? I can't even look at that much sugar without instantly getting a headache.

We were partners in crime. You and I. Always. I can't remember whose idea it was to sneak the candy and so much of it. I know I always led you into trouble, so it was probably me, but that was one of the happiest times I can think back on in our lives. Christmas was always a good time at home. It was cozy and warm, and Todd and Cheryl seemed to enjoy their lives a little more during Christmas. The music was always so melodic, and the white lights seemed to twinkle in a sort of reflective dew on the tree. I know adults have their struggles, but that time of year seemed magical for all of us.

I wanted to remind you of a happy time seeing as how you probably are not so happy right now and I hate that. You're going through a really hard time right now and I wish there was something I could do to make it better for you. We have always been there for one another, but I feel utterly useless to you right now. I only ever want to see you smile.

Why didn't we smile more? It seems like since the beginning, you and I felt like we had to carry the world on our shoulders. I know why I didn't smile, but now the burden is all on you and I know that it is heavy.

I told Matt to keep an eye on you while I am away. I love him so much, Alice, but I can't love him the way he needs to be loved. I am broken beyond repair that not even his love for me can fix it. In fact, it's just making things worse. I can't pull away from him, but I also can't give him what he needs. It feels so cruel to trap him in this way.

He should find a girl who can hold him and kiss him and tell him just how amazing he is. My selfishness is begging him to cling on to me for as long as possible, but I know in my soul that I want more for him. Is it possible to love a ghost? I feel like that is what I have become. I hope that made you laugh. Even in some twisted way. I always loved it when you laughed.

I need to tell you something though, hence the purpose of all of these silly letters. I write letters to you knowing you will probably never read them, but it makes me feel better to share my thoughts with someone I love. Even if it's all in my head.

Something happened. Something has been happening, Alice, and I didn't share it with you. I was afraid to tell you for real. I couldn't tell anyone. If I can't tell you then you must know I can't open up to anyone. I just wanted to make that abundantly clear. You are my person, and I can't decide if writing it all down to get every detail right is the best way to go or if I should just keep it all inside to myself, but either way I feel blocked. I have communication constipation. (Again, I hope that elicited a chuckle.) I feel like I can express it all much more eloquently on *paper. Even now though I am struggling to find the words and not just write down all the happy memories I have of the two of us. Maybe if I could document all the good in words, then maybe all our sins would be forgotten.*

Just know this isn't easy for me. I wanted to tell you in person, I really did. I just couldn't, but to start I didn't go to Europe for culinary academy. I didn't even choose to go to Europe. I was sent away, but that was embarrassing so I made it seem like I did, but there was another reason I was there.

Cheryl has some extended family in Italy (I don't know if you knew that) and I went and stayed with them for most of my journey. It's Cheryl's much younger half-sister and her husband. They are both in their early thirties, so they were kind of fun to be around, not old and stuffy. It wasn't rigid at all, which I liked a lot. I did some cooking while I was there and learned a lot. It just wasn't at a culinary institute.

The pictures and postcards I sent you were real. I never actually lied to you; I just didn't tell you everything. I guess that's called a lie by omission, but I am just trying to make myself feel better. I can't justify any of it. I hate not sharing everything. We share a face for crying out loud, shouldn't the rest just follow. Being a unit has been so easy until now.

I am so sorry I lied to you. I have never lied to you before about anything else I swear. At least not anything like this that changed my whole being. I never needed to withhold anything from you. You are always in tune with my thoughts and feelings. Call it a twin thing, but really, I just think it's because you are my very best friend. That will never change.

I thought you would pick up on my lying to you when I was gone, but I guess it's hard to sense that kind of stuff on a postcard. Plus, I think you were kind of jealous that I was supposedly having this amazing adventure of a lifetime and I left you behind. You must hate me for leaving you behind. Not to rub it in, but it was an adventure and if I could move to Italy tomorrow, I would leave everything behind to stay there.

Were you jealous? I was always pretty good at making things look better on the outside than they actually were for me on the inside.

I wore a mask. It was so hard to look in the mirror and see your face and know that I couldn't just wake up and be you. It was hard to look at you sometimes and see what it would be like to be a different version of me. What it would be like to be the better version of me . . . you. Don't try to argue with me.

You are amazing in all that you are. Remember that. I thought I could tell you; I thought I could write it down all at once. Maybe I will work up the nerve in the next few letters to actually share these with you. Maybe not.

I shared a critical part already. I lied. We can call this part one. Part one being I did not tell you the truth. Phew, that feels good to finally admit. Maybe admitting the rest will feel just as relieving even if you never actually know. My secret, private journal that I write to you, but never plan on actually showing you. I feel insane.

Will there ever be an escape for us? I know you are stronger than I am by far and you can find a way one day.

Wouldn't it just be easier if no traces of us were left behind? I think that ship has sailed. I love you Alice.

Love,
Katie.

CHAPTER 13

Alice
{ 2012 }

STARING UP at the ceiling in Katie's room is majorly freaking me out. Panic washes over me like the waters that almost drowned me, and I can hardly breathe. Cheryl made Matt sleep on the couch downstairs, and I am really hoping he comes in here to check on me. He makes me feel at ease, and right now I feel deep in between worlds. I want him to tell me what to do; I want him to help me.

I know I can't maintain this facade for too long and that I need an escape plan. Without Katie I need to get the hell out of here.

I am hoping that Matt lets me read the letter Katie wrote to him once more. I would love it if he offered it so I don't have to ask, but that doesn't seem very likely. He's hidden it like it's his most prized possession. Courage is something that will have to grow on me, but I feel like there are details I am missing and maybe comparing his letter to the ones I found in the car will help fill in some blanks. For both of us.

I didn't know Katie wrote letters. She mentioned in them that she wrote them to me in order to have a person to write to, but she never gave them to me. This is all just another contributor to my current insomnia. Weighted by grief and confusion, I don't think I'll ever be able to dream again.

Todd and Cheryl aren't particularly chatty about uncomfortable things or situations that reflect poorly on them. They have already made it clear that we are done talking about what happened and should never mention it again.

I have all the evidence of Katie's suicide safely tucked away. I anticipate a call from the investigator confirming it was an accident any day now. That lie will finally be put to rest.

I am wide awake and filled with anxiety, so I decide to start on the next letter from Katie in the pile of many to see what rabbit hole she sends me down this time. I may be going by Katie now, but I have never felt more like an Alice. Everything and everyone is mad here, but this is definitely not a Wonderland.

CHAPTER 14

Katie
{ 2012 }

Dear Alice,

 I promise I won't ramble on for pages and say nothing this time. I miss our conversations and deep talks. You already know that I have a secret and I will get it out eventually. However, the secret I am going to share with you right now isn't about me. Do you know why Cheryl and Todd adopted us instead of ever conceiving their own children?

 Cheryl always told us the farce that a fairy came down and showed us to Cheryl and we were gifted to her from said magical pixie. She said she loved us so much she never felt the need to have any children of her own (turns out that was the hard part to believe. Even more so than the fairy part). She was given fairy children and was perfectly happy with just the two of us.

 Now you and I both knew that that story was a bunch of crap for many reasons. We figured out really early in life that there is no such thing as magic. Way too soon for most children to stop believing in that kind of fantasy.

Nevertheless, the truth is our biological mother was fourteen when she had us and was in no place to raise a baby, let alone twins. Having been fourteen ourselves, I can't imagine having a baby. Can you? We never really talked about how much that would have sucked for her. I wonder if she ever believed in magic and at what age she stopped.

We did meet her a couple times. Do you remember her at all? All I remember about her is she looked really small and young and had the crazy blonde curly hair just like we do. I don't remember her eye color or how long her fingers were or if she had a dimple. Nothing truly stands out about her other than her hair was just like ours.

She stopped visiting when we were around seven. Cheryl never explained why, and I don't think you and I were invested in pursuing that relationship enough to ask. We were too young. It just ended.

I got curious and I looked her up on Facebook about a year ago. She is married now and has more kids. We technically have half siblings. That was a weird fact to stumble across. She never mentioned to us who our biological dad is. I get the feeling he was more of a detour in her life. He was probably someone she longed to forget.

Not knowing them personally never really bothered me. I had you in my life. You were always by my side. I never felt I needed anyone else.

Anyway, back to why we were adopted. Now you can't tell anyone because no one is supposed to know. You won't ever actually read this anyway, but for the purpose of this *letter, let us pretend.*

Cheryl confided in me that before she was married to Todd she was dating this professor from her college. He was about ten years older than she was and it was against school policy to have intimate relationships with students. She said it was kind of like Ross Geller from "Friends," when he dates Bruce Willis's daughter. Strictly forbidden, which only made it that much more tempting.

Most institutions have that rule in place for a reason, but they were both secretive and I guess madly in love. Not too long into the relationship though, she found out she was pregnant. I guess he dropped her like a hot potato and demanded she get an abortion.

Cheryl wept when she told me how much she wanted to keep the baby, but she wanted to keep her relationship with the professor more, so she went through with the abortion in hopes that things would go back to the way they were.

I guess there was a complication during the procedure, and she got really sick afterwards. She had to have a hysterectomy and Cheryl was never able to conceive again.

On top of it all, the dirtbag professor wouldn't take her back after that. Said she was damaged now, and he had already found another young freshman to sink into and manipulate. She lost her baby, her ability to have future babies, and the supposed, "love of her life," as she called him.

I knew Todd and Cheryl weren't openly affectionate, but I figured that was a lack of public affection and behind closed doors they were closer. I didn't know Cheryl had a greater love once before and I didn't know she couldn't have children until she shared all this with me.

My heart broke for her, Alice. I've never felt empathy toward her like this before. I almost pitied her. She was so minuscule when she sat next to me and divulged her soul. It made me feel closer to her briefly. She told me all this in confidence and I was very grateful to her for the first time since we were basically babies.

So yeah, a fairy might not have given us to Cheryl, but she did choose us, and I feel that means something.

I wish our childhood was filled with more understanding moments of closeness like that one and I hope one day you and Cheryl can connect on a level that is more mother and daughter than the coldness we have all felt for so long. It was a moment of warmth. Brief though it was.

I feel underneath a lot of hurt there is a woman who wants to be a good mom.

Anyway, that is enough shared secrets for one letter. As always, I love you and I am watching over you.

Your sister,

Katie.

CHAPTER 15

Alice
{ 2012 }

I HAD NO IDEA that Cheryl harbored such a tragic secret. I never really considered her life outside of being the woman who adopted us. I never thought to ask why, because I never assumed there was a specific reason. It seemed unimportant, but if Katie felt the need to write and share such a sordid secret on paper, maybe she was hoping one day I would actually read these letters.

And why did Cheryl feel so secure confiding in Katie and not me?

I hear Cheryl cry at night sometimes. Tonight she has gone into my old room to rifle through things and weep. I know she grieves for me—or rather Alice.

Does grieving equate love though, and how much more would she be hurting if she knew that Katie was actually the one who died?

All this is giving me a headache, and I find myself fitfully beginning to doze off when Matt sneaks into the room after two very gentle knocks.

"Hey" he whispers, "are you awake?"

"Uh huh."

"May I come in?"

"Sure." I don't have any confidence backing my voice up, so it comes out more of a tiny squeak than a whisper. I am immediately flushed with embarrassment, but it's dark so at least Matt can't see me.

"I just wanted to check on you. How are you?"

He has been in this room—Katie's room— so many times, but never alone with me. The realization is weird. There is no other word to describe it . . . just weird.

He sits on the bed noticing I have opened one of the letters we found in the car.

"Did you read that?"

"I just finished. I can only handle so much at once."

"Yeah, I know what you mean. I have read my letter from her about a hundred times now hoping that I read something different, or I can hear her voice in my head as I read it, but I never do. I wish it wasn't so cryptic. Why couldn't she have just been more upfront? All that letter contains is the deep dark depressing thoughts that I wish never existed in her mind in the first place."

He looks really sad. I mean, what else would be expected from him? Matt is loyal and kind and was head-over-heels in love with my sister. I think he is handling everything pretty well considering it all. Shock can make a person appear confused.

"Will you ever let me read your letter again?" I ask. He looks taken aback, but not angry. I have never actually seen Matt angry.

"I . . . don't . . . know." He stutters a bit, like he is ready to keep it all to himself or burn it all away. He doesn't want to disappoint me though. I have to remember not to exploit his desire to please.

"Do you want to read what I have read so far? I don't think there's anything in them Katie would have minded you knowing about. There are no rules from Katie that we can't share the contents with one another. That way we can kind of be on the same page about things."

He looks relieved when I offer, like he is grateful he doesn't have to ask.

Instead of reading them at the edge of my bed, Matt lays his head next to mine on the pillow and holds the first letter up so I can see. I don't really feel like re-reading them over his shoulder, so I gently nestle my face into his neck and close my eyes.

He smells like cinnamon, and Axe body spray. I've never been so close to him that I smell his body's scent. It's warm.

I start to get a little self-conscious about how I must smell. I brushed my teeth before bed, but that was hours ago and it's almost one o'clock in the morning.

The shower I took when I got home from the hospital was the best ever. I hadn't showered since the incident, and the mix of chlorine and hospital antiseptic was overwhelming. I used Katie's body wash, so I probably smell like her.

The house is so silent that I can hear Matt's breathing become more rapid when he reaches the parts about him, or the more dramatic moments Katie described in detail. I look up briefly when I feel something wet hit my cheek. I am nestled so deep into his neck that his tears are falling onto me instead of the pillow underneath us.

I reach my hand up from under the blanket to wipe his tears. I didn't even pause to think about it, but after the fact, it all felt too intimate. Seeing him cry is startling. He has such a strong and unflappable personality that I didn't think he would cry in front of me. If he could cry from his soul rather than his eyes that is where his tears would pour out.

When I wipe away a second tear, he grabs my hand. Not in a *don't touch me* way, but forceful enough to make me stop. I was getting a little too comfortable, but he started it by crawling in bed with me.

He doesn't let go of my hand. Instead, he stares at my palm, using his other hand to spread out my fingers in front of him. The letters are on the side table now and have lost all of Matt's interest.

I don't pull away. I am curious what he is looking at. Is he trying to see if Katie and I have the same fingerprints? Even though we were identical in every way, I know that having the same fingerprint is impossible.

I am looking at my hand when I notice his gaze has now turned to my face. Glaring at me with glass eyes. He changes his gaze from my face and back to my fingers and slowly, one by one, starts to gently kiss the tips of them. I can feel his lips on each of my nerve endings as he glides delicately over each one.

I can't swallow, I can't move. My heart is pounding. His kisses move from my fingertips, down my wrist and up my arm until they stop at the sleeve of my baggy T-shirt. The pause feels infinite, and my entire body is electric anticipating his next move. Where will the warmth flood too next? Which nerve endings will spark by his touch?

Neither one of us has made a sound. I haven't pulled back from him, not even an inch, and we are both staring at each other in complete stillness.

I can feel my heart racing, and I am afraid the sound of it thumping is so loud it's the only noise in the room, only matched by the sound of our labored breathing. We both go completely breathless when Matt finally breaks the stillness and kisses my bottom lip. He doesn't just slam into me though, but rather, like stepping into water one toe at a time, our mouths touch and then roll into one another.

We don't stir from this position. I am not sure if I should pull away or lean into him, but I am mostly just lying there completely stiff as a board.

I like what he is doing. I've never experienced this kind of rush before, and all of a sudden, my clothes feel like heavy foreign objects that don't belong anywhere near my body. I want his sweet cinnamon scented skin on my skin.

It's like he can read my thoughts, or maybe I said them out loud. But in an instant, he moves his body over mine and hovers for only a moment before laying all of his weight on top of me. This is a good kind of suffocation.

I am totally unaware of what is taking place right now. I'm out of my body and out of my mind, but it feels too good to stop. My desire for him thwarts all common sense. A voice in my head reminds me, *He isn't yours to have.*

Matt pulls his mouth from mine in a deep exhale that tickles my nose, then is rapidly sitting up and starting to pull off his shirt. When he lies back down, we are again face-to-face with our noses grazing. He kisses me softly again and again while his hand searches under the blanket. I've never been more annoyed to have such a large T-shirt covering my body.

The cold touch of his fingers prickle against my skin as he slides up my stomach. I get goosebumps from his fingers as they circle over my abdomen. I am not wearing a bra, so there is no hindrance between where his hands are now and my bare chest. His hand reaches inside my shirt and covers my breasts. I let out a soft moan unlike any before.

His kisses transform from soft pecks to deep and passionate that muffle my moans into hums.

When he slides his tongue into my mouth I moan again, only this time I moan into him so much it reverberates between us. The warmth of his tongue makes up for the chill of his hands and the hot and cold sensations are driving me crazy in the best way.

My shirt is now beside the bed and Matt's strong hands are working their way toward my underwear. I am grateful I chose to sleep in a T-shirt and underwear and nothing else.

My body trembles even though we haven't left the comfort of the covers. My teeth are chattering from nerves. Matt skillfully slides off his boxers without disrupting the duvet. I can feel all of him. The darkness is still a shade of blindness, leaving our sense of touch heightened and unafflicted. I feel him stiff against me as he slides down to kiss between my breasts.

I know Katie kept a single condom inside the drawer of her bedside table. I figured she and Matt were having sex, but I never pried. Sex was one of the things we refused to talk about. I pull away from him briefly to grab it and hand it to him to put on. This only confirms my willingness to go as far as he wants to. I beckon him to take the lead.

It isn't a struggle to get it on, and I feel his hands begin to feel around me. I try not to moan too emphatically. I have both hands on the pillow in tight fistfuls. My back arched to where our stomachs are touching, and I lift my hips to meet him.

He pushes forcefully into me then goes slowly because I think even in the dark he can see me wincing. After a couple of gentle thrusts, he is fully inside. It stings more than I thought it would, but the pleasure resumes, and the pain subsides.

Both of us are frozen in position and exhaling into each other. The breath that passes between us is shared and intoxicating. He places his lips back on mine in one final soft kiss before he begins to thrust again. In me, against me, all over me, consuming me.

The blend of gentle and intense is perfectly balanced. I feel like my mouth is begging to scream, but no sound is coming out. My lip stings when I bite down so hard in order to silence myself the subtle taste of blood fills my mouth. I can't stifle my body's urges. I can't help but pulse around him. My eyes roll back into my skull, and I feel dizzy.

It all feels deep, intense, and full. I didn't anticipate this moment, and knowing Matt, I don't believe he premeditated it either, especially not in this exact moment and not with each other.

It only takes a few calculated thrusts and a deep kiss for him to finish. I couldn't look away from him, but there we were. Done. Lying next to one another now naked and breathless. I want to cry, I want to laugh, I want him to hold me, but instead we both just lay silent until Matt stands, cleans himself up and slips away silently to fall back asleep on the couch.

What did I just do?

CHAPTER 16

Alice
{ 2022 }

I STARE AT the blossoms now cradled in my arms and am paralyzed by their intent. My heart begins to race as I frantically look up and down the hallway for anyone, maybe even a shadow to tip me off if I am indeed not alone. It is a brief second before I slam the door closed and lock it abruptly. I can feel the panic I felt as a teenager begin to creep into my throat and extend out until my fingers tremble, causing me to drop the lilies on the floor. My head swirls and seems to add another twenty pounds to my neck. I feel like I might faint, so I quickly put my head between my knees.

I can't breathe. I haven't had a panic attack in so long that I have forgotten all my tools to help me regain my composure. My first thought is that there is no Matt here to comfort me. I hate that he's my first thought. I haven't let the thought of him slip into my mind in a very long time. Overwhelmed, I open the door and collapse inside, weeping.

Who are these flowers from? Who knows that I am actually

Alice? How did they know to get lilies? Who has found me?

There are too many people from back then that I can think of. It's now a decade later and no one from my past is welcome in my present.

I am hyperventilating when I hear a knock on the door and am jolted to my feet. I am shaking trying to will my eyes to focus through the peephole.

Holy crap, it is Trevor! What is he doing here?

It looks like he is carrying something in a brown bag. I am in no state to see him. My face is beet red and my palms clammy from this panic attack. He did shake me out of my episode, but I am still lingering in fight or flight.

"Just a second," I yell and run to the bathroom to fix my face. I throw a bunch of cold water in the air and completely miss my face and soak my shirt. So now I am red-faced and wet.

I am just getting my neck through a clean dry shirt when I open the door, but my face still shows I have been sobbing.

"Hey."

"Hey, I had a moment to grab some dinner before running back to the office and I thought I would bring over my favorite Chinese food. It's a dive of a place, but I swear there is no better sweet and sour chicken in all of Miami. . . are you ok?" His voice turns from excitement to concern when noticing how red my eyes are.

I still haven't caught my breath from the trauma my body endured in the last fifteen minutes, and I am still swallowing air in chunks and my chest is heaving. Some of which is partly due to running around frantically trying to fix my appearance.

"Were you working out?" he asks but isn't convinced based on my jeans and the fact that I was practically shirtless when I opened the door. "Your shirts inside out." He starts looking around.

"Oh my gosh, you're not alone. I am so sorry I should have called. I'll go . . . I'm so—"

I cut him off and laugh hysterically, which seems to frighten him.

"Oh gosh no! Trevor, I am completely and totally alone." I may have said that with too much emphasis because now I feel like a truly pathetic single person who hasn't had a real intimate relationship. Worse still, someone who doesn't know how to have a relationship. *Pathetic.*

"I spilled some water on my shirt and was running around trying to change before I answered the door. I didn't want to leave you in the hallway."

I didn't lie. I just don't tell him that I was having a panic attack because someone from my past (and I have no idea who) sent me flowers saying that they found me and called me by my actual name.

My smile is genuine. I am really happy to see him, and the surprise is nice, considering I have never appreciated surprises.

"I love greasy Chinese food," I say as I grab the bag from him and turn to set it on my counter "Want to come in?"

I am hopeful that if I flirt a little we can move past the awkwardness. I am glad to see him step inside and shut the door instead of turning and running away. When I get weird, men tend to bolt. It never bothers me, but Trevor is just different from the others, and I don't wish to run him off just yet.

"I have about two hours before I have to head back to the office. It's going to be another late night for me, but I needed to eat, and I wanted to make sure you were fed as well."

He is coming off more and more considerate with each

passing moment. *He probably does this for every girl.*

"This isn't a date, by the way. I am not bringing you Chinese food to your home like a delivery boy for our first date. This is simply a pre-date where I gather more information about you. I'll learn a few things you like, and you'll learn a bit about me as well. We will have totally crappy and all so delicious food and then I will kiss you goodnight and go back to work. Then on Thursday I will come and pick you up and make that our official first date. How does that sound?"

Other than being totally paranoid that someone unknown is going to knock on my door at any minute, it sounds like the most perfect "non-date" I could imagine.

I like this guy.

Whelp. I finally admitted it to myself. I haven't felt this way in years. That feeling like clothing is a foreign entity that needs to be abolished has only happened to me once before. The sensation has been so rare that I had forgotten what it felt like to want sex. I crave a true intimate, skin-melding desire to consume each other, ravenous kind of sex.

Most of the time I don't even bother to remove most of my clothes during sex. It's never been worth it. I just want it over with, but simply looking at Trevor makes me want to bite his bottom lip. Somehow, I manage to control myself in his presence.

We both pull up a seat at my island countertop and I grab a few plates while he begins to open the takeout containers. The smell permeates my apartment, and I know it will last for weeks after tonight. I don't usually bring a whole lot of fragrant takeout home for that reason. Indian food is on the permanent no-go list, but it doesn't seem to bother me now. I like that when I come home for the next few days I will be reminded of this instead of those stupid lilies. I now prefer food smells to flowers any day.

I take charge of the conversation. I want to avoid questions that I don't want to answer. In my past, I would have been demure. I wouldn't talk unless asked a direct question, but I have too much to hide now. I've discovered Trevor is the only son in his family and that he works for his dad in one of the more major law firms in the city.

"I really wanted to be a musician, but Dad assured me I would never inherit a dime from the family fortune should I choose not to follow in his footsteps." He's embarrassed and must feel like a sellout for not following his dreams.

He chose stability and money. "It was the right choice because I wasn't that good of a musician to begin with." Or so he claims.

Trevor throws the question back at me. I take a minute to formulate my response.

"Dreams can be overrated. I chose to be a bartender. You probably made the right choice by being more practical."

My cynicism is showing, but I would rather tell him he probably was better at music than he thinks. That's just not what comes out.

He tells me he really enjoyed his college years and that is where he met Brady. He doesn't go into detail about their relationship now, but he does say that he hopes he isn't witnessing his friend's marriage fall apart.

Brady slipping so casually into the conversation is a little uncomfortable, but I understand why. Trevor assures me that I just caught Brady on a really bad night and not to judge him too strongly. He also confided in me that Brady has been staying with him the last few days because Bianca kicked him out. I am surprised. I feel a little sad about that. I don't want something so inconsequential to mean the end of a marriage for someone, especially someone close to Trevor, who I have come to care for so quickly. I find myself very forgiving when I am around him.

"Brady's kiss doesn't even hit the top ten of most traumatic moments from my life," I blurt, hoping to encourage him that it's no big deal. But now I am afraid that in one sentence I have said too much. Opened a window to more personal inquiries.

I can see Trevor raise his eyebrows, but I change the subject.

"Why is someone like *you* single?" I emphasize *you*, so I cannot so subtly indicate that I think he should have been snagged by someone and off the market a long time ago.

I love the look he gives me. He has no barriers. I have enough for both of us. No question is off limits for this man.

He feigns humility and smiles at his plate.

"I've only had one serious relationship. I almost married her, but she moved back to Australia after law school. I couldn't follow her out there due to familial obligations, and she wasn't willing to relocate to America permanently."

Apparently, she mailed back the ring, which seems really cold to me, but what else would you do? At least she gave it back.

"Was she the love of your life?" I don't really want to know.

"Maybe, but I won't know until the next great love of mine comes around so I can compare."

I love that answer. It feels honest. Being compared to another women seems awful, but realistic. I can't help but think of Cheryl and the letter that Katie wrote all those years ago confessing that Todd was not the love of her life. How depressing to know that there is someone else out there that can make you feel more alive than the relationship you are committed to.

Marriage is a covenant that is not broken lightly or without tidal waves of repercussions. It's best to attach to someone who consumes you, mind, body and soul.

With his honesty the conversation trails off as we digest what's been said and what's been eaten. We devour an entire container of sweet and sour chicken when he demands that it is now his turn to ask questions.

"What do you want to know?" I ask, hoping it's basic, like what is your favorite song, and do you sleep on the left side of the bed? Basic and shallow questions are always safe.

"I want to know everything, but we can start with how many siblings you have and what your family is like?"

Oh gee yay. We are starting off with a banger.

"I am adopted,' I say. "I don't have any family." This is my line for any time anyone asks me why I am always alone.

I have no one. It's the truth. I've gotten really good at moving the truth around so it isn't a lie, but it also doesn't divulge anything incriminating.

"I had a sister, but she died."

I cannot believe I just blurted that out. I have never told anyone in Miami that.

Now Trevor knows that piece of my puzzle, and I don't like how I feel just giving that tidbit away.

The only place my sister's memory has remained is in my mind. Now it is in Trevor's.

I start to recoil, and I know he can sense it because his questions start to ease into the superficial. He asks me things like what is my favorite color and what is my favorite climate, and what is my favorite food, and where is some place I would love to travel to but never have.

I tell him my favorite color is blue, specifically teal, and my favorite climate is tropical because I love the vibrancy and how the humidity feels on my skin. I share how I have never seen snow in my life and how I would love to visit Lake Tahoe in the winter and see Italy in the summer to eat the best foods and all that gelato.

Katie was in Italy, and in all of the postcards she sent me, she looked the happiest when she was traipsing around Rome and the Amalfi Coast.

This feels fun. I haven't had fun in a while, and I enjoy laughing with him as we clap our chopsticks together. He keeps touching my forearm, which springs me into attention. It feels more intimate than our kiss did.

I have paid attention to his every motion. I note how his lips graze over his utensils. I see how he reaches for more takeout containers and is constantly refilling my plate while I am talking, but never breaking eye contact with me. I see how he looks at me, like maybe he wants to consume me as much as I do him. Like the Chinese food might satiate our sexual appetites.

A timer on his phone breaks our trance indicating that the evening is over.

"I need to get back to the office."

He sounds incredibly disappointed, and even though he has to leave I like the fact he seems sad to go.

"Let me walk you to the door that is about five feet away from us," I say sarcastically as I get up and start closing all the takeout containers.

"You keep those," he says to me and pushes them back into my hands. "Just in case you get hungry and want a midnight snack when I text you around that time. Plus, I shamelessly eat from this place several times a week and still have leftovers in my fridge at home."

He winks at me, which I find hilarious, impressive, and incredibly sexy. I also did not glance over the fact he plans on texting me around midnight. That is far too late to get off work for a lawyer, but now I will be awake waiting for his text.

Saying goodbye is always the most awkward part of any date—even though he said this wasn't a date. I know he is going to try to kiss me because he told me so. And I want to revisit how I feel when our lips touch. If he doesn't kiss me, I'll kiss him, which is very out of character for me. Everything I do around him feels out of character.

He is grabbing his keys and phone off the counter when he notices the bundle of lilies placed haphazardly next to his giant bouquet.

"So . . . maybe I should be jealous?" he asks as he points to the flowers. "I guess I am not the only one buying you flowers. Those aren't from me."

"Oh no, those were delivered to the wrong person. You can look at the note. It's not even my name. Plus, I absolutely abhor lilies." I tell him only a half lie.

"Wow," he says with a chuckle, "good to know. Lilies are off the favorites list."

He doesn't bother looking at the note, a gesture of trust. He might be foolish to be so trusting right away. Yet, I envy him. I wish I could trust so effortlessly.

Trevor is a man true to his word. He opens the door to leave and scoops my waist in one solid motion pulling my entire body closer to his. He has one hand on the small of my back and another is behind my head as he draws my face closer to his. It feels like it all happens in an instant.

The kiss is anything but gentle, and as he pulls away, I find myself leaning into him for more. I brush my thumb over his lip that is now looking better and less pink.

"Glad this hasn't gotten in the way," I say as I tug on a bruise.

"Just wait until it's completely healed," he says like a dare.

"I have to go," he says softly without pulling away from me too far. "Thanks for dinner."

"You brought dinner here," I say smiling.

"Oh, that's right." He smacks his forehead gently pretending he is stupid. He is a tease. "I'll see you soon."

As I close the door, I realize just how safe he makes me feel. The flowers don't seem to trigger me anymore and I promptly throw them away in the trash. I don't care who has supposedly "found me." No one can find me if I am not lost.

At this point in time, I am Kat, and I am happy and have a major crush on this guy who seems to like me too.

I feel powerful and confident, that is until there is another *knock knock* on the door.

"Did you forget something?" I say as I foolishly open the door without checking the peephole first.

It's just Amber. She saw Trevor leaving, so of course she is stopping by for details. I think she was stalking in the stairwell until Trevor left. It's comical how invested she is in us.

I didn't look into the peephole. I got lucky this time.

The reality is that the person who sent those flowers could come knocking on my door at any minute. The thought paralyzes me.

"Girl what is wrong?" Amber asks, concerned, and my face goes white. I think I might fall. I wrap my arms around her, and tears begin again. I am a rollercoaster of emotions and I know I am scaring Amber. She closes the door behind us without letting go of me and slowly moves us over to the couch.

"*Mi Hermana,* come, let's talk."

My sister.

CHAPTER 17

Trevor
{ 2022 }

I'M FEELING PRETTY GOOD about myself right now. I gave this girl the largest bouquet of flowers that I could possibly buy and then went over to her apartment uninvited with Chinese food. Under normal circumstances I wouldn't have shown all my cards, but she seemed to like it. That kiss proves it, but what do I know? I have only known this person for less than seventy-two hours. I am risking the possibility of running her off before I even get a chance to see what this is and what I am feeling. I rarely come on too strong, but here I am doing exactly that.

I don't act like this around women . . . ever. I usually don't have to feign my confidence. I've been told my arrogance is a strength and a weakness. The last thing I want is for her to think I am playing her. I've never wanted someone so badly in my entire life and that feels sudden and scary.

Isn't there a rule that you aren't supposed to talk to a girl you just met for at least three days? I have broken so many of the so-called rules.

Who makes these stupid rules?
I haven't been someone's boyfriend in a long time.
Do I even have it in me?
She makes me want to.

I head back to the office all while banging my head against the steering wheel. I also told her I would text her tonight when I am off work. I think I saw her smile, but something was definitely bothering her. She dodged a lot of my questions. Once again, I am left hoping it wasn't me, but this girl is impossible to read. Should I back off, should I not? She liked the kiss. I know that. You don't lean into a kiss you want to stop. The road feels like it stretches endlessly like in a Looney Tunes cartoon. I am having such a hard time focusing on the road.

We kissed pretty passionately the first time we were ever alone, but if that were an indicator of deep affection, I would have been more invested in several girls from my past. She could be under the impression it was some random night with some random guy. To play the game right, it is important to know when to fold.

I'll figure her out eventually. This is where my arrogance is my strength. I am always up for new challenges and don't give up easily. She should know this about me.

Make a note to tell her.

I am late for work, where I know the look of disapproval will be written all over my father's face.

My dad and I could not be any more different if we tried. He is constantly dabbling in things around the community and always says the more of a presence one has in public, the more power he can obtain. He is not wrong, but it is his egotism that makes him insufferable.

"Take on the family business son. I am leaving you my dynasty." I mutter under my breath while rolling my eyes. "Doesn't matter what you want in life son. I bred you for this." the tone of disgruntled mockery continues.

Anyway, there is a fundraiser for the largest hospital in Miami and it ends up being a really big deal. Every year there is a different theme. It's a ball. We call it a gala because we aren't in a Disney cartoon.

I have an extra ticket and have yet to invite my plus one. I don't want to ask another girl to come because I feel so intensely about Kat. Love at first sight has always felt like such a load of crap, but this has got to be as close as one can get. Maybe I am fooling myself. I could just be lusting after her.

Brady was hoping to smooth things over with Bianca at the fundraiser, which might make Kat feel uncomfortable. Regardless, I am going to text her and ask if she will come with me. It's not until next Saturday so hopefully that is enough time for her to request it off from work.

When I get back to the office, Dad and Brady are standing in front of my office door. Both with their arms crossed.

There is that disapproving look I knew I would get. Times two.

Brady isn't blood, but he may as well be my older brother the way my dad has taken him under his wing. I think he is the son he wished he had and part of me wishes that he could assume the whole succession role that, apparently, I was born for. Brady obeys everything Dad requests and doesn't ever question his authority. Passing the bar wasn't good enough. Neither was graduating at the top of my class. I am still such a disappointment to him, even though he will never admit to me directly.

"That was a long dinner break."

I can tell I am in trouble.

"We have a lot of work to do on this case and you decide to dine in somewhere?"

"Can you say table for one?" Brady snarks.

The tone of my dad's voice is part exhaustion and part aggravation because he thinks I ditched our busy "burning the midnight oil" session to dine at some swanky restaurant alone.

Who would do that? He doesn't know me at all.

I am going to let him think that's what happened because I am not sure the alternative would please either one of them. Dining alone seems like the option that will get me in the least amount of trouble, rather than the truth that I brought dinner to a girl and dined with her instead. I can't exactly lie and say there was a long line for takeout because I didn't bring any food back with me.

I say nothing while the lock on my door unclicks, leaving space for us to all pile inside and start throwing papers around in silence. Each one of us with a highlighter in hand hasn't said a word in over an hour.

I am the first to make a noise other than the profusion of sighs that have echoed endlessly. "Does anyone want a coffee?"

Fatigue is starting to seep into all of us. It is a little past midnight, and I am not convinced that a jolt of caffeine would even revive us, but the air in here is stiff. The criminal case we are working on is particularly depressing, so any excuse to leave for a moment I take. The whole thing tugs at my mental health, and without frequent pauses I might go insane. I think we are all just going to curl up on the floor of my office tonight. Dad specifically keeps a cot in his office for nights like this one.

"Just get one from the kitchen this time and don't drive to Starbucks to enjoy your latte there."

Brady thinks that he is so funny, and he gets such validation from my dad who has never laughed a day in his life but smiles out of the corner of his mouth when he hears Brady's sarcastic retort. I think he likes how much of a bully Brady can be. It honestly makes him a far superior lawyer than most. His snide remark isn't even clever.

"Ha ha, you're so funny," I say halfheartedly, clutching my sides as if he left me in stitches. I don't have plans to ditch and go to Starbucks, but I do plan to check my phone and text Kat like I said I would. I want her to know that I am a man of my word.

> **Trevor:** Hey, I hope you are sleeping, but I told you I would text you and I want you to know that I always keep my promises. I had a really great time with you tonight. Feeling the repercussions a little bit because we still aren't done at the office, but how great I feel when I am around you is keeping me more awake than the third cup of coffee I am about to consume. Sleep well and I will see you Thursday for our date. It can't come soon enough. Goodnight.

I don't expect a text in return. It is a quarter past midnight now. I am a man of my word, just maybe not punctual. I am truly hoping that she is asleep, but before I am even done pulling a shot of espresso out of the expensive machine that Dad had to have, I hear my phone ding. I smile when I see it's her. Who else would it be at this hour, but still it makes my heart rate elevate a little knowing that she's awake and maybe she was waiting for my text before going to bed.

> **Kat:** You forget that I am a bartender and I work pretty late from time to time, too lol. This is still early for me

on a regular night. Amber and I are up and attempting to binge Grey's Anatomy and a pack of Oreo's. We are about two episodes in, and she has already fallen asleep on my couch. I had a really nice time with you too and you are right this is the best Chinese food in all of Miami. I shamelessly made another plate after you left. Amber had some too and she agrees that it is far superior. Most dives are though. She also thanks you for dinner.

Kat: Also, I am sorry (not sorry) if having dinner here kept you from finishing work at a decent hour and getting a good night's sleep. I hope you finish up soon. See you Thursday for our "official" first date. Can't wait. Night.

Kat has a way of zapping all logic of priority out of my brain and my espresso is now dead because I let it sit too long. I respond quickly because I don't want Brady and Dad to think I am sipping my coffee in the kitchen to avoid more work. I would just keep digging myself deeper in a hole and I am ready to call it a night.

Trevor: Worth it.

Two words, but very impactful. Every minute with her has been worth it to me. Even getting punched in the face by my best friend was worth being around her. I spill my coffee when I hear Brady enter the kitchen. Some which got on my phone. Hastily I reach for a paper towel and my smirk vanishes. I don't have time to shop for a new car and I definitely don't want to shop for a new phone either.

"Man, you are jumpy," Brady says in response to me spilling my drink the minute he walks into the room, "and you are taking forever again."

"I barely pulled one espresso." I'm a little too defensive.

Brady cuts me off with a hand in front of us.

"We decided to call it a night. Your dad just left and offered either one of us his cot. He wanted to sleep in his own bed tonight I guess."

"I can make it home, I think. I am tired but not *that* tired. Why don't you go home to Bianca tonight? It hasn't been that long, but maybe you both need to sleep in your bed tonight."

I would love to get Brady out of my house, but I mostly just don't want to see his time spent at my place cause more of a division between him and his wife. If I believe in the concept of "meant to be," I believe it for them.

"I can't yet. She needs some more time to cool off I think. I'll just sleep here on the cot and I will see you tomorrow."

"Sure thing man, but hey, I am going to ask Kat to the fundraiser next week, so maybe you can patch things up before then?"

Brady looks betrayed.

"Plus, a week and a half is a long time to be separated over something you are apologetic about. Put your tail between your legs and go home begging."

Brady laughs at this metaphor. I'm sure it's because he has never felt more like a dog in the doghouse.

"I messed up, sure, but you have no idea why we are where we are man."

With that cryptic cliffhanger, Brady spins on his heels and heads to my dad's office to set up the cot. He still hasn't been open with me. I don't pry. Number one, it is really late. Number two, if he wanted to share with me right now he would have. He still hasn't explained himself from when we were at the marina, but I'll add it to my to do list to meddle in their business some other time.

I only wish the best for Brady and Bianca. I hate to see them hurting. That is an issue for another day however, and I am glad to see he didn't put up much of a fight about my seeing Kat again. I'm sure he would like his mistake to evaporate into thin air. However, with Kat around, she acts as a constant reminder.

I have yet to ask her to attend, but I plan to do so on our date Thursday.

CHAPTER 18

Alice
{ 2012 }

I *JUST HAD SEX with my sister's boyfriend. I just had sex. I just had sex with my dead sister's boyfriend.*

What the hell just happened anyway?

Matt and I have barely ever been in a room alone together. We have spent little to no time alone at all. Katie was always around, as she should have been, as his *girlfriend.*

There has been no opportunity to develop a crush or feelings for one another. My mind never went there. He has always been a great boyfriend to Katie and nothing more.

Everything that has happened between us since Katie died has felt elevated and electric and comfortable, but I told myself that it was because we were grieving, and we literally only have each other to lean on.

Maybe that is why we crossed the line. Maybe he is grieving and just wants Katie, and I am a warm body in her bed, and I look just like her. I even used her shampoo. I probably smell like her.

The tears are starting to fall now, and no matter how many times I try to blink them away, I cannot stifle them.

The stark nakedness feels ugly now. My arms wrap around my middle like maybe I could hug myself so tightly I dissolve.

Shame. It's all too familiar.

I never desired to have sex with anyone who wanted my twin sister over me. Despite the last few days and all its confusion, I am not my sister. I never have been, and I never will be. Even in her death I feel greatly insignificant by comparison.

Matt just walked away. He just got up and left. He didn't say a word. He just put his clothes back on, covering up his vulnerability, and went back downstairs to the couch where I assume he just fell asleep. Not a word. Not a sound. Not a kiss goodnight. Not even an apology or explanation. He didn't cry. Nothing. Just cold like stone.

After tonight I feel like I literally have no one left in my corner. Having sex with Matt has created a deep divide. Obviously, neither one of us thought this through. We didn't think about it at all, and it alienated my only support.

I was in the heat of the moment. It felt good. It felt good to be wanted by someone, to be touched and kissed and loved. Having Matt desire me took away my sadness, briefly, but when it was over, the sadness flooded back in, even more so than before. Guilt was now the overpowering winner in my lineup of unwanted feelings.

Yet, in some twisted way it made me feel closer to Katie. It briefly satisfied the jealousy I had of her. I had something she took pleasure in. I had the boy who loved her, and it felt special, in the moment.

Now all I can think about is what Katie would feel knowing

that Matt and I crossed that physical barrier. She even said in her letter that a piece of their love will live on . . . forever.

Well, Katie, he aches for you so much he came straight into your bed to find you. Settling for the hollow representation he found in me.

He searched for little pieces of you all over my body. I am sure he could tell the difference. I probably don't kiss like you did, and I probably don't make love in the same way.

I look up at the ceiling like I am trying to talk directly to heaven in hopes that Katie can hear me. It is all so futile. If her ghost has lingered, she surely doesn't respond in any way. The silence of her bedroom is deafening. Not even my cries make noise.

I cover my face with the pillow to soak up my sobs. The tears are a torrent and I let them run their course. I feel they may never cease, but I don't really care anymore. I want to purge it all. Of course, the tears do let up eventually, and I sit up in bed to pull out the notepad in Katie's bedside dresser. I know I am not getting any sleep tonight, so I shouldn't even bother to try.

I flip through her notebook. If Katie didn't write down her secrets in the letters just yet, I highly doubt that she wrote anything of value in her notebook. I do notice that the back is covered with numbers. Tally marks that have no title or indication for what they are for. But there on the back of the pad are about thirty to forty tallies. I would have to count them to be sure, but my brain is more interested in diving into Katie's mind than it is in trying to figure out yet another cipher of hers I need to decode.

I feel like I didn't know her at all. She carried a lot more secrets than I realized.

I take out a pen and start writing a letter to her. The same courtesy she bestowed upon me. Even though it was never meant for my eyes.

Dear Katie,

You're dead and I just had sex with your boyfriend. Sorry for the blunt delivery, but it's the truth, and unlike your letters, I am getting to the point in the first sentence. You are taking me along for a ride and quite honestly, I want off the rollercoaster. I know you never meant for me to read your letters, but I did and now there is no going back.

I hate myself and I hate you a little bit too, and I hate Matt a little as well. I feel like I have no one to turn to. I am totally alone, and it is all your fault. You shouldn't have died. I was drunk and scared. I should have been smarter. You should have been smarter. Suicide is never a good idea.

I have to know . . . did he kiss you so gently when he touched you? Did it make you feel like melted metal going completely liquid? Like all the molecules in your body have softened.

I hate that I let him have me so easily. I am so sorry. No words will ever be able to convey the amount of shame I feel. I miss you and I wanted to have something of yours besides your freaking name. You're dead, and now so is Alice. Both of us were successful in ending the life of one another. However, one victim still has a pulse.

I am still alive, even though the name Alice is no more. I hate this scavenger hunt for clues in the letters that you have left. Wherever you are, are you pissed I found the letters? Do you hate me for sleeping with Matt?

You could have actually given them to me, you know. I would have read them and kept your secrets. I always kept you secrets. You could have told me in person. Somewhere quiet. You could have told me how important the contents were. You knew I could be discreet. We shared the darkness with each other all the time. What happened to you that made you feel like you couldn't share with me?

Why did I go along with getting this stupid tattoo? It hurts, and it is a constant reminder of you, and I am pretty sure it is getting infected. I always allowed you to take charge of my life because I wanted to be you so badly. I wish I had more of a spine. Even now, I am not strong enough to stand up. I don't know who I am anymore? Maybe I never did. My identity is so wrapped up in you.

I hate that I am lying here in your room as if I were you. I hate what I just did with Matt. I hate that he has that part of me, and I hate that I liked every minute of it until it was over. I hate how it ended and it turns out I hate being you. Maybe that is why you wanted to die. Because being you absolutely sucks. I always wanted your life. Being you will be my saving grace though. It's all I have to cling to.

Everything in this room is just a reminder of how much I didn't know you when I thought I knew you better than anyone.

You knew me. I shared all my hardships with you. We were twins. I am a liar and I have turned your life into a lie as well. I hate myself for that.

I hate you for a lot of things, but mostly I hate that I

don't actually hate you for any of this.

I miss you and I am afraid if you could voice how you feel about what just happened with Matt, that you might never be able to forgive me. I don't think I can forgive you for your part, so I couldn't blame you if you were not able to forgive me too.

Did Matt just up and leave when you guys had sex, or did he hold you afterwards? None of that really matters. I don't actually want any answers to these questions. What's done is done, but I want you to know that I am crippled with guilt over so many things that have transpired in the last couple days.

So, if you are around here somewhere and haunting me or watching over me and are able to read this, just know I am sorry. My only excuse is that I miss you so much and I don't actually hate you, but I hate this nightmare that's been manufactured for me. I love you and that is why this all hurts so much.

How funny that we both write letters to one another that neither one of us was ever going to read.

Forever your sister,
Alice, (Now Katie.)

※ ※ ※

I finish my letter to Katie and my eyelids are finally heavy enough that I might be able to fall asleep. The desire comes and goes, but putting my thoughts on paper has stilled the endless hamster wheel spinning in my mind. I put the pen and paper away and make sure the letters from Katie are well hidden before I drift off to sleep. I have to see this through if I ever wish to move on.

My sadness over Matt has transitioned from tears to rage, but at least I am not crying anymore.

It's funny how anger can be such a motivator. I thought that maybe I would stick around for a few more days and play detective into Katie's life a little bit, but that was when I felt like maybe Matt would be in my corner. Now I feel like I have no one.

I had hoped maybe I could bond with Cheryl like Katie had shared in her letter. I had been curious to see if Cheryl thinks that I am Katie if she might continue some of those revealing motherly moments with me.

I'm honestly pissed that Cheryl can't figure out that I am actually Alice. Did she not know her daughters well enough by now to be able to tell us apart? How bad of a mother do you have to be to not know who your children are? If I ever have children and I am blessed with twins it would be so easy for me to tell them apart. Even if I adopted twins, after years of being around them and raising them, I would never have a doubt in my mind which one is which.

I am seething. I feel like the pillow will melt under my head. I am so hot with fury. All my tears have evaporated. I resemble a cartoon character that has a tomato red face and can hear a train whistle when steam comes out of my ears.

Light bulb moment. That gives me an idea; Katie said in her letter to Matt that she loved taking the train and watching the scenery pass her by. That is how I will escape this hell, never to be seen by anyone in this life ever again.

I pull out my phone and start researching train tickets that leave late at night.

Katie also mentioned a desire to get as far away as possible. I think about the farthest place possible I can go to in the United States. I don't have a passport, so my options are limited.

Katie does. Is it expired by now?

New York seems like a good destination. It's on the opposite coast and when Cheryl took us to see *Phantom of the Opera* for our thirteenth birthday; it was really enjoyable.

I loved Broadway. Maybe I could start over as some sort of theater protégée. Sadly, my name in lights seems kind of counter intuitive for someone who never wants to be found again. And, quite honestly, no one would choose to live in Manhattan unless they aspired to be known for their artistic craft, whatever it may be. I also don't have the talent for show business. I am far too introverted and shy.

So, New York is out. I could always not go as far and make a life for myself somewhere in the middle, like Colorado. The mountains always look so pretty in pictures, and I could hide out in some hipster hiking shop and be nameless and go skiing. I would first need to learn how to ski. I have never seen snow, and now that I think about it, I really hate being cold and wearing layers. California is so temperate when it comes to weather.

Where can I go that is warm and far away from California yet doesn't have a sea of people all searching for super stardom?

Georgia seems nice and I have heard an awful lot of good things about Southern charm. However, I am allergic to peaches and that might be against their religion in the state of Georgia.

I finally looked at what seemed so obvious from the start. The very southern tip of Florida is perfect. There is ocean and warmth, and I am not allergic to oranges, so I am good when it comes to the state fruit. It feels as far away as possible from here, which I need. Being on the opposite coast sounds like a dream.

There is a girl in my Spanish class who moved here from Miami, and she always said how much she misses the culture. Everything is brightly colored, and the people are kind, and the food is incredible.

Not to mention Florida has Disney World. I have lived in Southern California my entire life and have never been to Disneyland. We are so close, and Todd and Cheryl never took us as kids. They said it was too kiddy for them when we were young, and then we were too grown to care. Or so they assumed. I never spoke out and told them that it was something I wanted to do because I didn't want to come across as immature. I think Disney sounds fun, a piece of a childhood we never really had.

Florida is feeling more and more like home by the minute, and I make a point to take myself to Disney when I get there. I can feel a bit of excitement in all of this. I am not sure that would have been there had Matt not had sex with me. I think I care for him more than I should. I'm afraid to admit I like him more than as a friend who is also grieving my sister. I let him touch me. I wanted him to.

I've always thought Matt was special, but not in a romantic way. I was glad Katie found such a gem. He treated her with so much loyalty and chivalry that he seemed like the perfect gentleman. I wanted that for me. I didn't necessarily want him just someone like him. He belonged to Katie, and I didn't think twice about that.

No, I just wanted someone *like* him for myself. Someone to listen to me and dote on me and look at me the way Matt looked at Katie. He always gazed at her and walked ever so slightly behind her so that he could stare at all of her with an adoration I have never experienced.

Todd and Cheryl never display any sort of affection. On occasion I have seen a side hug, but that was rare, and I think once at Christmas I saw a brief peck on the lips under some mistletoe.

Breathing air was enough justification for Matt to display his emotions toward his girl at all hours of the day. Being in her presence was enough of a reason to touch her.

Sometimes it was a bit much and I thought to myself often that at some point they must get sick of being this close to one another. I guess Katie never let that time come. She stopped it all very abruptly.

Matt's love didn't die with Katie. His affection simmers and needs a home. Like a junkie in need of a fix during a rough detox. I guess it showed up with him when he crawled into bed with me.

That bed for him is familiar. He has curled up next to Katie in it many times, but for me this bed is completely foreign. It smells like Katie and the entire room is enveloped in her memory. He probably feels more comfortable in this room than I do.

Katie's room feels like some sort of weird vortex that is sucking me into another dimension, to a place where I am no longer Alice and I have to adopt all of her secrets. It's hard to internalize someone else's dark thoughts and not share them when you only have pieces of the whole. I still hope that Katie fills in the blanks with her letters, but at the same time I kind of hope I never learn what was so dark that she felt she had to die. I am not sure that if I find out, that I can keep that darkness inside me and all to myself. I carry the weight of my own secrets. I might drown. The irony of that thought isn't lost on me.

I found an overnight train schedule that leaves tomorrow at ten, but instead of using a credit card to book it, I simply jot down the time so that I can buy a ticket when I get to the station. I'm sure Matt will drive me. It is the least he can do.

If I can even bear to face him in the morning.

I am starting to feel calmer, less mad at the world, and I know that I have all day tomorrow to pack and figure out everything else. Maybe I can steal some of the cash in Todd's drawer to pad my budget a little bit. He'd be pissed, but I would be too far gone to care about any repercussions.

I have no idea what I am going to do once I get to Florida, but I am just going to take it one step at a time.

I have a big travel day ahead of me and won't be getting a whole lot of sleep tomorrow either, so I set down Katie's notepad and place it back in her drawer. I will definitely be taking that with me. The mystery of the tally marks in the back piqued my interest.

I close my eyes and start to drift off when I hear the door crack open. I figure it might be Matt coming to make amends for running out of the room so quickly, but I don't want him to think that I was upset as much as I was. I don't stir or open my eyes to check. I pretend to be asleep, and whoever is in my room stops when they reach the bedside table. Their shadow hovers for a moment, but then I can hear their footsteps leaving and the door closing tightly behind.

I immediately open the drawer to see if the journal is still there. If someone were to grab that after I just divulged my soul onto paper the truth about who I am I would be caught and may never find any redemption for both Katie and me.

Much to my relief there lies the journal. Closed. There is something on top of it though. I know that Matt and I used the one condom Katie had on her bedside table, and yet now there is another one sitting right there on top of her journal like the old one was never used.

CHAPTER 19

Alice

{ 2022 }

"Are you going to be sick?"

Amber is looking over my pale appearance like she might need to run for a bucket for me to throw up in. This is not the mood she expected me to be in after Trevor left.

Amber looks at me with anxious eyes, holding me on the couch as if I might shatter into a million pieces. She's never before shown such concern and delicacy, as if I am made of glass. Her nurturing is soothing. I can feel it seep into me as she runs her fingers through my curls. She makes this shushing sound as she whispers to me gentle notes of comfort in Spanish.

I can hardly inhale let alone use my small amount of Spanish to translate what she is saying. She could be mumbling phrases and calling me the biggest basket case she has ever seen, and I wouldn't care because her body language is so reassuring.

I do know what *hermana* means, and it has been a long time since anyone has called me sister. It triggers more tears that make me feel like Florida is going to need another flood warning because Hurricane Kat (Alice) is about to blow in.

Amber allows me time to compose myself before she starts her interrogation. I am just now starting to catch my breath, and she slips off the couch really quick to grab me some tissue and a glass of ice water. For the first time I feel like I don't want to be alone in my thoughts, and I am glad that Amber knocked on my door tonight. We are close enough to be able to have occasional meltdowns with one another.

"What happened tonight?" Did Trevor do something? I saw him leaving here. You were so happy when you left work, I am honestly stunned to see you like this? Did he do something to you?"

Her last question makes me laugh and shakes me out of my last few tears. As if Trevor would hurt me. I feel like I know him well enough to know he isn't the type. I blow my nose and take a sip of the icy water, which settles my stomach.

"No, he is so amazing. He brought Chinese food from this hole-in-the-wall place that he discovered, and shared dinner with me. Then he left to go back to work. It was a really nice evening."

"Okay, none of that seems like it warrants a panic episode."

She's right. Trevor's actions don't warrant a panic response because he wasn't the one who started any of this.

I don't exactly know where to go from here or how much to share with Amber, but I just start talking; it feels good to confide in someone, but I am cautious.

I tell Amber all about how I was adopted by a couple with my twin sister, and it wasn't the warmest home to be a part of. When I turned seventeen my sister died, I disclose, leaving out the more heinous details on how she died. I maintain the pretense that it was an accident.

"She left me all alone and I ran away to Florida, and I have been here ever since."

I keep all the darkest moments to myself. It's going to take more than a bundle of lilies to draw those demons out.

I can still see a bit of confusion on Amber's face, like she is trying to figure out why I was panicking.

"Oh, and someone from my past, when my sister was alive, sent me flowers today and I just never want to go back to that time of my life. It triggered a lot of emotions for me that I haven't felt since I was seventeen."

Silence sits between us as Amber searches for the right words to say.

"I am so sorry your sister died."

No one has ever said that to me before. No one has ever acknowledged the supreme loss it was for me to lose my best friend and twin. I can feel the tears starting to surface again only this time they are tears of gratitude.

"Have you made any progress watching *Grey's*," she asks with feigned annoyance. But I am glad she has changed the subject.

"When would I have had time?" I ask a little pointedly.

"Oh, that's right. You have a boyfriend now."

"I do not have a boyfriend." I huff.

I fix the blanket over us and settle into the couch. "I have a date, but not a boyfriend."

"Uh huh, sure. You are in the stage of denial. Whatever."

Amber is so unconvinced it makes me want to ask her what *her* love life's been like lately, but she flips to Hulu and presses play on the episode we left off on before the yacht party.

"You are in *love.*"

"Shut up Amber and watch the hot surgeons save another poor idiot's life."

※ ※ ※

Amber barely makes it twenty minutes before she falls asleep with her head in my lap. I am so not the reason we have made little progress watching this show.

I forgot to turn my phone on silent, so when it notifies me of a text a little past midnight, I am certain she is going to stir awake. When she doesn't, I wonder if I will be able to move her so I can at least get to my bed.

Amber has slept on my couch many times, but I don't feel the need to pull a "Ross and Joey" and cuddle together on the couch for a nap.

Friends is a show that I could watch all night long on repeat and binge, but *Grey's* is so dramatic that I find myself recoiling from it sometimes.

I feel like my entire past is a soap opera. I have been steeping in normalcy for so long I don't want to see the drama unfold at fictional Seattle Grace. I don't want to watch death occur anywhere. Not even in a made-up reality.

It's a little triggering for me, but Amber swears by it, and I like that we watch it together. I am going to be seventy-five by the time we finish nineteen seasons though!

I snatch my phone and silence it. I am glad I wasn't glued to my phone waiting for Trevor to text me, but I am noticeably lighter when I see the notification is indeed from him.

We text briefly, and the TV becomes a distant hum in the background. I am all in on what Trevor is saying. He is still at work, and I feel bad for keeping him with me later than he probably should have, but when he ends the text conversation with *worth it,* my body goes warm.

I don't know if I believe his words are true. I can't imagine a simple meal with me is worth hours of extra work and disapproving looks from your boss, who happens to be his father. I want to believe that it is all worth it. Like we are destined to have found one another, and I find myself wanting to prove to him that I at least could be "worth it."

I've never been good at believing in fairytales.

I gently lift Amber's head off my lap and slide one of the couch cushions under her head and I lay her back down. I know she is awake because she moves a bit, but it doesn't seem like she has any interest in leaving. Maybe because she is exhausted, or it could be because she wants to stay and keep an eye on me throughout the night and into the morning.

Sleep eventually finds me as well and I welcome dreams of Trevor and Chinese food and not a single unwanted lily.

❀ ❀ ❀

When I awake the next morning, Amber is in my kitchen making French toast with cinnamon sugar on them.

"Hey there sleepyhead. How did you sleep?"

I salivate, but I desperately need caffeine first to combat the headache I woke up with. I have had hangovers that feel better the next day.

I need a solid two to four cups of java just to feel human. I drink it hot and black. It's efficient, and unlike the patrons at Starbucks who need a ton of caramel to combat the flavor of real coffee, I actually enjoy its bitterness.

I head to my broken coffee pot to pour myself a cup before diving into the cinnamon magic that Amber has whipped up. I didn't even know I had all this in my fridge. I probably didn't, and she either woke up early to go to the store or slipped into her apartment above me for supplies. She is literally going to make someone the best wife and mother someday. Maybe when she is done playing matchmaker with me, I can find someone for her. Maybe Trevor has a friend who isn't a sloppy drunk and is actually single.

"I slept great, and you didn't have to do all this." She doesn't need to know that I have a headache from sobbing last night, and I really did sleep well. Trevor's text had an awful lot to do with that, I'm sure.

"Are you kidding? This is really nothing. I am hungry and I just want to make sure you are okay. Last night was a doozy. I don't think I have ever seen you like that before."

"I know. I am sorry for scaring you. I'm fine really. I think my emotions were just heightened from being so tired or I am probably premenstrual or something. I swear I'm okay." I take a few sips. "Man, you make a good cup of coffee. You have to tell me how you do this."

Amber wiggles her finger at me.

"Nah nah. I will take that secret to my grave." She says as she places her hand over her heart, and all I can think of is, *I know the feeling.*

CHAPTER 20

Alice
{ 2022 }

I HAVE BEEN ANXIOUSLY anticipating my *real* date with Trevor. The days have felt like they lasted an eternity, but it is finally Thursday, and I have changed my outfit about seven times in preparation for tonight. I even FaceTime Amber at work to get her stamp of approval. My choices are between a really cute floral mini dress, or jeans and this billowy top that ties in the front and has a deep V. One is cute, one is sexy.

"Wear the jeans and the sexy top with your blue heels and leave your hair down. It's a date, not a night at work. Let those curls fall." Her advice leans toward the seductive. She's right; my appearance should look like I am going on a date and not trying to keep fry grease out of my hair.

I have no idea how to tame my mane of curls. The humidity is extra heavy tonight with the possible chance of summer rain. Without even stepping outside, the volume and frizz in my hair is so intense it could create its own orbit. I throw some product in and try to smooth it out, but it doesn't seem to make much difference.

I remember Trevor saying he likes my unruly yellow curls, so I don't bother with it much more and just let it hang naturally around my face. It's grown quite a bit this year, and the ends of my hair stop just before the top of my breasts. I wonder if I straightened it just how long it would be?

I slip my heels on. They are a teal blue and open toed shoe with a chunky heel. Very 2010's, but I felt very Miami when picking out this color at the store, and I am obsessed with them. They make me happy. I love how they make me feel taller and my five-foot three frame could benefit from a little extra height, especially around Trevor who is most definitely over six feet tall.

I am ready before Trevor arrives. Even when I am excited, I am usually running behind schedule. I grab my small sparkly purse that literally only holds my phone and one credit card and maybe a lipstick and sit on the couch and check my phone. I am careful not to lean back too far, otherwise my hair might get even more static in it, and I would have wasted the product I used trying to keep it down.

Trevor texted last night that he would be by around ten to pick me up. It's a really late first date, but it is better than having to wait another week.

I check my phone and the time reads fifteen past ten. I don't know him well enough yet to know if he is prompt or likes to text when he is running late, so I turn on the TV and wait for either a text or a knock. I figure I would watch a few minutes of *Grey's* because Amber is begging me to get to the season finale. I assume I only have a few minutes. Then he will surely be here. He did say he likes to keep his promises.

To my surprise I get through an entire forty-five-minute episode before I hear a knock on the door. He never texted to say he was running late, and I am notably a little frustrated by that. It's an hour past when he said he would pick me up, and he didn't even bother to mention it.

I checked the peephole this time. I am not making that mistake again, and sure enough it's Trevor.

"Oh, so you didn't stand me up," I say, a little more sarcastic than I meant to. He looks a little beaten down.

"I am so sorry, I couldn't get out of my office, which feels like the lamest excuse. I should have texted, but I was rushing and . . . you look amazing." He trailed off when he stopped looking at the ground and started to look at me. My cheeks flush when he pauses at my breasts. I like how he looks at me. I can tell he is sincere. He probably wasn't able to text me for a good reason.

"Shall we."

Trevor offers his arm to me, like a perfect gentleman, and I lock my door before he leads me arm in arm to his car.

This all feels a lot more rehearsed than our Chinese takeout dinner. I think I like the relaxed version of our non-date more than the formality in his posture. The date has just begun. I try not to get too discouraged.

He walks me to his car, and I stop dead in my tracks. When I see his beat up Prius, I can feel the panic in my throat. It isn't something I feel I can control anymore. Recently, if I am triggered by something, there is no stopping my emotions. It is a wave that just needs to pass, only I don't have the time to allow for it now.

No, no, no this can't be happening.

How is it that he drives the same model car Katie and I had growing up? The color is the same, the seats feel the same, and I am afraid to breathe too deeply in case it smells like the

Bath and Body Works body sprays that we would spritz on everything. If it smells like "Twilight Woods" I might literally ask if we can Uber instead.

"Oh, this is your car?" I couldn't have sounded more repulsed.

"I've been meaning to get a new one, but I just haven't found the time yet."

I hate that he feels he needs to justify his car in front of me. I couldn't care less what he drives. He could have picked me up and taken me to dinner on a donkey.

I've already put him on the defensive, twice. He opens the door for me with so much chivalry I just don't know how to respond.

"Thank you," I mumble as I slide into the passenger seat.

I can feel the panic start to creep into my chest, and I am desperately trying to fend it off. If I let the panic win, then it really is all over for me and for my date. I take a few calculated deep breaths, and when Trevor slides into the driver's seat, I purse my lips. I don't let any tears escape.

"Are you ready for dinner?" he says as he puts the car into drive. I simply nod and look straight ahead. I am acting so weird, and he can absolutely sense my mood. I am not hiding my emotions as well as I would like to.

"I am taking us to a great little Italian bistro. I know you said your favorite cuisine is Italian and the owners of this place are actually from Sicily."

"Wow, that's great." My lack of enthusiasm is appalling, and I am not very conversational. I remain silent on the fifteen-minute drive to the bistro. The only noise is my fingers tapping on my thigh. It's an old technique I picked up to help with panic attacks. I am not sure if it works, but I am trying.

Trevor is trying to break the awkwardness by asking a few questions, but I just simply nod or "mmmmh" in agreement.

When we pull into the parking spot, I ask curtly if he can give me a moment. I don't even wait for his response before I tear out of the car and run to the other side of the building where I know he cannot see me.

All that panic is finally letting out and I am gasping for air still fighting back tears. *It's just a car. It's just a car. Breathe in and breathe out. Don't panic.*

I wish I had a paper bag to breathe into. Maybe if I take some of my dish home, they will put it in a paper bag. I take a solid five minutes before walking back to the car. I see Trevor's silhouette as he leans against the car with both of his arms crossed. I was too busy with my own thoughts to notice that he too is wearing a nice pair of jeans with a button-down shirt open at the collar and revealing the tiniest bit of chest hair. Sean Connery was my childhood crush. Who am I kidding, he still is, and the little bit of chest hair is a turn on. I want to take a minute to really appreciate how nice he looks, but I don't think complimenting his appearance will change the atmosphere around us.

"The restaurant is closed," he says stoically.

"Oh," is all I can manage to say.

"Yeah, I checked to make sure they would be open late, but with getting stuck at the office, time went by a lot faster than I calculated for. Sorry."

"No problem, do you want to go find someplace else or . . ."

"You know it's late. Not a ton of places will be open right now on a weekday. Why don't we try to do this some other time?" Trevor doesn't say this with much conviction, and with that, the date ends.

I am crushed. I know I ruined it, but I am not going to admit that out loud, so I just agree and we get back in the car. Once again, I go silent, needing a paper bag to hyperventilate into.

When Trevor drops me off from our date, I hope that I don't have to invite him up, but rather he would offer to walk me to my door.

"I had a really nice time being with you tonight," I lie.

He smirks but continues to look straight ahead at the road while he drives in the general direction of my apartment.

"Tonight was awful. I am so sorry," I say, almost laughing at how preposterous the last hour has truly been.

"My sister and I shared a Prius in our teen years . . . before she died."

I blurt it out like vomiting words.

"It was the exact same model—the same color and everything. That is the *only* reason I feel uncomfortable in your car. Oh, and I am not mad about you being late. I am rarely ever on time, and I mean *never* on time."

I emphasize *only* because I got the sneaking suspicion that he thought I was upset because his car is old and dingy and not at all what I thought a lawyer would drive, which is true, but I would never hold that against him. Especially not a successful lawyer like Trevor who has so humbly not mentioned or bragged about it. I know because I Googled him.

"Oh . . . my . . . gosh," he says when he finally looks over at my direction. "I am a jerk."

He reaches for my hand and gently squeezes.

"I just assumed you expected something a little more upscale. I thought you were disappointed, and maybe you were a gold digger. I also feel really bad for being late. I am really *really* sorry for judging you so harshly, plus I am sorry for everything else that transpired this evening. I was just going to wash my hands of it all. I mean, I'd think about it. Truth is I am a fighter, Kat, so I was going to go home and mope about it for a bit and then call you. I don't really like to quit on things."

He gives my hand another squeeze. I don't think anyone has fought for me before. I don't think I've ever fought for anyone, either. I am good at running away.

"I will say my pride is a little hurt. I usually don't feel like such a failure after a date."

"The date doesn't have to be over yet . . . does it?"

We pull into a parking space in front of my complex when it begins dumping rain. Florida is known for its random summer storms and this one is no exception, but the timing of it couldn't be worse.

To my surprise, Trevor throws open his door and strides into the rain to open the passenger side. He grabs my hand and pulls me out into the warmth of the summer storm. He looks me deep in my eyes as the rain instantly soaks our hair and clothes. Yet another cheesy romantic moment. I catch myself leaning into him to kiss him, fully committing to the moment. I fully anticipate his lips to touch mine when he leans in really close, but to my surprise he doesn't kiss me; instead he yells, "RUN!"

His voice reverberates between my ears. Next thing I know I am being drug through the rain and up the stairs and straight to my apartment door. Nothing but sloshing of puddles between our bodies. We both laugh hysterically, clutching our sides when we reach my door. Even just those few moments in the rain have us sopping wet. Nothing like a Miami summer storm to wash away everything.

"I don't believe I have ever taken those steps so quickly in the entirety of me living in this apartment, especially not in heels!"

We are both breathless, and the constant laughter is not helping us recover. When I inevitably catch my breath we are still laughing, but I open the door and ask, "Would you like to come in and dry off."

I watch him saunter past me. He somehow looks even hotter all wet. His hair is even darker and looks like the most perfect melted dark chocolate swirling into a confectionary. Every part of him seems to glisten and is magnified by the raindrops on his arms and forehead. He glimmers like he's been bedazzled by nature's tempest.

We might as well have gone swimming in our clothes. Our jeans are sagging at our waists and start to tug with every step. My favorite pair of shoes are soaked through, and I hope I can salvage the suede, but even if I can't, Trevor's words, "worth it," come to mind.

It doesn't take me long to close the door and I instinctually lock it. In a spin of dampness and frizz, Trevor has managed to turn me around and press me firmly against the doorframe. I can feel his energy in his stare, his desire for me, a desire that feels oddly familiar. This time I don't misjudge when his mouth touches mine.

He kisses me like he is trying to drink all the raindrops from my face. Even when we were making out last week, it didn't feel as primal and intense.

All the other kisses I can recall in my life have been gentle and sweet. This is neither gentile nor sweet.

His hands roam simultaneously all over my body all at once, even though I know that isn't possible. He would have to have the arms of an octopus for that to be true, but how he glides effortlessly over my wet skin, it makes me wonder.

His kisses move from my mouth to my neck. He works his way down my body, and I am still stiff as a board as he presses me against the door. I collapse in his arms, forcing him to hold me up. I might crumple to the floor otherwise.

The struggle to unbutton my very wet jeans is like trying to peel tape off my skin. Yet, he manages eventually to unclasp them; they slip slowly down my thighs and he wastes no time as they drop to the floor, plopping with a splat, leaving my legs red from the abrasive friction. I step out of them in order to free my feet from the shackles of the heavy fabric, and he slides his tongue up my stomach as he works his way back up toward my mouth. Water from his hair trickles down my arm as he moves from my ankles to my chest. In one fluid motion, he grabs the hem of my shirt and pulls it over my head where his wonderfully warm tongue presses into my mouth. The heat overwhelms me yet sends goosebumps to the rest of me exposed.

I am now standing in my underwear in front of him. There is no bra. The deep V in my shirt wouldn't account for a bra, but the wet white shirt hid nothing from him anyway. The way the date started I would not have bet that he would have gotten me to expose my undergarments to him. Even before the terrible date, I wasn't sure if this is where we would end up. Hopeful as I may have been.

I start to pull away from the door to remove his jeans and shirt, but before I can even set my hands on his clothes he presses me back against the door and holds my hands above my head.

"It's not my turn yet." The sound echoes in his throat like a demand for me to remain still.

He keeps one hand on my wrists to keep them in place above me, his lips are pressed firmly on mine, I have no limbs to cover what has already been left bare. He doesn't kiss, doesn't roam. Trevor keeps my arms in place with one hand and pauses, glancing over my body with his eyes. I've never felt so naked. Not judged, not vulnerable, just naked.

"You're beautiful."

He sounds so sincere I don't know what to say in response. His wet shirt feels cold against my bare chest and my nipples perk up to meet the buttons of his shirt. I desperately want to feel his skin on mine and think it is completely unfair that the only thing between stark nakedness and me is a pair of light pink lace undies, the only halfway decent pair of underwear I own. I am so glad I put it on as a precaution.

He is still donned in his date night attire, but I can't rectify the inequality because I am still his willing hostage backed up against the door.

I can feel him in the fabric of the wet denim, and I know he is anxious to be free of them. I enjoy being dominated by him and having him make all the decisions.

"Is it your turn now?" I ask timidly, like I must follow the rules of conduct he has set in place.

He releases my hands and I throw my arms around his neck. He wastes no time scooping me up and I press my hips into him when I wrap my legs around him. Not an inch of him stumbles under strain as he continues to hold me up. The release of my arms is confirmation that I now have the freedom to unbutton his shirt. I do it slowly even though I am sure he would prefer me to rip the buttons clean off. It's a nice shirt, and after tonight I hope he wears it again on a more successful date.

This night is feeling pretty successful all of a sudden.

I push the fabric down over his shoulders and he slides his arms out so he doesn't drop me.

With the shirt finally gone, it feels like this barrier between us is finally removed. I press deeper into him as he holds onto me tightly; it's almost like we are conjoining into one being, or forcefully trying to.

Still lifted in his arms, he carries me to the couch, where wet jeans and all he sits on my blankets and places me purposefully on his lap. My knees sink deeper into the couch cushions next to me as I lower myself onto him. I don't know how much longer he can remain in his jeans before throwing me off him and tearing out of them.

I'm too engrossed to care that my couch is getting all wet. A moan escapes me. My body is begging him. One more calculated groan, and he is up and out of his jeans. I can see him standing before me, and even though I may have been mostly naked for longer, Trevor beats me to it; he is laying me on my back on the couch and slipping my panties off before I can even stop to appreciate the glory of all of him naked.

"Do you have a condom?"

"Oh shoot."

Trevor throws himself off me and runs over to where he threw his jeans next to mine and pulls a condom out of his front pocket.

"You were that confident you'd get lucky?" I ask half sarcastically, half seriously.

It's a little funny to think that he had a plan or hope for tonight and it wasn't just me, but I also think it's kind of ridiculous that he was walking around with a condom in his pocket this entire time. He was probably ready to chuck it out the window on the drive home.

The only thing I can think of that sparked the mood after

such a horrible failure of a date is that we were honest with one another. If brutal honesty leads to this kind of sex, I might just bear my soul to Trevor before the night is over.

There is a moment of awkwardness while Trevor slides the condom on, and I am naked on the couch. The wet fabric underneath me is starting to itch.

Pretty soon, Trevor is back on top, covering me like a moist, warm blanket. My hips are pressing into him, pleading with him to enter me. He uses his fingers to spread me, and with one push he thrusts inside me.

It definitely doesn't hurt like my time with Matt had, and I only wince with the anticipation met and not in any discomfort. I let my knees fall open to make more room for him. He starts off slow, but promptly picks up his rhythm. It's aggressive and intense and I have no idea where to place my hands. They need to hold onto something. I reach for anything above my head, but nothing is stable enough to grip on to. Both arms cover my eyes and yet still I have to move to match his energy. I feel everywhere all at once.

When I place my nails into his back and claw at him, he stops. I think maybe I hurt him or my matching aggressive energy was a turn off.

"If you want me to finish instantly, keep doing that."

Oh, so he liked it.

I make a note, but I remove my hands in a large gesture that shows I am not ready for this to end yet.

Trevor takes a deep breath and resumes more methodically. His eyes shut tightly, like he is straining to control his passion.

I kiss his neck and use my tongue to trace over his vein. It is popping out more than usual and I am obsessing over every inch of his body.

"I need a break."

He says as he pulls out of me.

"Oh . . . okay . . . yeah sure, no problem." My tone cannot hide my disappointment.

"I said *I* need a break. I didn't say you did."

I squeak a little as he slides his fingers into me and places me back on my back. His tongue glides over my nipples. I am far from quiet, and I am so glad that I don't feel the need to stifle my noises. I want him to know just how much I am enjoying this.

"If you want me to finish instantly," I say, "keep doing that!"

Trevor continues, and with every one of my moans his fingers get deeper. His thumb is brushing the outside of me. I am on the precipice of the largest orgasm of my life and with a few more impactful touches. I fall over the edge.

I can feel myself contract around him and my back arches in complete and total pleasure. I feel weightless.

"Okay, break over."

I am barely finished throbbing before he is back in me. This time I have nothing hindering me from doing everything I can to drive him crazy. He turns me to my side and is spooning me from behind with both hands cupping my breasts. The rhythm is fierce again and I am a little sensitive, but it doesn't take long for Trevor to join me in euphoric bliss.

All his weight crashes into me. I can't help but joke, "If this is us on a bad date, I am so curious what a good day would look like?"

We both laugh and neither one of us feels the need to get up and put our wet clothes back on.

"Before we do that again, next Saturday is a fundraiser gala supporting the hospital. We annually host it at my firm, and I was wondering if you would like to attend it with me."

"Sure." I like when he asks me out, and I especially like it when he asks me out while holding me so closely. "We could call that date our *official* first date."

"Or we could just day we are dating now." He says things so earnestly and with such sincerity.

I spin around so he is no longer spooning me, and we are facing each other so I can kiss him.

"I'd really like that." And I give him about fifty small kisses just to show how much the idea of being his excites me.

"You're mine," he rumbles in my ear.

I don't want to be anyone else's.

"Do you want to go take a shower?" I ask.

"Oh absolutely!"

CHAPTER 21

Katie
{ 2012 }

Hey Alice,

Did I ever tell you about the first time I had sex? Who am I kidding? I know I didn't, but I wanted to share it with you now. Matt was so gentle and kind, and I was awkward, stiff and absolutely freezing. Matt and I stayed late after his soccer game and snuck into the school. If you think sitting in those desks all day is uncomfortable, you should try having sex on top of one. (Just kidding. I highly don't recommend it.) It was very weird, and my tailbone was pretty sore by the end of it. Luckily, it didn't last long.

It was special though. However, once that door was open it felt like there was no closing it. There really is no going back and I would never tell this to Matt because our first time was so raw and intimate, but I kind of wish we would have waited. Waiting until marriage seems like an archaic concept these days, but honestly Alice, I get the appeal. I believe there is a reason God asks us to wait.

At some point it didn't seem to matter though. I knew

that I was never going to get to marry Matt. I was never going to get to marry anybody, but if I had reached that milestone in life, I would have wanted it to be Matt. I felt very loved by a boy and that meant something, but sex turned it into something I just wasn't capable of. I stopped enjoying it completely. I want Matt to know that it wasn't his fault but will never tell him.

I stopped being an active participant in our lovemaking. I started to recoil every time Matt touched me.

Can you imagine how wonderful it would be to lose your virginity to the one person you are with for the rest of your life? Does stuff like that even happen anymore?

I miss you. I don't know how I can miss someone who is sitting in the next room. I feel so distant from you, and you seem to be pulling away from me because of it. I hate that I don't think we will ever mend everything. I should have shared more with you. I should have shared with you the first time I had sex. You were the truer sister and I should be doing more for you. You have your troubles and I have mine and it would have been better to battle them together. Stronger in pairs, right?

Matt was an excellent lover. Pretty sure he is as good as it gets for an eighteen-year-old boy but remember that sex is less about individual pleasure and more about intimacy. This is a lesson I wish they taught us more about in school. It is not something we have ever understood.

We knew how to not get an STD, but no one shared with us just how it really feels when two souls come together, and not just a bunch of genitals smooshing.

Sorry I said genitals smooshing. That was icky, but you know what I mean.

I am very indifferent to sex. It feels like something men just do to you to feel pleasure and nothing more. Like you are just a vessel to be filled to please them and there is very little or rather nothing in it for you. That's my two cents and take on life for this letter.

Lots of love.
Katie.

CHAPTER 22

Alice
{ 2012 }

I WISH I HAD READ that letter literally a few hours sooner. I probably would have visualized Matt and Katie on that desk and wouldn't dare add myself to the mix. The sun is high, and I am just rising after sleeping for what feels like only a few minutes last night. Matt is curled up and asleep like a dog on the floor at the foot of my bed.

When did he sneak back in?

I check the clock next to the bed and see it's a quarter past one. I am guessing Matt didn't sleep much either. That makes me feel a little bit better, like maybe Katie's letter was embellished and doesn't have a whole lot of truth to it.

Despite how last night ended, I definitely felt the pleasure in it and didn't feel taken advantage of—until Matt walked out so abruptly. Perhaps I have an inability to say no.

In fact, I know I do.

I don't intend to wake him, but I also have lost half a day of packing, and I need to be discreet and punctual. Throwing myself out of bed and methodically tearing through Katie's room looking for goodness knows what to bring with me causes Matt to stir.

"Hey." His voice is like gravel in his drowsiness.

It bothers me that his sleepy head hair, and the way he rubs his eyes with the heel of his hands in the morning, makes me soften toward him.

"Hey." Mine comes out as one quick staccato.

If my heart softens too much for him, I may not follow through with my plan. I don't look at him when I respond and keep going about my business. Very obviously with a new guard up against him. I open Katie's closet to look for her luggage bag. It is on the top shelf of her closet, and I am struggling to reach it when I feel Matt's hands above mine pulling the bags down. The warmth of his previously blanketed body radiating against me. I just keep staring straight ahead into Katie's clothes, my back to him as he towers over me.

My entire body jolts when I feel his arms wrap around my waist and his head fall into the side of my neck.

"I'm sorry."

The words themselves seem meaningless, but the hug is most sincere. I place my hand on the side of his head and start to rub his nappy hair between my fingers—too intimate of an interaction. More affectionate than any friendship.

"I know."

It's the only response I can think of in return. I know he is sorry. He isn't a monster; he never has been.

He lets my waist go and begins to help rummage through the room without question as I put in the bags anything needed or important. I found her purse in the corner of her room under a pile of jeans and a top she was wearing only a few days ago. I guess she didn't bring her wallet to the party.

"I could probably use her license now. It will confirm my identity in case anyone was to question me." I am looking at her DMV picture and trying not to cry. I hope never to be found.

"Where are you going?"

"Maybe I should keep that to myself. The fewer people who know the better and you and I are about to part ways."

Matt looks in the opposite direction when I say, "part ways." I can't tell if he is relieved that this mess is almost over for him or if he is sad to see me go. I don't have time for juvenile drama.

I found money Katie had stored in her room and put that in the bag right next to her purse. I figure I can rummage through her purse on the train, but most everything inside will come in handy.

"I think Cheryl keeps my birth certificate in the safe in their room. I am going to go get it and I will be right back."

I leave Matt looking through an old scrapbook Katie made, and while the nostalgia is priceless, it doesn't seem like something I should bring with me. I give him a moment to absorb it all and leave for Todd and Cheryl's room. I can hear Cheryl downstairs talking to some friend on the phone that is offering to bring us dinner tonight. I assume Todd is at the office by now.

It's not like him to take time off work. I even saw him head to the office when he had a nasty flu. He had a fever and I think wore his slippers, but he went in, nonetheless.

I type in the code for the safe in the back of their closet and luckily find Katie's birth certificate right on top. I grab it, and the one that says Alice, and start to head out when I hear the master bathroom door open.

"What are you doing Katie?" Todd stands in the doorway of his bathroom, with questioning eyes. His arms are crossed as he waits for me to turn around and explain why I am digging though their closet, let alone in their bedroom at all.

I guess he *is* taking some time off. It would probably look bad at the office if he didn't take at least a few days to grieve the death of his daughter.

"I am looking for a sweater I let Cheryl borrow. It's not here though so it must be in the laundry."

I am getting better at lying. I hate that. Todd walks toward me and places his arm on the back of my triceps and gives it a little squeeze.

"I think you and I need to have a little chat tonight."

I am a box of jitters and completely on edge as it is, but this conversation frightens me. What could he possibly have to say to me? Todd and I haven't had a meaningful conversation in years. The fact that he is touching my triceps is unwelcome. The squeeze around my arms is tighter than I would like.

Does he know I am Alice?

"Yeah, sure."

My voice trails off a bit and I walk out of the bedroom, knowing full well that talk will never happen. It makes my plan a little harder to leave if Todd is anticipating a conversation at some point. He might be more observant of my every move, and I need to be a little more intentional about how I go about today.

"Todd wants to talk with me later," I say as I close Katie's door behind me. Neither one of our bedroom doors has ever had a lock.

"I wonder if he knows about last night?"

Matt just brought to my attention the second most obvious reason why Todd wants to chat.

"Awkward question."

"Shoot."

"Did you replace the condom in the drawer last night? I heard someone come in and open the night table, but the only thing out of place was there was another condom there like we hadn't used one at all."

Matt is looking at me with really big eyes like he has just been caught doing something unforgivable and is about to be in big trouble. For an eighteen-year-old boy who shaves, he looks awfully young and pensive.

"No, I didn't. Do you think it was Todd, and he knows?"

Todd may know we had sex, but if he does it may work in my favor. He needs to believe I am Katie at all costs. If it wasn't Matt who replaced the condom, then the most likely answer is that it was Todd. If so, he probably wants to give me a talk about what he heard us doing last night.

"I need to ask for a favor from you. Again."

I look at Matt and plead with him to snap out of his fear and spring into action mode.

"I am leaving tonight and never looking back, but with Todd wanting to talk *later* and suspicious of what we did, I need you to take me to your house for dinner with your family." *Later* could be literally any moment. "I need an excuse to get out of the house, and then I just won't come back. You can say I left your house after we had a fight, and I got a Lyft ride home. You won't even have to lie when you say you don't know where I am, but really, I need you to take me to the train station."

"Why the train station?"

"I can't just take the car. I figured it would be the best form of travel to do at night. It's not a straight shot, but at least it will get me moving in the right direction." I say, not really paying attention to what I am throwing in the duffle.

"Depending on where you are going, I would take the bus. It's cheaper and it doesn't necessarily get you there faster, but it is a lot more flexible on location. Plus, they usually stop near places to eat. Or you could fly, but that is a lot more expensive and requires documentation, so never mind that one."

I don't like his interjection into my plan, but anything sounds good enough as long as he drops me off somewhere.

"The bus sounds fine. Just take me anywhere I can get a ticket out of here."

"We should get you packed then, and we can just say you were planning on spending the night."

"That sounds good. Thank you."

※ ※ ※

We finished combing through Katie's room and took everything of value, and I packed about a week's worth of clothes. I can use laundromats along the way, and I need to refrain from overpacking. It's harder than I anticipated to leave so much behind.

Leave everything of mine behind.

Matt confirms with the more lenient parent, Cheryl, that I can go over for dinner and can possibly stay the night. Cheryl is falling back into her migraines, so she doesn't seem to care one way or another, and we make a point not to ask Todd. It's all about timing. A manipulation Katie and I had become adept at over the years. Todd is keeping to himself a lot today, but I know that at any moment he could strike, insisting we have a talk tonight before I leave with Matt.

We slip out and place my bag in Matt's truck that has been

living in the driveway for the last day and a half. As we pull out, I feel relieved knowing that the hardest part of leaving is finally over.

It was easy to say goodbye to that house. I've hated everything inside for a long time and had no qualms about not looking back. The only thing I regret leaving behind are the belongings I had as Alice. To leave it all untouched is excruciating. I never even glanced into my old bedroom and regret not at least grabbing one memory of my own to cling to. My breath is rapid and my heart races, but just in time Matt reaches over to grab my hand.

I need him to stop doing that.

I have never experienced panic like this, and it is happening so frequently now. I always had Katie to lean on. My body is so deep into the attack that I don't notice we are headed in the wrong direction.

"Where are we going? I need to get to the bus station."

"We are headed to my place for dinner. My mom made us her famous chicken piccata. There is no need to rush off without eating a homemade meal. You are safe with me, plus it would be great to fake an argument in front of witnesses. Right?"

He makes a valid point. I do feel safe with him, despite last night. I have chosen to pretend it never happened.

"The more of this ruse we can sprinkle the truth with, the better" I shift uncomfortably in the passenger seat. Crossing my legs underneath me.

I relax a bit thinking about having a home cooked meal by Matt's mom. The few times I went over there with Katie were pure bliss. No one has the perfect home life, but Matt's seems pretty close. His dad is emotionally available and home for dinner every night, and his mom is a preschool teacher who has infinite patience. Some people might find her demeanor toward adults a little condescending, but I find her soft-spoken and kind. She was made to be around children, and I like that she isn't duplicitous. It would be nice to have a constant mother figure in the home and a dad that you didn't actively avoid. It's all very cozy and welcoming.

Matt's home is only about a twenty-minute drive, and I think those twenty minutes alone with just him, sitting in the passenger seat of his truck, is the most at peace I have felt in weeks.

"Did you make Katie feel this calm?" I blurt. My insecurities are showing plainly. Matt and I may have been intimate with one another, but he is absolutely clueless about how I feel toward him since he came to my bedside in the hospital. I still find myself questioning my feelings.

He catches on to my admission and is smiling as he looks at the road ahead. He hasn't let go of my hand since the panic attack and is now using his thumb to brush over the top of my skin.

"If I did, she never said anything, but I like to think that she felt safe with me in a world she clearly felt very unsafe in."

That is exactly how I feel, like the world is out to get me and Matt is my safe space even though I am still a little hurt by what happened last night. I have nothing to lose. I am about to put him and all that I know behind me, so I ask him the questions I really want to know.

"Why did you leave so quickly last night?"

The energy shifts, and I can tell I made him uncomfortable even though I haven't felt more assured or at ease. I am confident that whatever answer he gives me I can simply take it at face value and then move on.

"Um . . ."

I am almost amused at how uncomfortable he looks. Tears swell in his eyes.

"I really miss your sister, and it all just felt so familiar. It was almost a reflex, and I know that is the worst excuse of all time and I feel so terrible about using you to assuage my grief."

Wow, this boy is honest.

"I kind of figured that was why. Is that why you left right after too because you were disappointed I am not her?"

"No! Oh gosh is that what you thought? No. I knew it was a dick move. I mean who initiates like that and then leaves the second it's all over?"

His voice trails off a bit, like he is mumbling to himself. What was such a deep emphatic *no* has now turned into a whisper.

"Umm . . . I liked it."

"What?"

"I left so abruptly because I felt guilty for liking it. I liked it so much."

His answer further shakes me. I look out the window and watch the palm trees whir by.

I was not expecting that. I knew his body was into it for obvious reasons, but I thought he was immediately overcome with guilt and disappointment. I know I felt immediately guilty, like I took something from my sister that I shouldn't have. I wasn't the warm body he knew so well, and he couldn't quench that longing he had so he had to leave. I wasn't wrong about the guilt, he felt guilty for sure, but not because he was thinking about Katie, but because he was thinking about how much he enjoyed me.

It feels sinful to smile at this moment. To find any pleasure in what we did is despicable. I feel so good and so bad at the same time.

In addition to feeling guilty, all my anger toward him has now disappeared. I was using that emotion to propel me to leave. Now I am softening, so I need to be angry with him.

I take his hand back in mine and give it a little squeeze. Nothing else is said until we pull into his garage. Summer in California means that there is daylight until nine, but pulling into the garage makes it feel like the sun has set. The darkness masks the emotions that are written all over our faces.

Matt leans over the center console and pulls a stray hair that fell from my ponytail out of my face. When I turn to meet him, he is a lot closer to me than I expected. His eyes are so hypnotizing and the most intricate in-depth compilation of blue. There is a little brown, a little green, a little gold and just a hint of gray on the outside of his irises. They look teal. It's my favorite color. I can't help but stare.

He doesn't have to lean much to kiss me. This kiss feels normal, and this time meant for me. It's soft and gentle and light. It isn't a passionate kiss, but it says more than words could in that moment.

"We should go inside."

CHAPTER 23

Alice

{ 2022 }

I DON'T HAVE a lot of fancy dresses. They aren't exactly a staple, and my closet isn't big enough for a ball gown. I haven't had a night of dress-up in so long I am surprised I can scrounge up anything formal enough. There was no time to shop for anything new. I found a floor length halter red dress that I wore to a Valentine's Day party several years back, and I think it's as good as it is going to get for tonight. Red feels like a brighter color than I want to wear in front of a bunch of strangers, but it's either this or a white mini dress.

Trevor is on time tonight. I might add that he has been on time ever since our first date was bungled. It's made me more punctual as well. My anticipation to see him is the best alarm clock. We have only seen each other a handful of times since our night out, but Trevor has been sure to text me every day. Some may find it clingy, but I am thriving off his attentiveness.

I decide to straighten my hair for tonight. Turns out it really is very long when straightened and I am running a million miles a minute trying to get myself together. Half of my head is curled and the other is in progress. Sweat is starting to tickle my forehead with all the running back and forth, and I don't want my dress to stick to me. Part of me feels the need to shower again, but then my hair will instantly curl. It would be an endless loop of getting ready.

I finally have my hair straightened and in a high pony much resembling Arianna Grande's iconic ponytail. I didn't expect my hair to be *this* long when straightened, but I am kind of obsessed with it. I barely have my mascara slapped on when I hear a knock. I am running around in my bra and flesh toned shorts when I answer the door rather embarrassed.

He has seen me naked. I don't think he will mind seeing me in my underwear . . . again.

I run to the door and throw it open and then run back to the bathroom. This is a ritual of mine. I'm on time, but I didn't say it wasn't chaotic.

"I'm almost ready," I shout from the bathroom.

I blot my armpits and add my third round of deodorant. It all feels pointless because my nerves are not going to allow me to stay dry.

What was I thinking?

This dress feels all wrong now, and I literally have nothing else even remotely appropriate. Maybe I should wear the white mini because of the heat, but it gives off beach vibes and is not an upscale hospital fundraiser hosted at your boyfriend's prestigious law firm.

Okay, no going back now. This is as good as it is getting. I slip the dress on from the bottom up and tie the straps around my neck. The front fabric hangs perfectly in a cowl neck and the back also swoops and teases in the best way. The fabric hangs in the back just enough but doesn't go too low as to expose my shapewear. I don't feel confident until I walk out and see Trevor's face.

"This is the fanciest dress I own. Is it okay?"

Based on the fact that his jaw may as well be directly on the floor, I am assuming the answer is yes, but I just want to try and make him verbalize it.

"Red is my new favorite color."

It might be mine now too.

He pulls me into him with a hand on the small of my back, just where the fabric stops on this fiery beauty.

"As much as I love this dress and can't take my eyes off you. I'd really like to remove it."

"I don't think the theme tonight is nudist."

It's stupid banter, but my joke makes him laugh.

"Your hair looks incredible. I like your curly chaos, but this is beautiful as well. Personally, you could have walked out in jeans and a band tee, and I would have still been excited to show you off tonight."

For someone who is so intense in the bedroom, he sure is tender most of the time we aren't tossed in the sheets. I don't know how well that bodes for a lawyer, but he is definitely not hardened from his career.

Todd was hardened. Every lawyer I have ever met has been calloused in some way, but not Trevor.

"You ready?"

"Yup." I say as I throw my lipstick for the night in my little purse. "Let's go."

He leads me by the hand to the parking lot and we stop in front of this *new* Range Rover.

"What's this?"

Beep beep.

"It's my new car," he says with the biggest grin. "I couldn't have you upset in my old car, and I needed the right push to get me to the dealership so, *voila*."

My heart feels like it might burst. A *thank you* does not feel good enough. I could make a joke about how I'm glad my panic attack spurred him to go shopping. He made a snide comment about being lazy, but he is so far from being lazy. He is busy and he took time out of his busy schedule to do something so grand just because I couldn't handle the trigger in my life. The only thing I can think of doing is to show how much this means to me with a kiss.

I throw both arms around his neck. My hands are in his hair, and I love that he is on my bare skin. I love this dress more and more every minute.

He gestures for me to take his hand and opens the passenger side door.

This is going to be the best drive of my life.

✺ ✺ ✺

When we pull up to the event, there is complimentary valet parking. Trevor hands the keys over to the driver and struts around to open my door. I can't believe the amount of chivalry I am privileged to experience. I hope that I can rise to the occasion with my own manners.

I must be on my best behavior. I know I will be meeting Trevor's father tonight. He mentioned his parents are divorced, so I am assuming Mommy Dearest will not be in attendance. Also, fun added pressure, Bianca and Brady. Cue the spotlight.

Trevor was kind enough to warn me about them. I guess

Brady went home a few days ago begging for forgiveness, and Bianca took him back, but the whole topic surrounding what happened is sensitive, and I am going to try and steer clear of them as much as I can. I don't feel like that is completely fair because I didn't do anything wrong, but I definitely can be sensitive to triggers. I hate that I am a trigger to someone, especially Bianca, because she was so nice to me. I hope we can all be friends one day and use it as an anecdote at parties like this, but regardless I don't think we are there yet.

Walking into the establishment is like walking into a fortress. I cannot believe this is where Trevor works. The building is impressive. The theme of the evening is Under the Big Top, which was derived from the movie *The Greatest Showman*. Twinkly lights and several yards of fabric hang from the vaulted ceiling to emulate the inside of a circus tent, and the Miami zoo has brought several animals that are roaming around casually through the sea of people. A giant Boa snake is being carried right beside me, and I inch into Trevor to avoid grazing up against it. I do not care for snakes. The monkeys on the other hand are a hilarious delight.

There are hundreds of people attending, many of whom have decided to dress up in full circus costumes. Everywhere I look I see various shades of red, so I am not sticking out as much as I thought I would. I like to be invisible. I have spent the last ten years of my life succeeding at that, and the seventeen years before that honing the craft of invisibility in many other areas of life. I've never been one to want to stand out. I like to blend. Blending in is good.

I hang on to Trevor's arm and let him guide me through the maze of people, gently nodding at those he greets and says hello to.

"Hey Dad."

Trevor has stopped us in a circle that has a tall and distinguished looking man in a suit with white hair and stubble. He would be what Amber would call a "silver fox." Apparently good-looking genes run in the family. It is a shame Trevor's parents didn't have more children. Such a waste. If Trevor had a brother I would instantly set him up with Amber.

"I'd like to introduce you to Kat, my girlfriend."

"Oh, so you're the flavor of the week, my dear. Hello. You look like a strawberry." He says to me pointing up and down at my red dress.

Oomph I didn't like that. Strike one.

Trevor looks appalled at his dad for saying something so condescending even if I was just the next girl in the apparent lineup of women parading in and out of his son's life. His strawberry comment makes me wish I had worn something else. However, I doubt anything I decided to wear would have been satisfactory enough. It also wasn't an insult. Loads of people like strawberries. Maybe I am just being sensitive, and a strawberry is actually his favorite fruit. Or he could just be hungry. Most likely the drink in his hand has impeded his filter to not be rude.

I had not paid close enough attention to the circle, but Brady is standing next to him and snickering like the best friend to the bully in every old school movie.

"Dad!"

"Dad, what, what, you're so sensitive. It was a joke, I am kidding, hi hun, I am Howard Daniels."

He reaches out his baseball glove sized hand to shake mine. I do so and try to remain confident in my shake and not quiver. I've never met a more intimidating human, but remember I am a good liar.

"Hi sir, Kat Clemonte." I shake his hand back with enough

confidence to somewhat impress him. I am sure none of the other girls had approached Howard so directly.

It looks like Trevor is impressed that I stood my ground even though I feel like the earth might fall away. He places his arm around my side and pulls me to him. A welcome gesture to stabilize my quivering knees.

"We are going to go get a drink. Dad, can I top you off? Another Manhattan?"

"Two cherries."

Howard hands Trevor his empty glass and he gracefully turns me away from his dad and Brady, who still looks like the little imp of a sidekick he is. Even if we all mend fences one day, I don't know how much I would really enjoy being friends with someone like him.

"I have to apologize for my dad's behavior. We don't have the best of relationships, and he is just jealous because I brought a beautiful date, and he couldn't get the woman he is seeing to come with him."

I don't care how many insults Howard throws at me. All that matters to me is that Trevor is proud to have me with him here tonight. I could care less about Brady and Howard.

Not true. I wanted to make a good impression.

I did hope to make a solid first impression with someone so important in his life, but Trevor doesn't seem embarrassed by me, so I am trying not to take it too personally. And I have no idea what is left to salvage with Brady. I haven't had a whole lot of experience with parents and even my own were probably the worst relationships I had in my youth. The only parents who seemed to like me were Matt's, but they liked everybody, so the bar was low. Besides, they thought I was Katie.

I grab a glass of champagne and we head back into the fray to take on more verbal blows with Howard's freshly made cocktail in hand.

Howard and Brady seem to be thick as thieves, and I am starting to notice that their personalities match each other's a lot more than Trevor and Howard's seem to. It makes me curious how Trevor turned out so sweet. I've known his dad for a grand total of fifteen minutes, but I feel like that sort of cynicism is learned and runs deep inside him.

Trevor is making his rounds through the crowd and taking time to converse with those he has personal connections to. It's fun to see him so charismatic and in his element. He is good at what he does.

I've always felt that I am more of an introvert, but Trevor has proven to be the opposite. He is definitely exuding extroverted energy. It's not a side of him I have seen before so up close and personal. His professionalism is quite the turn on. Who doesn't love a man in a suit?

I humbly take my position as his shadow tonight, and I don't mind one bit. I simply grasp onto his arm, sip my champagne, and nod at the appropriate people and follow alongside him.

There is a moment before we all sit for the decadent feast where Trevor and I are solely conversing.

"You have a really nice office," I say as I look at the architecture in the brilliant lobby.

"This isn't my office, this is my *office building*." His reply is smug and playful.

"You know what I mean . . ."

The champagne has gone to my head, making me feel a little sultrier, and the silk against my skin feels like butter. Everything feels soft and airy. I am far from drunk. Being drunk once was enough for me to never want to feel that way again, but I feel good tonight with a subtle buzz.

"Would you like to see my actual office?"

The look in his eyes tells me that I am about to see much more than just his office, and we both quietly excuse ourselves from our seats.

The elevators to the individual law offices have a velvet theater rope draped in front of them, but as soon as Trevor gives his ID to the guard, he steps aside and allows us up. No mere mortals are allowed up to Mount Olympus.

It takes a few minutes to get up there and we enter his office. I am surrounded by floor-to-ceiling windows and a very modern minimalist style glass desk. All of Miami seems to be illuminated below us, and you can see way out into the horizon. Much like Zeus. I guess Howard would be Zeus; Trevor is Hercules.

"I think you may actually have a better view than I do? I also think this room alone is bigger than my entire apartment."

I feel him slide behind me and start to kiss the nape of my neck. When he nibbles on my skin, just enough to tease and not sting, I get chills all the way to my shins. Trevor then switches to the left side and I instantly crumple with giggles.

"Are you ticklish?" It's a rhetorical question.

No, I made that noise voluntarily. Yes, I am ticklish!

"Where else are you ticklish?" Trevor is using both of his hands to scour my body like a "tickle monster." It is the least fun game when he finds all of them, but it also sends me into a fit of hysterics that make me want him more.

"*Mmmm,* I love when you laugh." His voice rumbles as he puts his mouth on mine before I can respond to how immature playing the tickle game is. There is no fight in me. I love every minute of his hands on me.

The playfulness is over though as Trevor lifts me from my rear and places me on his desk. The drop from his arms to his desk startles me. It was quite a distance onto a glass desk.

Slowly, he slides his hands up my dress and brushes the silk against my newly shaved legs as the fabric piles around my hips, and his head darts from my mouth and kisses me all the way down until his head is below my hips. I regret the tan shorts I put on to make my stomach flat. It comes up so high that Trevor has to reach up to my breasts from under my dress in order to slide them off. The man is determined.

My shapewear slides off my feet around my heels with a snap, and Trevor throws them clear across his office.

"You don't need those." Trevor has a look that isn't quite mischievous, but also isn't hungry. I fully expected him to undress me and then tear me apart, but instead he stands, leans in for a kiss, and then abruptly spins around before giving me the tour of his office, Vanna White style.

"So, this is where I work for a horrible number of hours in a day," he says as he points to various corners of the large room.

"Are you kidding me," I gaspe, still winded from being plopped on his desk. "What was the point of riling me up and taking off my spandex if . . .?"

"Oh, did you think we were going to have sex? What kind of man do you take me for?" Trevor smirks and clutches his tie like I have just offended him by insinuating such a thought.

"Seriously Kat, I am a professional, and there is way more to me than just a hard body." Trevor runs his hands down his chest in false humility, but we both laugh with every flex of his hard muscles.

"You are such a tease."

"Diddo." He smirks. "I am making my life easier tonight when I get you back home and out of that completely evil dress. I need easier access and those stupid shorts were just going to slow me down."

Neither of us have moved, I am still sitting on the desk, and he is still in front of me, but while I continue to laugh from our playfulness, Trevor has stopped. His face falls, looking at me. He looks almost sad.

"Are you okay?" I ask. Mere minutes ago it was all childish banter, and the next was solemn and serious. I hardly caught the change of emotion in time.

"What's wrong?"

"You're just . . . incredible. You're incredibly witty and incredibly beautiful and that handshake you gave my dad was more impressive than I have seen most peers give. You're so strong and unbelievable, and I look at you and want to know why? You carry yourself with such intensity. It is a sight to see. You're quite something to behold, Kat, I just . . . I just want to know what or who hurt you. What made you so soft and so impenetrable at the same time?"

"Well, we both know I am not impenetrable," I blurt, trying to lighten the mood.

"Come on Kat." It's not a challenge. It's a longing.

There is no breaking his trance, his stare, his hyper fixation on me.

"I've only known you a short while, and yet you have somehow consumed me. My every thought is of you. I can hardly put two words together without trying to slip you into the conversation. It's a borderline obsession." He guffaws like it's insane and runs his hands through his dark tousled hair. His eyes bulge like he is trying to keep the crazy at bay.

He is insane. It's all insane, but I understand. I feel the same way.

If this is how feeling seen feels, I am not a fan. Girls are always gushing about how he "sees me." I conclude that it is way overhyped, and invisibility is far more comfortable.

Trevor places his body next to mine, our knees touching, and gently brushes the base of my tricep with the back of his fingers.

His touch feels like it could sear me. I recoil, removing myself from his hovering, slide myself off his desk, and just stand at his giant windows. The vastness of the city below me. The power it gives is unquestionable. He wants to know me, but am I willing to be *known?* The last person who knew me so well was Katie. Then Matt. All ending suddenly and ripping me apart.

"How do you get any work done?" I sigh, changing the subject, but not the mood. The atmosphere is still heavy, though his sincerity and concern I can tell are not burdening him. He wants to meet me where I am.

Trevor walks to the window and joins me, looking straight ahead, yet I can feel him trying to peer into my soul.

"Ironically, it helps me work." He places his arm around my waist to draw me in. "It reminds me that the world does not center around us. There's a whole hive of people down there, living their daily lives, going about their business. Out of many we are all one entity. One humanity. No man is greater than another."

How can we be so different? He is so open while I am so closed off. He sees the world below him as his anchor. I see it as an escape. What makes me feel invincible, humbles him.

"I feel like Cinderella. This girl who doesn't belong here but is completely taken with the prince and waiting until midnight for the other shoe to drop."

"What if there is no drop, Kat. What if there is no pumpkin and no spell ending. What if there is just this?"

I covet his optimism, but I know better.

"There is no such thing as happily ever after, Trevor." My words are hurtful. I don't intend them to be. The warmth of his body against mine, never wavering. I may have been mean, but Trevor seems unphased.

"Not sure why you think that, but I am going to make it my life's mission to restore your faith in fairytales."

Trevor places a tender kiss on the side of my temple, takes my hand and without looking back walks me out of his office. He may not have looked back, but my gaze is still glued to the immaculate skyline. I'm glad he doesn't look back as I wipe away a tear that has been pooling at my lashline and finally fallen.

I didn't mean to cry.

✻ ✻ ✻

The rest of the evening goes exceptionally well. Even Bianca came up briefly to say hi. I take it that her maturity level exceeds that of her husband, and I am glad she doesn't outwardly harbor any ill will toward me. We don't have to be best friends, but it is nice that we can be in the same room and be friendly considering her close relationship with Trevor.

Brady, on the other hand, seems to have consumed a little too much whiskey (again) with Howard, and it doesn't feel like a snap judgment anymore to recognize that this is a pattern for him. Surprisingly, he's honestly more tolerable when he is drunk.

It reminds me of Todd. If it weren't for Trevor, I would say attorneys are all just inbred alcoholics.

We give our dutiful goodbyes.

"I want to thank you for coming with me tonight," Trevor says as we exit. "I would not have had as good of a time had you not accompanied me."

"Well, I should hope not," I jest.

"Okay, I wouldn't have enjoyed the event like I did. I wouldn't have enjoyed it at all. It's always filled with really stiff people and tends to drag on, even with all the entertainment around. You, however, made all that much more illuminated. You lit up the entire building, a temptress in that mean red dress, but I actually enjoyed myself for a change."

The valet drives the Range Rover up and opens the door for me to step inside. I completely forgot about the compression shorts that were left on the floor of Trevor's office, alluding to an activity we did not partake in. I probably won't need them any time soon.

"I am also very sorry about my dad and Brady. I have brought girls around them before and they have never behaved so atrociously. I've been so frustrated by both of them lately. Dad doesn't shock me too much. He is always kind of a dick, but Brady has been like a brother to me for several years, and I just feel so distant from him. He's acting so strange, and I can't seem to get to the bottom of it. His behavior with you was the worst I have ever seen, but since then he is just bitter and angry all the time."

I don't know how to respond. I ran away from any of my relationships that got complicated, romantic and not. I have done it more than once. It is honorable that Trevor doesn't just write off his struggling friend. Yet another way he is my exact opposite.

We arrive at my apartment, and I assume he is dropping me off for the evening. I wonder why during the last almost three weeks of getting to know Trevor he hasn't offered to take me back to his place.

"One of these days we should go back to your place. I just realized I've never seen it. You don't have a secret wife or live with your dad, do you?"

"No," he laughs. "I haven't taken you to my place yet because Brady had been crashing with me, and then lately it just seems like our time together begins and ends with me picking you up and then dropping you off, but you are more than welcome to come over any time. Should I turn around and take you there now?"

"Now that we are here, I would rather you *take me* in the back of this car. You know. . . to christen it."

I straddle his lap in the driver's seat, and we are finished with all of our clothes having never left our persons. This time no tears from me. This is only the second time I have had car sex, and both times were an immense challenge. However, mission accomplished.

"Now can I take you upstairs and take that dress completely off?"

"Yes please."

CHAPTER 24

Alice
{ 2012 }

"Dinner was lovely Mrs. Fields, thank you very much." I say as I lay down my fork. I haven't been able to eat much, but Matt's mom does make a killer chicken picatta, and it makes my stomach finally settle since I was in the hospital. It's my first full meal in days. My nerves have been shot, but I think the main reason why my stomach has ached so much is because Cheryl is a terrible cook, killing my appetite. She wasn't always this bad, or at least not to my recollection. Katie was the better cook, by far.

Masquerading as Katie would be shattered the minute someone asked me to prepare something in the kitchen. Yet another reason for my impending escape.

Cheryl has called my cell phone tonight a couple of times, but I have chosen not to answer. If she is calling on behalf of Todd and our scheduled *chat*, no thanks. I am not interested in anything Cheryl has to say now or ever again.

I thought that we might be able to bond a bit based on

Katie's letter, but Cheryl's momentary desire to be more motherly left just as quickly as it came. She lapsed into her old lazy patterns. It was yet another reason I feel little to no remorse in leaving.

Matt has had his hand on my thigh under the table throughout the entire dinner, and I feel like it is a little too comfortable of a gesture to do around his parents. I must remember that he was always affectionately open with Katie. He must be keeping up appearances for my sake. I have entered the unknown territory of trying to decipher what of Matt's embraces are for me and which ones are to keep my lie unquestioned.

"It was the least I can do, Katie. Nothing subdues the sting of grief like a good homecooked comfort meal. I am terribly sorry about your sister. What a tragic accident. How are you holding up?"

How am I holding up?

It is such a simple question, and yet I have no ability to answer it. The phrase that comes to mind is from *Alice in Wonderland* by Lewis Carroll:

"'I can't explain myself, I'm afraid Sir', said Alice, 'because I'm not myself, you see.'

'I don't see,' said the Caterpillar."

No one can see me. My world has turned upside down. I may as well be talking to a caterpillar, but I am Alice, though I cannot confess that out loud. Fortunately, I am talking to a preschool teacher, and she can tell that I am not able to articulate my emotions right now. Tears are welling, begging to bridge over the edge of my eyelids, and Matt's mother reaches over to touch my hand from across the table.

Why couldn't I have a mom like her? Nothing would be as it is. Everything would be what it isn't.

Matt excuses us from the table and walks me to his room with his arm over my shoulder. I am putty in his arms. The only safety I feel is nestled into his scent. When he sits me on the bed, I just start weeping. Matt says nothing while I sob. Like a shadow, just a presence surrounding me when I simply need him to just exist.

I wouldn't say he always knows when to hold me, because last night he failed miserably, but I think I've stopped faulting him for that one already.

"We should probably get on with that fight so we can make a scene for me to storm out on," I mumble when the tears are ceasing just a bit. "I already have the tears."

"I am coming with you."

"Is that you trying to start an argument, because the goal is for your parents to hear us, and they can't know I am running away?" I haven't taken him seriously. "Let's try something else like—"

"No, Alice, I am coming with you," he sternly interrupts. "Wherever you are going I want to go to. I need to be with you. I can't just let you go, and I know why you can't stay here."

"Matt, you have no idea why I can no longer stay here. Katie may have told you most of her secrets, but she didn't tell you mine." Of this I am certain. "You can't come. It defeats the whole purpose of disappearing. You can't follow."

"I think she told me more than you realize. I understand your pain, Alice. I can go with you, and we can figure it all out as we go. You still have your cell phone, and you need to ditch that. What are a few days in my car if I tell my parents I am taking you on a road trip to take your mind off things? We can go in the opposite direction. Where could I tell them we are going?"

"Seattle," I say bluntly. "You can tell them you are taking me to a Mumford and Sons concert in Seattle." It comes to me instantly. Something I wanted to do had I been asked last week.

His face turns into the largest grin. The Cheshire Cat would be jealous. It makes me smile too. I like to see him happy, I always have, even when he was with Katie, and they would fight.

"So . . . we're doing this?"

"We are doing this." I confirm.

"So where are we going?"

"I'll tell you when we get there."

I have never been able to trust anyone. Even Katie, the one person I thought I could trust, but I don't trust anyone, anymore. Not even Matt.

"We can leave in the morning after a good night's sleep. I'll talk to my parents about it later."

I curl up in bed completely unaware of how exhausted I am and rapidly doze off watching Matt pack a bag. I don't think he has taken into consideration that this means abandoning his family and his life. I guess it's not that I don't trust him. I don't trust that he is ready for that kind of commitment.

Even though I am less on edge at Matt's house than I was in Katie's room, my rem cycle remains scrambled. Though I do fall asleep, I do not sleep as well as I am hoping to before leaving town. His sheets hug the curves of my body in a haven of new morning warmth and crispness, while the window blinds become a filter for morning light, creating a soft diffusion of pink blush at war with the lingering darkness. Matt is no longer beside me. I can hear the hum of the coffee machine just outside the door.

The aroma entices me, like a siren call to the kitchen.

Sure enough, a fresh pot is sitting on the counter and without any awareness of my surroundings, I pour myself some of the beverage that will revive me.

I went to bed in his T-shirt last night, nestled safely in the crook of his arm and totally forgot to put pants back on this morning. It's really early, so I didn't think anyone else would be up besides him. I am all kinds of shades of red when I enter the kitchen and hear Matt's dad speak, "Good morning, Katie."

We both just take a sip of our coffees and I slink back to Matt's room, tugging the oversized tee down with one hand and a chorus of giggles trailing behind me. I close the door behind me and throw on my pair of PINK yoga pants and UGG slippers. Thank goodness the coffee is strong. Though my half-undressed entrance to the day was enough to jolt me awake. I grab my mug and head back out to join the conversation, this time fully presentable.

"Cream and sugar Katie." It isn't a question. Matt's dad scoots the creamer to me. He knows how Katie takes her coffee from having served it to her in settings much like this time and time again. I appreciate pretending nothing just happened. I too know Katie loved more cream than coffee in the morning. I have always felt like that defeats the purpose.

What lies before me is a crossroads. Do I dump the creamer in like Katie would and keep up the charade, or do I make up some excuse to keep the integrity of the coffee that I am most definitely going to need today.

"I am trying a new diet. Black coffee only."

I guess I am going with the excuse. This might be the best cup of coffee I have ever had, and I don't want to pretend that

I enjoy a bunch of sweetened creamer in it. Matt's dad salutes good luck to me as he enjoys his morning cup across the table from us. And I make a note to make a sour face every once and a while like it is a struggle to swallow.

"Katie and I were going to ask if we could go on a road trip for a concert in Seattle. We were talking late last night about what would take our minds off the tragedy of losing Alice and I was able to snag tickets late last night."

Matt's a decent liar. That surprises me a little. I know the boy can keep a secret, but I never pegged him as a good liar considering how honest he is.

"I hope you can get a refund," Matt's dad says casually not looking up from his incoming sip. "Did you really think that your mother and I would allow you to take off on a several days road trip out of state with your *girlfriend,* after you were just caught underage drinking at a party with the same said *girlfriend,* resulting in the death of her sister?" He gestures in the air between him, Matt, and me.

He's talking like I am not in the room, but with a soft, emphatic candor. It's a side of parenting I have never witnessed. I feel like a fly on the wall.

My face flushes and aches from being embarrassed. Even in all my insecurity I have never experienced the amount of humiliation I have had in the last few days.

"I wasn't drinking Dad, you know that. It was a really messed up situation, but I have never given you a reason not to trust me. Can we go?"

"When will you be back?"

"Four days. Two to drive there and two back."

"Where will you stay."

"A hotel near the concert hall," Matt lies.

Matt's father reconsiders after a few moments of silence.

"I'll tell your mother you will be back *no later* than four days."

I swallow my coffee and inhale incorrectly, causing me to choke for a few minutes, bringing way too much attention to my reaction. The way this conversation began, I am shocked we actually got permission to go.

"Oh, do Todd and Cheryl know about this?"

"Yes, they are cool with it," I lie.

Matt and I make a good team.

We plan to hit the road right after lunch, and Matt's mom gives us bags of fresh baked cookies and some popcorn for us to snack on.

"Thank you Mrs. Fields." Yes, *Mrs. Fields* made us fresh cookies for our trip. I always thought the name was perfect for her. She has the warmth and softness of a cookie just out of the oven. My heart breaks that Matt and I will never see them again, and that they have no idea. Yet another crippling brick in my wall of mourning.

Matt isn't giving off any signs of regret, but I think that may be because he doesn't grasp the reality of it all yet. Even I had a twinge of sadness leaving Todd and Cheryl. It was easy, but I at least felt something.

"Are you ready for our next adventure?"

He makes it sound like the world is waiting for us, and everything is going to be okay. I love his optimism and nod unconvincingly, looking straight ahead at the road. I think I have lied all I can for one day and I hate lying to Matt. It drains me, and I am nervous.

※ ※ ※

We make it to Arizona without much trouble. It takes a little over seven hours with a couple stops for bathroom breaks and food. The only money we have, except for Matt's credit card, is the cash that Katie had in her room. She only saved about three hundred dollars, but I also happened to snag the four grand stashed in Todd's sock drawer, which puts us in a better financial position than penniless. I barely had two dollars in change in my wallet, so I am grateful to Katie for saving anything. She was always the better saver.

Matt is just over eighteen, so I am not worried about him being able to get a job. I don't turn eighteen for another six months, so I am hoping once we get to Florida I can find someone who will hire me. So much for finishing high school.

Matt's convinced it shouldn't be too difficult for us to survive on what funds we have. But just in case, I plan on eating popcorn for dinner and having a cookie for dessert. "Don't worry about it. We can use the credit card as long as we aren't at our final destination. They can't track us if we don't make any purchases where we settle."

He has a point.

We find a campsite for the night and set the truck up under the stars.

"I left some sleeping bags and a foam pad from my last camping venture. I figured they would come in handy in order to camp in the bed of the truck tonight."

I didn't consider where I would be sleeping. I love that he was thoughtful enough to pack what we needed, and it is such a beautiful summer night. I can't think of anything more romantic.

"We aren't in a huge hurry, right? Why don't we head

over to the Grand Canyon before dawn to see the sunrise?"
"I really like that idea."

I have never seen the Grand Canyon, and it was on a travel bucket list that Katie and I had made. It was part of the reason I was so jealous that she was able to go to Europe and see so many things without me. We were supposed to do all our adventuring together and we had plans, after graduation.

Matt throws the foam pad down in the back of the truck and I hand him all the blankets and pillows. I should have packed warmer pajamas. I figured Miami would be warm, and I packed really light. Matt can tell that I am chilled even though it is a very warm desert night. My arms are crossed, and I have goose bumps up my forearms and down my legs. I never changed out of his shirt and my leggings this morning. It seemed like a really good travel outfit, cozy, and smells just like him. Like cinnamon.

Matt goes into the back and pulls out his soccer team sweatshirt that he had packed earlier and places it over my shoulders.

"I don't know how you're chilled in this desert heat. Are you sick?"

His hands palm my clammy forehead. Honestly, I do feel feverish, but I think it's just nerves and a lack of sleep because no healthy human could be cold in this kind of climate. Maybe I am getting the flu. I'd rather be violently ill than admit that Matt is starting to make me nervous.

"I'm fine."

Now that our comfortable friendship has become admittedly romantic, I am unnerved by everything Matt does. His smell sends me spinning, the way he smiles when he looks at me. He has that perfect Christian Bale smile that's tight and creases the indentations of his cheekbones. I completely melt when it is directed at me. His sandy brown hair is always tousled as if he just woke up from a nap. Soccer has made him lean but muscular. It doesn't take too much effort for an eighteen-year-old active boy to stay fit, but it is an attractive trait, nonetheless. I like it. I like him. A lot.

He climbs up into the pickup bed first and gives me a hand. We both are settling in a little earlier than usual, but the sky is dark, and the only source of light is the moon and a few campsite lampposts. We agree to get up well before dawn to see the sunrise over the Grand Canyon.

I feel like I haven't slept in a year. My body aches with fatigue and all the stress of the last several days. At this rate, we are only going to get a few hours of sleep before the three-and-a-half-hour drive to the Grand Canyon.

"Have you ever been there?"

For how much time I have spent around Matt, I know surprisingly little about him. I don't know what his aspirations are or what he plans to do now that he has graduated. I also know shockingly little about his past.

"My dad brought me when I was about eleven," he starts. "I remember the drive feeling like I was never going to get out of the car alive. It went on for ages. As a kid, I couldn't quite grasp the distance we were going, and it wasn't even that far, but I remember falling asleep and then Dad waking me up as we got there. We were going on our annual father-son trip and that year we planned specifically to see the Grand Canyon. My eleven-year-old brain couldn't comprehend just how grand we were talking until I saw it with my own eyes. It is the most spectacular view I have seen. I told my dad one day we should go back at sunrise. I'd like to see the Grand Canyon the way the world does when it wakes up, not just me waking up from a long car journey."

I can hear his breathing deepen and can tell he is feeling nostalgic and sincere. His relationship with his family is so pure, and I find myself green with envy because of it. I also dislike myself for taking him away from it all—for me.

"I cannot wait to take you there."

I can feel him reaching for my hand under the blankets and I make it easy for him to find. This moment radiates with even more intimacy, and I feel it's because he opened a window into who he is. He is allowing me to view his soul.

"I've never been anywhere." There is immense regret in my voice. "Katie and I were never even taken to Disneyland, and we lived so close by. We had plans to travel the world and see everything, starting with Disneyland when we graduated. Then we wanted to kiss Southern California goodbye. I don't know if she ever shared any of that with you. I didn't handle my jealousy very well when she went off to Europe without me. I know it was a really good opportunity for her, but I was angry she started exploring without me and we never did any of it together."

Matt wipes a tear from my cheek and gently slides his other arm beneath me until I am back nestled in, using his bicep as a pillow.

"She did tell me, Alice, she told me all about your plans, even the Disneyland part. She was really excited to have these adventures with you. As much as I like to think I could have kept her alive, I had no chance."

We are both crying at this point.

"I feel like Alice in Wonderland from that scene where she cries so much she creates a flood."

Matt chuckles. I always felt like Alice was a name that suited me.

"You truly are Alice in Wonderland, aren't you?"

"This nightmare doesn't really feel like a Wonderland, wouldn't you agree?"

Matt inches closer and is now mere centimeters from my mouth.

"There are moments that feel like it could be."

His kisses under the stars feel like a Wonderland moment, and I fear that is exactly what he meant.

CHAPTER 25

Alice
{ 2022 }

Ding...

Trevor: Good morning beautiful. I wanted to see if you had any plans for Christmas?

I love waking up to texts from Trevor; they definitely rouse me out of bed. This winter has been chilly by Miami standards, and people have been flooding into the bar for a drink to warm them up. It's funny how hot climate cultured people panic the minute the thermostat reads less than seventy-five degrees.

Christmas time in Miami is incredible though. I love how the palm trees are all adorned in lights and Santa is usually dressed in a more tropical ensemble rather than his typical red furry coat. The vibe is very chill, rather than chilly.

Kat: I don't have any plans for Christmas per se except maybe working. The owner hasn't decided yet if we are going to be closed on Christmas. He says it is turning into a moral issue. He wants to give us all the time off, but also doesn't want to lose out on the profits for that day. It's nice to work for someone who is so honest.

Trevor and I have been going strong for a little over six months now and it is starting to feel serious. It's the longest relationship I have ever had, and aside from Trevor's brief fiancé in Australia I think the same goes for him.

Not much has changed on the Brady and Bianca front, although Trevor is still actively trying not to lose those friendships, and Amber found herself a man who looks like Idris Elba. She's been frequenting my apartment for late night *Grey's* episodes a whole heck of a lot less. She is busy, I get it. Most of my free time has been spent with Trevor anyways, but I feel like I am perpetually going to be stuck on season seven and never make it to the finish line of this never-ending television series.

We still gab and gossip when we are on shift together, so I don't feel like I am missing out on my girl time with her too much.

Trevor: Have you ever been skiing?

Kat: If you are talking about skiing on water during the summertime, the answer is yes, albeit very poorly. However, considering I have never seen snow except for in Hallmark Christmas movies and my bucket list Pinterest board, I think it is safe to say the answer you are looking for is no. Miami doesn't hold out for a lot of snow skiing this time of year, or any for that matter."

Trevor: YOU HAVE NEVER SEEN SNOW! What rock have you been living under?

Kat: I thought I told you this. I will try not to take offense and assume you are wanting to whisk me away to some magical winter wonderland?

I may be jumping the gun a bit here, and I sincerely hope that I am right, and he isn't just asking me if I have ever been skiing to place some sort of gauge on my athletic prowess.

Kat: Pretty please whisk me away.

I cross my fingers behind my back. My thoughts cannot be calmed. Trevor has made me feel like I can branch out of my self-imposed cage just a little bit. There haven't been any more flowers since those lilies showed up on my doorstep six months ago, and I haven't bothered trying to figure out which ghost from my past sent them. No more intrusions means I won't be looking for it.

I did invest in a heavy-duty deadbolt for my apartment door and was contemplating a camera, but I didn't want it to turn my apartment into someplace I found myself most afraid. The lock was enough peace of mind.

I still haven't shared too much about my past with Trevor. He knows I had a sister and she died. He doesn't know her name, (or mine still for that matter), and he doesn't know how she died. The longer we are together the more I feel him wanting to ask more questions. It's only fair to want to know the life and history of the person you have been seriously dating for half a year. I know one day that bomb will go off, but I am holding it at bay for as long as possible. I can hear the ticking growing louder each day.

What's the worst thing that could happen? Well, for starters, he could leave me, he could condemn me, and based on if there were any criminal findings in the investigation into Katie's death, I could put him in a compromising ethical position. I never stuck around to see if the cops ruled it an official accident. I knew it wasn't.

> **Trevor**: Of course, I want to whisk you away. How does Vail for Christmas sound? Fair warning it's a family trip, but I promise you that there will be lots and lots of snow. Plus, I will be there. I like to think that's an added perk.
>
> **Kat**: You can't tell right now, but I am drooling like a dog. I am SO EXCITED . . . to see snow. lol.
>
> **Trevor**: Lol you are mean. Maybe we should FaceTime so I can see your drooling dog face?
>
> **Kat**: Lol I would love to, but my break is almost over.
>
> **Trevor:** Ah I see, well better pack soon, we leave tomorrow.
>
> **Kat:** Tomorrow!?
>
> **Trevor**: Don't worry I already cleared your schedule with your boss. Christmas is canceled for Salut. I may have sweetened the deal a little bit and believe me your boss had no moral conviction in taking the bribe. Merry Christmas indeed. Everything you need is waiting for you at home, so don't panic. I'll see you tomorrow love. Have a good rest of your shift and don't tell Amber, she'll get jealous. Lol.

Of course I am going to tell Amber, and Trevor knows that. Her jealousy is also inevitable, but also I assume she will be happy for me. As great as her Idris Elba boy toy is, he isn't whisking her away on a fancy vacation at a ski resort for Christmas.

"Hey Amber!"

I sing in a whistle-like sort of tone. Let the taunting commence.

※ ※ ※

My shift felt like it lasted an eternity. I officially aged forty years with the anticipation of going home. I was acting dramatic, but I swear the clock was laughing at me. It grew a big fat mouth of mockery and slowed time down all over the world just to prolong my excitement. I may be tired from a long day of work, but it is a good kind of exhilarating tiredness.

Amber left hours ago and literally laughed at me on her way out. I deserved it for how much I was razzing her earlier and for how much I rubbed my amazing Christmas plans in her face.

I basically levitated to my apartment when I clocked out. I was under a hypnotic trance. I don't remember getting in my car to drive home, I just remember arriving.

A few months ago, Trevor had delivered a box of chocolate-covered strawberries and flowers, just because, and they were left by the front door. The reaction was not what he expected when I called him in a rage. It was a really unfair reaction to something so well intentioned. I gave him a key to my apartment and told him that I just don't like things left at my front door. I told him it stresses me out, and that I might have bad neighbors who would steal my stuff. I don't. I have the best neighbors, but regardless we were at the point in our relationship where it became appropriate to give him a key anyway.

A lot of my triggers bark their way out of me and latch onto him in the worst ways, but instead of prying or getting upset, he responded by giving me a key to his place as well, and we just let my overreaction go. Pretty sure I blamed it on my period and then thanked him for the chocolate because the antioxidants help with the mood swings. I am a master at making excuses for outbursts that I don't wish to explain.

I've kind of gotten over the fact that I lie to all the important people in my life. I've made the lie my reality, so it really doesn't feel like lying anymore.

I open my apartment door to see brand new luggage stacked against the base of the island and a note on the counter.

Hey Kat.

Surprise! I know you've never seen snow. I was pretending that I forgot so you would be more surprised. Gotcha! You mentioned it pretty early on in our getting to know each other, and I have seen your Pinterest board over your shoulder when we are watching TV together. I watch you mindlessly scroll through all the images, daydreaming about the future and I want to be the one to make all your dreams come true. I know you fantasize about all things snow and cold weather activities, but I also know that you have made zero plans to fulfill those desires. I don't think you even own a jacket that isn't made out of denim. That is where I come in.

Inside the luggage you will find all you will need. I got a metallic teal hard-shell suitcase for you, because those are honestly the most durable and it's your favorite color. Great for how much you desire to travel. It is an investment in the future trips I hope to take with you. Let this be the first of many.

Since you have also never seen snow and have lived in Miami for the last decade, (see I pay attention), I know that you have never had a reason to stockpile winter clothes, especially when your space is so limited. I'm sorry, it's not limited, it's cozy. We are going to be gone for a week, so inside are a week's worth of ski clothes, snow boots, warm loungewear and a few other fun things just for me . . .

I know I told you to pack, but let's be real, what on earth were you going to pack? The warmest thing you own is a loose knit sweater. So . . . no need to pack babe, I did it for you. The plane leaves at seven in the morning and I will be there by around five-thirty to pick you up. Get a good night's rest. Inside the carryon is an outfit marked travel day. It is a perfect combination of layers, so you don't get too warm in Miami and aren't too cold when we land in Vail. By the way, I had help shopping. Women's fashion is so confusing.

I cannot wait to have a white Christmas with you. Get some good sleep. I love you.

P.S., this is not your Christmas gift. That comes later.
Trevor Daniels.

We have said "I love you" many times by now. It was simply a regular Tuesday night for us. Loaded with cuddles and great Chinese take away, but those words meant everything. I love hearing him say it. Makes me feel like I just took a shot of whiskey, and my entire body warms with the sound of his voice uttering those three little words. I even said it back the first time he whispered it into my ear overlooking the view from my balcony. I never tire of it.

The urge to resist tears is futile. I throw open the suitcases and unload all the surprise outfits he has bought and packed away for me. Even on top of the carryon is a new Louis Vuitton and matching wallet.

I can hardly breathe. I have never been this spoiled in my entire life. I immediately rip my phone out and FaceTime Trevor even though I pray he is sleeping. He is coming to pick me up in about five hours.

He answers anyway. I can hear the gravel in his voice as he palms his eyelids, urging them to lift from their heaviness.

"Hey beautiful, did you get all squared away for tomorrow."

"I wanted to show you my drooling puppy dog face. If I thought I was drooling earlier I was clearly mistaken."

I put my hand under my chin and tilt my face downward, opening my eyes really big and panting like a dog that just got done playing fetch. Pretty much anything this boy does makes pant.

I can see his face perk up a little as he starts to wake more with each passing moment of my excitement. I also make him laugh from a dead sleep, so I am pretty proud of myself for that.

"You have to be prepared. The snow is no joke. You may have hyped it up a little too much."

"Even so, I can stay inside by a fire in my new lounge sets and hug my brand spanking new Louis Vuitton, like are you kidding me?" The volume inches upwards with infectious energy. "Are you sure that's not my Christmas gift, because all of this is way too much, and I am obsessed with it all! Are you my Christmas gift?"

You're my miracle.

"Get some sleep Kat, and I will see you in a few hours. I love you."

"Yeah . . . yeah . . . yeah . . . like I can sleep now. I love you too."

I throw my phone on its charger on my night table and begin to pack my toiletries. For as thoughtful as Trevor is, I am sure he didn't pack an electric toothbrush and my twenty-step skin care routine. I don't even have a bag to put them in, so I grab a gallon sized Ziploc and throw it all in there. At least this way if there is any explosion of lotions from the high altitude of the Colorado mountains, I will be able to protect all my precious new stuff.

I am going to the mountains of Colorado. I can't believe it!

I never felt like gifts were particularly high on my list of love languages, but Trevor is starting to make me reevaluate. He spoils me and I don't feel deserving of so much.

I know I am getting zero sleep tonight, so I set up my coffee pot to start the automatic drip at five in the morning. That way I have a good thirty minutes of time for the caffeine to soak into my bloodstream and make me feel human.

I want to go through all the bags even more but would hate to repack it all before having to leave and risk forgetting something. So, I leave most of the luggage untouched except for my new travel outfit he told me to wear.

I am so antsy and just staring up at my ceiling. The last time I blankly stared at what was directly above me was that night with Matt when we slept in his truck. Only I was outside back then with a view of crystal-clear skies. Right now, all I see are the weird bumps in the texture of my ceiling. Both kind of look like stars if you squint enough.

It still unnerves me that Matt randomly pops into my head. It is getting more and more frequent, which frightens me. Could it be that my brain is remembering all these stupid little nuanced details so that when the time comes to spill my soul to Trevor I have a fresh recollection?

Who knows? There was no real ending with Matt. I let my feelings for Matt drift long ago. I had no other choice.

All I can really fixate on right now is that the man of my dreams is flying me to see snow in the morning and time is still being a fickle fool.

❊ ❊ ❊

I didn't sleep a wink, but the buzzing of my coffee maker and my immediate joyful disposition gets me out of bed in an instant. Being a bartender keeps me up late, so I have naturally adapted to become a night owl, but today is an exception. I am sure the adrenaline will wear off at some point, but for now I feel like I am five years old and full of expendable energy.

Trevor knocks on the door, and I about bowl him over when I greet him. I didn't expect him to have hot coffee, but he hands me a red holiday to-go cup and looks at me like a stranger has just assaulted him.

"Who are you and what have you done with my girlfriend?"

"Oh . . . ha, ha. Come on, let's go," I say as I grab my collection of new and gorgeous luggage. I take a swig of the coffee he brought me and completely ignore the pot on my countertop.

"Mmmm black and hot, just how I like it."

"You always act so surprised when I know things about you. We have been spending every waking moment together for six months now. I know how you take your coffee. You made sure that was one of the first things I knew about you."

"I feel like Princess Diana," I beam as we walk to his car. "Did Princess Di have a Louis Vuitton? I am stroking the bag like it is a small dog.

"I am sure she did. Wow you are awake this morning. Let me drink my extra sugar sissy latte as you so lovingly nicknamed it and let me catch up."

I can see the sleepiness in his eyes. Trevor isn't much of a morning person, much like myself, but he is better at this than I am, usually.

"You order a sugar free hazelnut latte with almond milk and no foam extra hot. It's a little girly if you ask me. Whatever caffeine is in your latte needs to hurry up and get on my level! We are going to the SNOW!"

I know I am annoying him with my caffeinated, erratic behavior. Much resembling a squirrel with ADHD, but I just don't care. He probably finds it adorable. Maybe just a tiny bit.

"I am this close to taking your coffee away." I know he teases. So, I tease back.

"You wouldn't dare." His threat is playful, but I cannot take a chance on anyone taking away my liquid energy. I am afraid for myself. With any more excitable energy I may not be allowed on the plane. I am like a bomb that could go off at any minute, and the airports don't take too kindly to bomb threats.

"Where are you going?" I am thoroughly confused, "The airport is in the other direction, and if we are driving to Colorado, we are going to hit the ocean before we get anywhere close to snow."

I can see the smirk inching across his face like he knows something I don't, and I know I haven't annoyed him too much this morning because he still is relishing having the upper hand.

"Yes, *one* airport is in that direction, but we are going to another one. This is surprise number two."

I didn't realize how much I like surprises until last night. Usually they send me into panic, but Trevor has a knack for making it fun.

"Oh . . . I get surprises. Okay . . . so luggage was one, and weird off-the-beaten-path airport is two . . .not sure why. . . how many are there?"

"Several, although I have to warn you some of them you may not like."

What does that mean? Is he going to present me with lilies? Are we going to a lily farm? Is there no coffee in Vail? Are we camping in an igloo where I will never be warm again?

I have no idea what a bad surprise from Trevor even looks like, but I guess we shall see.

CHAPTER 26

Katie

{ 2012 }

Dear Alice,

Remember the time that we successfully switched places for an entire week, and no one noticed? We got the idea from one of the Olsen twins movies. One of their early ones, when they were really little, and their movies weren't completely driven by which boy gets which twin. No judgment on those movies, we watched every single one of them and devoured them for material. It felt like we were seen by Mary-Kate and Ashley, like there was someone in the public eye who understood the challenges and joys of being an identical twin.

I was really impressed that we got away with it for as long as we did. We probably could have gone longer, but you had that big test coming up in algebra class and I wasn't smart enough to take that for you, so we decided to tell everyone we had traded places for a week.

Cheryl and Todd were so mad. I think they were mostly

angry with themselves for being so detached from our daily lives that they had no clue. They told us that if we were ever to do that again, that we would be in big trouble.

Seeing as how we were in eighth grade and pretty young, their threats still scared us, but it didn't take long to realize that it would be more of an inconvenience for them to punish us than it was for them just to ignore our wrongdoings. I think Cheryl took away my phone once, and the duration of my punishment was supposed to be two weeks, but after one day of my boredom and nagging her incessantly, she caved and gave it back to me.

That was the moment that I realized we could manipulate and be practically untouchable. That is until the ground from beneath my feet seemed to crumble away from me, leaving me suspended in midair and fighting for a foundation. (Wow I can be dramatic, but that is exactly how it feels, constantly, never ceasing, floating.)

You were always more self-satisfied, and I know that I sought out the validation of others a lot more than you did. I like the popularity and the laziness it allotted me. I didn't feel the need to excel in academics when my looks could get me places, and I never really understood why you dove so hard into academia when we have the same face. You could get just as far without all the hard work you would put in.

I didn't understand until I learned the critical lesson that you cannot trust a single soul, especially those closest to you. People in general will just always let you down.

The exception is you, Alice. You have never let me

down. You have always been there for me, and I need you now most of all. I know you won't let me down.

I remember that week that I got to pretend to be you. I had never felt more comfortable in my skin. I felt like I had no pressure in the entire world. I am sure it is because I wasn't constantly seeking popularity and status, but I was also not too worried about my grades like you were. I was suspended in a limbo, but being able to wear my same face, and yet feel completely unburdened. It felt like I was given a beautiful mask to wear.

I felt this way when I was you in public. When I was pretending to be you in private, I realized why you hated being you so much. I wanted to fix it, but I couldn't. I was better at being myself in private and fake in public. You were fake in private and your true self in front of the world.

We never did swap places again. I also think we grew out of watching the Mary-Kate and Ashley movies. I don't know about you, but I think they didn't have their lives together like we thought when we started seeing their anorexic bodies in the tabloids and magazines. They suffered too, just in different ways.

I sort of stopped idolizing them, and I think that maybe it is just the fate of all blonde identical twin sisters to deal with a lot of hardships. It's probably not appropriate to make such a blanket statement, but when my world crumbled, I didn't feel I could turn to you or the Olsen twins for guidance, I felt truly lost and hopeless. I still do, which is why we are here and I am writing these stupid letters.

Did you know that when I was in Italy I went to a

small Catholic cathedral for mass and sat in during the sermon? Remember that time we went to church with Cheryl? We were so engrossed in the message we scared Cheryl into never taking us back. We always plotted a way to go back, but never did. Well, in Italy I was in a deep moment of desperation. I am told that desperate people often call out to God, even if they don't necessarily know God, but I was a person under the category of desperate and reaching out to the heavens for help.

It was intense.

There was a lot of standing and kneeling, which was very different from the Pentecostal church we went to back home all those years ago, but it felt relatively the same and I think they worship the same God. Catholics just have more rules on how to commune with God, or so I gathered.

I spoke to the priest after and told him all my darkness, all my secrets, and asked him how I can get into heaven. He was kind and gave me what felt like homework.

I don't know what I was hoping for. Maybe I wanted God himself to come down and cleanse all my blackness. I wanted him to deliver us from our shame. Didn't the pastor talk about Jesus washing us white as snow? Maybe I should have gone back to see him, and maybe I still should.

For now, though, it is cathartic to write these letters. With every page and with every line I write, I am pouring out all the sisterly love I have for you.

Love,
Katie.

CHAPTER 27

Alice
{ 2012 }

M ATT'S KISS LINGERS on my lips under the Arizona sky before he leans into me and climbs on top. His body dominates mine in every way possible. I like the strain in his biceps as he keeps his upper body elevated.

"Are you sure?"

I have to ask. Last time I didn't say anything, I just went along with it, and it had an emotional consequence, both of us riddled with guilt the minute it was over. I don't want to shame him, but I also don't want to add to our collective grief.

"I am not Katie." I have to make sure he understands this.

It comes out more like a statement than a threat and my voice is barely above a whisper, so I know Matt isn't detecting animus in my tone. It's just a fact. *I am not her.*

Matt stops kissing my neck and looks down at me.

"I know you're not Katie. You're Alice, and you're kind . . ." he kisses me, ". . . and beautiful . . . ," he kisses me, ". . . and the most amazing and bravest person I know. I am shocked, just as much as you are. I never planned to feel this way about you, and I thought at first it was just because you remind me so much of her, but you are her opposite in so many ways. You are nothing like her, you are stronger, and you have completely enraptured me. Wherever life takes you, Alice, is where I want to be."

I am too afraid to ask him what he knows.

"Okay."

That's what I say *Okay?* You have got to be kidding me. I feel so inarticulate and stupid. Here this amazing boy is telling me how much he adores me for me and not that I have the same face as my sister, and all I can say is *okay!*

Thank goodness what follows doesn't involve talking.

I reach for Matt's hands. The full weight of him is now on top of me as we make out. I slide his hand slowly up my shirt until the warmth of his palm relaxes my chilled skin. I want him to know that I want him to touch me.

The first time we touched, we didn't really stop and savor what was happening. It felt more like an itch that needed to be scratched. It was fast and meaningless. This time feels different. We take more time to stop and appreciate each and every sensation.

My hands trace over every scar. The one on his chin from when he fell over his handlebars as a kid. The one on his thumb where he cut himself in the garden at home.

Matt kisses my dark purple under eyes that look more like a bruise by now, and his fingers encircle the piercing in my navel.

I notice that his back is perfectly rounded with muscle and the sides of his obliques are perfectly rigid. I really enjoy moving my hands over them so that they fall into the grooves. It's all very California of him, and his body looks like the sun enjoys kissing every inch of him as well.

The one thing *not* California about Matt is the way he talks. He's way more articulate than the average surfer dude, avoiding the overuse of the words "like" or "bro." I always thought that he was too smart to be categorized as some dumb jock.

His hands are timid around my body, and I am curious if he feels the need to conduct a deep exploration of every crevice like I am to him. I slip my fingers into the waistline of his boxers and the elastic gives only a little around his taut abdomen. He has no body fat. My touch seems to drive him crazy, and he inhales sharply.

I think I like teasing him. In fact, I know I do. I slowly drag my one finger that is in his waistline and move it across the front of his pelvis, just below his belly button. I make sure not to touch him down there just yet. I tease and relish in the reaction I get, based on how his abdominal muscles flex with strain and anticipation.

It is fortunate I am not wearing any buttons. Everything I am wearing can slide off with the simplest of ease. I guess Matt was planning on sleeping in his jeans, which is just the most uncomfortable thing I can think of, so I let him know what a terrible idea it is by trying to unbutton them for him. He just has to slide off my leggings, but I am tasked with removing his jeans. It's unfair.

"Do you have protection?"

It seems like a fair question, but why would he have initiated sex with me had he not brought protection? But also, why on earth would he have brought a condom into the bed of his truck?

Both seem like answers I wouldn't fault him for, but I don't know how I feel about having unprotected sex. I know I won't stop regardless.

He answers very confidently with an, "I do," and resumes our interactions without pause.

"Were you planning on getting lucky?" I chuckle nervously. Who says *get lucky* anymore. I have absolutely no idea what I am doing.

"I never dreamed I would get this lucky."

Ah, the cheesy one-liner comebacks that sound like Ryan Reynolds in some sappy romantic comedy. I wonder when men grow out of those, and I hope it isn't anytime soon. Every girl deserves to feel like the main character at some point in her life. I hope that I can have the lead role many, many more times before the cheesy lines stop. That sort of thing might turn off some girls, but with Matt it doesn't feel stupid. My face heats from blushing.

I like how his hand trembles a bit when his fingers glide over my nipple, which reacts like it wants more. Here I am under the stars in the desert, losing all of myself to a boy in the back of his truck.

I can feel him sliding my leggings down as we both remain still under the blankets. He keeps my shirt on but lifts it up to my chin to see all of me. I have a bra on this time, and I can see his allure as well as disappointment. I reach one hand back and unhook it effortlessly from seven years of practice.

"That was impressive," Matt remarks as he pushes it out of the way to join the T-shirt fabric around my neck. I like that he is impressed by something so simple as unclasping a bra. I like that he is easy to please and that I am the one doing the pleasing.

He reaches his head down and begins to drag his tongue over the peak of my chest, conjuring an involuntary groan. I can feel myself opening for him and longing for that pressure.

I wrap my legs around him and drag his body into mine.

Luckily, no one is around us, so I don't have to be too concerned about being quiet.

My moan is like the checkered flag at a race. It means green-means-go, and Matt is sitting up and completely undressing himself still on top of me. My leggings are somewhere under the blankets in the bed. Bra? Who cares? I never want to put them back on because it means this will be over.

Neither of us takes the time to look at our naked and vulnerable selves. It's dark out anyway, and I think we both are satisfied with the touch component of the evening rather than the visual. The blackness of the night heightens our senses. Every touch is electric, and every sound is more instigating. I don't need to see him to feel what he wants.

I didn't even see him put the condom on, but I know he has because I can feel it. My limited experience has told me that sex is not like it is in the movies. There are moments for sure, but mostly it is awkward and a little uncomfortable, and condoms do not feel good when they are inside you.

You wouldn't want someone to finger you with a rubber glove on and I cringe at the concept of all that latex inside me at once. I'd like to feel him. Just him. Bare and beautiful, but the thought of getting pregnant dampens my passion.

It's over almost before it really began, but I have heard that about teenage boys. I have so much ahead of me I am not in any particular hurry to rush anything. I like that I drive him so crazy that he explodes.

Now comes the awkward part. I wonder how he will react this time. Last time he left me to interpret my emotions alone, but other than locking himself inside the cabin of the truck I am not sure where Matt would be able to run off to. That is until he throws on his jeans and leaves the truck without saying a word.

Here we go again.

I put all my clothes on, including the soccer sweatshirt he let me borrow, and wait alone for what feels like an eternity. But then Matt returns and plops down next to me, spooning me incredibly tight. A short burst of air escapes my lungs. I actually get winded for a second.

"Oh hey, wow." My words are breathy from being plopped on.

"What, you didn't think I was going to run off . . . again?"

"I mean you just got up to leave and didn't say anything, so yeah I kind of did."

Our conversation is playful, even though the topic at hand is heavy. He kisses my earlobe and whispers into it, "Never again."

I am sorry for a lot of things. I am pretty much sorry for everything that has happened over the last few days, but mostly I am sorry that I am not sorry about how I feel for Matt and the relationship we have fallen into.

"I am sorry I lived, and she didn't."

"I am sorry she didn't survive. I am not sorry you did instead. I often think I could have done more, but I didn't have all the pieces. Katie was like that. She liked to play games and keep you guessing. Whenever we fought, I had to play twenty questions just to figure out what I had done to upset her. She liked to watch me squirm. She liked to mess with my head for her own amusement."

You would think talking about Katie in the context of her relationship with Matt would be distressing, but I like hearing about his relationship with my sister.

"I think for as much as she knew how to love, she poured all of that into you. She was broken. I keep racking my brain trying to figure out how we are here right now and how the entire world went up in hypothetical flames in such a short period of time. It's unfathomable to me that one person can have such a detrimental ripple effect on others, especially in the lives of those you loved so much during your time here on earth. She is dead. She doesn't care about the mess she left behind. Maybe the only way to not leave a trail of wreckage when you die is to not love anyone at all."

My mind has trailed off into the mirk as it so often does when I am in deep affliction. I find myself floating in my own thoughts. I forget that I am saying any of this out loud until Matt interjects.

"That's a lot of darkness Alice."

His deep, gravelly voice snaps me out of my trance and back into reality.

"You're right, that was too much. It is of course incredibly meaningful to love, I just don't know how to mitigate great love also equating great loss . . . we should change the subject."

I can feel Matt breathing on my hair and inhaling deeply as if to store the memory of my scent mixed with the dry desert night. *Bath and Body Works* should monetize it and call it *Desert Blossom*. It can smell like orange blossoms, lilacs, and cacti. They can also add shimmer to make it look like the night sky tonight. I don't think I have ever seen so many stars.

"What do you think happens when we die? Do you think we become like stars and can look down on the ones we love while we shine?" Matt asks as he brushes my hair back from my face.

"Matt, that isn't exactly lighting the subject. But I have my beliefs about what happens when we depart this world."

"Oh really . . . do tell."

I think Matt is expecting some sort of sci-fi imagining, like we transform into the force from *Star Wars* or something completely bleak like *ashes-to-ashes and dust-to-dust*. It would be an appropriate conclusion considering our desert surroundings are dust.

"Cheryl took us to church once. I literally think it was an isolated event because I do not remember ever going back, but the sanctuary was large and there was a big stain-glass window depicting the crucifixion of Jesus behind the pulpit. I thought it was the most masterful piece of artwork I had ever seen.

"Everyone there was really kind. We were greeted at the door and given a Bible so we could follow along with the sermon. Katie and I took one, but Cheryl didn't bother. She always painted the church as some sort of cult, but I think she had just had a fight with Todd and didn't know what else to do. I hear the church is a great place for desperate people.

"The sermon was all about how Christ came to die for us so that we can live eternally with Him in heaven. The preacher explained how heaven is paradise and better than any tropical oasis here on earth, and more peaceful and full of fatherly love. It sounded like everything I have ever wanted in my entire life. Plus, the idea of someone loving you so much that they die for you was overwhelmingly beautiful, and I wanted to claim it. I wanted to be a daughter of Christ and feel purposeful and chosen.

"Todd and Cheryl never provided the sort of parental love I felt in that room. Everyone had their arms raised in worship. Tears stained their cheeks. I wanted to know this God, so when they asked if anyone would like to secure their destiny in eternity and claim Jesus as their Savior, Katie and I raised our hands. I knew I wanted to secure my fate. Especially when the afterlife seemed a million times better than life here on earth.

"I don't think Cheryl expected us to eat it up as much as we did, which is probably why she didn't take us back. I think it scared her. Katie and I thought about going by ourselves several times, but this was before we had a driver's licenses, and then we just never did. Maybe for Christmas a few times, but nothing regularly.

"However, it just kind of always stuck with me, and I think Katie too, and there is still a part of me that would like to know more. So yeah . . . I think I believe in Jesus and heaven, and I believe that's where Katie is right now. Unburdened and free. Probably sipping a Mai Thai in paradise . . . I don't know."

Matt doesn't say anything for what feels like a long while. I think maybe he fell asleep, but then he comes back with his considerate sincerity and tells me that my idea of the afterlife sounds way nicer than his star idea, and how maybe when we get to where we are going we can find a church and start attending regularly on Sundays, just to see what all the fuss is about.

Tufts of fluff fall off into my hands as I fidget with the blanket a little bit as the night carries on. Small pieces of fabric torn away as I just bore my soul to Matt. My ears have been burning all night to learn more about Matt and his plans. I may have derailed all of his hopes and dreams by allowing him to follow me into the unknown.

"Okay, I am going to change the subject again. I have to ask, what were your plans now that you graduated, you know, before this amazing camping trip." I gesture to our lovely surroundings.

"Well . . . I applied to join the military, and in a few weeks I was to set off for San Diego to join the Navy. I thought about joining the Marines like my dad did when he was right out of high school. He built his entire career in the military, and I am not sure I want to do that, but it could have opened doors for me. I am, I mean *was*, very excited about that.

"Dad shared with me some of the difficulties of being in the Marines and the immense challenges to the body and mind that it brings. It was overwhelming, and while the Navy is definitely not for wimps, I think I'd prefer my focus be on boats and water-related militia, instead. I have always had a thing for ships.

"For family game nights we would play *Battleship*. Other than the fact that I think Dad let me win, I was undefeated. It was a real confidence booster. Mom is really proud of me even though I know she is scared to see her only son go off and join the Navy. It's a risky move for sure, but I think she is also kind of used to it by now. She has had to deal with all the deployments my dad has gone through during their marriage. My baby sister might grow up to do the same thing, but she is only five, so Mom has a long time before she has to worry about her.

"I thought about maybe being a cook in the Navy and getting a job as a chef in one of those elite restaurants in Los Angeles when I was done living at sea, but I had no official long-term goals.

"Katie didn't want me to join the Navy. She said I was selfish for thinking about doing something so dangerous that could maybe kill me. It is completely ironic how hypocritical that is now. She didn't want to be a military wife, and I get that. She didn't really have the demeanor for it. My mom has patience oozing out of every pore in her body. Katie, on the other hand, couldn't be patient enough to wait for a red light to turn green."

"Oh, I know she was the worst at that. Do you know how

many times we almost were crunched like a soda can because she ran a red light or a stop sign? I almost refused to get in the car until she promised to follow the rules of the road better."

We both laugh, which makes me wonder why borderline slandering Katie and her memory seems amusing. Is it us trying to satiate our guilt, or is it simply because it is easier to despise her for her faults than it is to miss her and all her goodness right now. It is starting to wear on me a little, though and I like to think of Katie more in her bright shining qualities rather than the ones that drove us crazy. No one is perfect.

Matt starts to ask me about my hopes and dreams, but a yawn slips from his lips just after the sentence comes out. It is way later than it should be for us to be awake if we are still planning on seeing the sunrise over the Grand Canyon.

"We should get some sleep. We need to be up in about three hours if we are to hit the Grand Canyon by daybreak."

I don't even think I am finished giving permission to fall asleep before I feel Matt's breathing change and turn into a subtle snore. I've heard boys can fall asleep faster than girls, but this feels like some kind of record. I am exhausted, understandably, and yet I still will most likely lie awake for another hour contemplating everything until I pass out.

※ ※ ※

Next thing I know, Matt's phone is blaring "Reveille" to wake us. A deafening boom of trumpets. He would do well in the military with this kind of rousing. I, on the other hand, have never hated a sound more in my entire life. But Matt is kind enough to jostle me awake with a small kiss on the cheek and a nudge. The tip of his nose is cold on my face.

He is still spooning me when I crack my eyes open. I have never slept next to anyone before the last few days and the warmth from Matt was like sleeping in the embrace of a giant teddy bear. He never let go of me all night. We never stirred. I was grateful to have his sweater, and I think he was chilled and used my body for warmth. He makes me feel safe.

"You are really pretty when you wake up, you know that."

"Coffee. . ." My voice is garbled. I am a complete zombie.

Matt's expression went from lovesick puppy to *what the hell* in a matter of seconds.

"Coffee," I repeat, emphatically.

Why that's the only word I can verbalize right now is beyond me. I feel like I might be having a stroke, but also my throat feels like sandpaper in this ridiculously dry desert climate. I never want water. Always coffee. Coffee is just bean-infused water anyway.

Matt has an insulated tumbler that he filled with water for us when we were on the road, and he hands it to me to take a swig.

"Sorry," I sputter. "I am not a morning person, and am in desperate need of coffee. Can we get some when we hit the road? Do we have time?"

Unfathomably, Matt thinks I am adorable in the morning. It's all he can see, and he gives me a kiss on the mouth before he confirms that we can indeed grab a cup before we hit the Canyon.

I am a little self-conscious that I haven't had an opportunity to brush my teeth and I have on occasion disgusted myself with my own morning breath, but if Matt noticed it doesn't deter him from kissing me again. Coffee will make my mouth feel so much worse. I will just brush my teeth in the Starbucks bathroom.

"We better hit the road, we are going to be pushing it as it is, sleepyhead."

Sleepyhead? I haven't slept in about three days straight.

Haphazardly, we throw the blankets in the backseat and jump into the cabin of the truck. The vibration of the road causes me to instantly fall back asleep on my pillow propped up on the side of the door. I wanted to just stay in the back of the truck all cozy in bed, but I don't know the laws here in Arizona, and I am sure it's not legal. It was also unfair to make Matt drive alone.

Regardless, I fall back asleep so it's not like he has someone to have a great conversation with anyway. I am comatose, only to stir awake when we pull into a Starbucks. Matt goes ahead and orders our drinks and I rush to the bathroom with my toiletry kit. I have now officially been wearing these leggings and his shirt for well over forty-eight hours going on seventy-two. The grime is growing, and I am due for a change, but we don't have the time to gussy up right now, so the pajama look is going to have to fly a little bit longer. Thank goodness for toothpaste and deodorant to make me feel human again.

Matt is considerate and bought me a venti off his credit card. He figures his parents aren't watching where his transactions are coming from just yet. We aren't technically missing for another three days.

He sips his matching venti black Americano and takes a call outside. The only other person I can fathom who is awake at this hour is his dad. Matt heads to the patio to take the call, clearly out of earshot from me. Something feels off and the hairs on my arms stick straight up.

I give Matt some space and I savor the warmth of my coffee to calm my goose bumps a bit. The air conditioning in Starbucks is at full blast so I attribute some of my shivers to the rapid change in temperatures. I am excited to go outside and feel the heat. I am presently the only one standing in Starbucks, minus the two employees and the silence is so loud. I could really use some noise to drown out my intrusive thoughts.

A quick blow of the milk-frothing wand on Starbucks' automatic espresso machines startles me and my body jolts in a spooked little hop. I think I can hear the baristas snickering like I just gave them a little entertainment in their early morning before the rush.

When Matt returns, I can tell he is a little perturbed but trying not to let the emotion show.

"You ready to get back on the road? We are about two hours out."

"What was that about? Your dad was calling really early?" I assume.

"Oh nothing, he was just checking on how our night went and how travel is going. He knows I am an early riser." And now I am confirmed.

Matt grabs my hand and my toiletry kit from me as we walk back to his lifted behemoth of a red truck. I can't help but recognize that this is the first time he has blatantly lied to me, and I have to say I don't care for it, at all.

CHAPTER 28

Alice
{ 2022 }

Surprise number two is equal if not better than my first as we pull into a small airport right onto the tarmac. Before us is a gorgeous gossamer white aircraft with Trevor's firm's logo in big bold letters on the side. *Heathrow and Daniels* are just staring at me in huge font, and it is so surreal to see Trevor's last name on a jet.

"I knew you were good at your job, but this feels like a privilege only the mob or Taylor Swift gets to relish in. Holy crap!"

"I told you we weren't driving to the snow-covered mountains."

How he can joke at a time like this is beyond me. I have never felt a more serious moment in our relationship.

"Does it have a matching yacht to go with it?"

"Yes . . . you were on it the second time we met."

Okay, I wasn't being serious, but Trevor actually is. I knew he was rich, but this sort of wealth feels surreal. Suddenly I feel very insufficient, and thanks to Trevor, I at least look like I belong here. All my new clothes now feel like costumes to play the part and I am relieved to wear them. It's the person inside all the fancy new stuff that I am not sure will fit in so nicely.

I am a bartender and ran away from a broken home life when I was seventeen. I have no idea which fork to use first when there are multiple of them in front of me and if I am quizzed during this trip, which feels likely, I know for sure I will not receive a passing grade.

Trevor can sense my nervousness.

"It's going to be great. Just remember the snow."

I can feel his hand on the small of my back inching me forward as someone comes to collect our bags out of the Range Rover and load them onto the aircraft. We are the first to arrive, which gives me a sense of relief. I am never the first person anywhere. It gives me a chance to openly gawk at the cream leather seats and fiddle with the windows like a child before it would be totally inappropriate to do so in front of others. I assume more people are coming. Trevor did say it was a family vacation. Apparently, this is an annual endeavor where several members of his family go as a tradition.

What luxury, oh my.

I am startled when the first newcomer to join us is a bubbly voice greeting me with squeaks and giggles.

"*Ahhh*, Kat! Hi! Are you ready to go on an adventure?"

My head perks up instantly. I mean how could it not. Then I notice the tuft of brunette blur that is Bianca whose face now matches her voice. She has her small Pilates toned arms wrapped around my neck in a hug before I can even utter a response to her warm greeting. She has my arms pinned by my side. I can't even sit up from my seat in enough time to hug her back.

"I see you are wearing some of the clothes I picked out for

you. When Trevor said he wanted to surprise you and was going shopping, I knew he would be totally hopeless, so I told him I would step in and get the job done for him. His heart was in the right place, but a new winter wardrobe needed a woman's touch, don't you think?"

Bianca has bounced onto the jet like a tornado and is basically having a conversation with herself even though she is directing her questions at me. She doesn't pause for a minute for my response. Thank goodness because I have no idea what I would say back to her other than a tepid thank you.

Like a feather caught in a breeze she floats down in the row next to us and has chosen the window seat, same as me. It's nice to have Trevor in between us as a buffer. Bianca may be alone right now, but I have a strong hunch Brady is not that far behind. So, this is what a bad surprise feels like. I feel a little ambushed and the magic from my new purse and the plane is starting to wear off just a bit.

"I thought you said this was an annual *family* trip. Last time I checked Brady and is just a friend."

"He is, but he is also my brother-in-law. Bianca is my sister."

Wow, okay, that feels like a detail that should have come up a little sooner. There have been a million moments where he could have mentioned this to me. The least appropriate of all is when I am not allowed to have an honest reaction.

"I thought you might reconsider coming if you knew Bianca and Brady were invited as well."

I feel really bad that Trevor thought that my decision to come would waver knowing who else was attending.

Despite the awkwardness of the familial ambush, I take pleasure in knowing Trevor isn't as much of a saint to my sinner as I anticipated. The only thing I fixate on at this moment is the view out the window of my boyfriend's private airplane. Snow on top of the mountains is well within reach. I will see snow before I am able to touch it for the first time ever. The excitement overwhelms me. I may parachute out of the plane to get to the fresh powder faster.

※ ※ ※

Bianca has been really sweet during the flight and is still holding a one-sided conversation over her husband and brother's laps toward me. I am sure the boys would have preferred we sat in the aisles to converse less obtrusively, but I desperately need to be at a window. It feels like my life depends on it.

Florida has everything I could ever want; the ocean is a true spiritual experience for me. Though, I have a suspicion that snow might hold the same spirituality for me. Everyone has a climate they prefer; maybe mine are the mountains rather than the beach. Who can say until I experience it?

Trevor and Brady have been awfully quiet as Bianca blathers relentlessly. I have heard several species of birds chatter less. The lack of pause means that there is no room for awkward silence, which is such a relief.

Trevor and Bianca's dad, (so weird now that I know they are siblings,) is already in Vail awaiting our arrival at the house.

Trevor hasn't given me much to go on as far as what my expectations should be. When he originally said *cabin in the snow*, I envisioned a tiny log structure where we would be sleeping on the pullout couch or a sleeping bag on the floor with a cozy wood-burning stove that someone would have to teach me how to light. Now, based on my attire and the private jet, I am thinking I may have been led astray by the words "cozy cabin."

Maybe there is a butler to stoke the fires for us. That wouldn't be the craziest thing. All I know is I am going into this with an open mind and my expectations for a cabin like the one in the movie *The Holiday* are very low.

Landing is a little bumpy coming in over the mountains. It has been a while since I have been on a plane, but the weather is perfect with only a slight flurry. I quickly realized that I am not a fan of turbulence. However, it is an excellent excuse to hold my boyfriend's hand and have him "protect me."

When the bumps cease, the ride is more comfortable than any form of travel I've experienced. That, coupled with the lack of sleep and my waning caffeine buzz, I find myself drifting to sleep with the hum of the engines as a lull. Before I can completely claim my snooze, Trevor covers my eyes with both his hands in a mad dash and startles me.

"What are you doing?" I am laughing, but I am also trying to pry his hands off my face so that I can see out my window. *We must be getting close.*

"Are you ready?"

Boy you have no idea how ready I am.

"Yes, yes release me you mad man! Let me see! I've been waiting my whole life for this!"

Slowly he releases his palms from my eyes, and I can finally take in the view several thousand feet below. The purity snatches my breath away. Untouched beauty that is pristine and glistens as the mountains dance with the sunlight. I have never seen anything so immaculate and sparkly. It is beyond anything I could have imagined. The feeling that swells in me is so overwhelming that a tear falls and pauses on my cheek.

Trevor wipes it with care and consideration before Brady notices, sparing me embarrassment and possible mockery. Bianca has fallen asleep, and the plane is quiet for the first time since takeoff. I think we all are taking advantage of the silence.

"I can't wait to feel it." I am giddy. "I want to jump into all of it and just sit in it like a cloud."

"You do know that snow is just ice, right, and that ice is really freaking cold." This is the first time Brady has said anything to me directly, and it comes across more as a shout than whisper. His attempt to lower my thrill is futile. I am too excited.

To me, snow is more like cotton candy than ice, but I could turn into a Popsicle and die a very happy woman. They would unfreeze me a thousand years from now and I would still be smiling.

"I don't think I have ever been this happy," I whisper to Trevor, wrapping both arms around his one resting on the armrest between us.

It's hard for me to admit out loud, but I want Trevor to know just how much I appreciate him right now. He has done more for me in six months than any other living soul I have encountered in my entire lifetime. For the first time in my life, I feel like I might be able to find a way out of my darkness. Maybe even find happiness.

My heart is bursting for him and for snow, and I kiss him passionately right then and there. I didn't plan on too many public displays of affection, especially on a family trip. When I knew Brady was going to be like a dark shadow, I hesitated a bit, but I just can't help myself. The only thing that snaps me out of my rose-colored lenses of love is Bianca taunting,

"OOOOOOOOO" from a few seats over.

"We thought you were asleep." Trevor says as he releases the suction from our pucker.

Trevor doesn't look embarrassed, though, and it makes me want to kiss him again.

"Oh, and also . . . get used to it."

I like how he says that.

And he does indeed kiss me again and again and again. It's more silly than passionate, but I love his confidence not to hide how he feels.

I may have been a little too excited to disembark the plane, even though the comfort of that jet was nicer than my home, and I want to move into it and just fly the globe in a constant circle.

I ran out the door, completely forgetting my jacket that was meant for layers when we took off from Miami. It hit me all at once.

When I say that I have never had a chill up my spine like that chill ran up my spine I mean it. Maybe I wouldn't have a smile if I was a Popsicle unless I had a massive parka on and some gloves.

My nose is instantly splotchy and red, and my cheeks feel flushed. My limbs are probably trying to retain any ounce of heat my body has left. The skin on my face feels tight, like all the moisture has vanished. Not leaving the Miami climate for a decade has left my body with zero ability to warm itself up when necessary. The snow will have to hold on a second, but as I turn around to grab my coat, Trevor is already behind me beckoning my arms into the sleeves, amused by my sporadic behavior. I am acting like a toddler or a dog or both, but I am everywhere all at once, next level excited. I don't even think Disneyland, as a kid, would have elicited this kind of reaction.

"Have you ever been cold before, Kat?"

"Not like this I haven't. If I open up those suitcases and find nothing but bikinis in there as a joke, I am going to be pissed."

"I promise you I would never do that to you."

Once I have the jacket zipped up and the fur-lined hood protecting my frozen ears, I head back out into the winter wonderland. If I truly am the Alice that Lewis Carroll depicted in his book about "mad" things, then this is my Wonderland, and I too am blissfully and wonderfully "mad."

It's all very short lived though. There isn't a whole lot of snow on the tarmac and a Lamborghini SUV is here to drive all of us to our next destination.

What an incredibly nice car. Sheesh! It even smells like money. The newly printed kind.

Vail may be the cutest thing I have ever observed. It is like a tiny little town that should belong in Europe, but rather is plopped here in the middle of Colorado.

Part of me wishes we were staying in one of these amazing hotels in the quaint streets of downtown. They are so spectacular, and right in the heart of it all, but I forget all that nonsense when I pull up to the Daniels *cabin*. The only resemblance it has to a cabin is the material used to build this five-thousand-square-foot masterpiece. It belongs in *Architecture Digest* and wouldn't be caught dead on an app like Zillow.

This house is as much a cabin as Marilyn Monroe or Elizabeth Taylor were Plain Janes. You would look at whoever made that nonsensical comparison like they had lizards coming out of their ears. Well, right now I am looking at Trevor like he has lizards coming out of his ears.

There are several feet of snow on the ground. I can't believe it. To me it looks like perfect white plush towels stacked on top of each other in a tower. I still want it to envelop me, but I also want to be plopped in front of a fire with a spiked eggnog right about now. My very first white Christmas thus far has not been disappointing.

"I'm dreaming of a white Christmas," Trevor croons, with an awfully good impression of Bing Crosby.

When we pull up to the ever-humble estate, Howard is standing outside donned in snow gear and waving us down with a warm greeting. I don't know why I expected him to look more like Ebenezer Scrooge in slippers and a robe this time of day, but I was anticipating a *"bah humbug,"* rather than a "Merry Christmas." He seems downright jolly and places his arm around a woman who looks like a snow bunny straight out of *Playboy*. Blonde as can be with boobs larger than the circumference of her head and a waist so tiny I think I could wrap my hands around it and touch my fingers to each other. She looks significantly younger than Howard, but it is hard to tell because of the Botox.

"Welcome, I am Monica!" She beams and throws her arms around me in her soft white and very poofy fur coat. "How was the trip? Was it comfortable?"

Comfortable?! Sheesh, I have never been more comfortable in my life.

I am a small person and Monica makes me look like a giant. She is as petite as a mouse. I never expected the Daniels to be huggers, but to be fair, I don't think Monica has been in the Daniels family very long.

"Let's go inside, it's ice cold out here," Monica says.

Of course, the inside is even more immaculate than the outside. The foyer has a large crystal chandelier that mimics its cousin the icicle just outside, but glistens with equal if not more brilliance.

I get the cabin vibe for sure. There is a stuffed bear towering over the guests in the entry, and there are floor-to-ceiling windows that look out over the glorious, white landscape. This home puts the houses I grew up around in Malibu to shame. Every room has its own fireplace, the kitchen is off to the right of the foyer, and to the left is a large living room with a giant stone fireplace with a walnut wood mantle and a fourteen-foot Christmas tree regally dressed in red, gold and silver bobbles. It is centered in the middle of a wall of windows. As tall as it is, the tree still doesn't touch the ceiling, which has several large wooden beams across the top.

Imagine the house from the movie *The Proposal* times two, only more Christmas in Colorado and less Alaska as a backdrop.

I really enjoy home design, especially in movies with castles and chateaus and cabins alike. A girl can daydream; it's not like I can do much design wise in my six-hundred-square-foot apartment, but the amount of area in the home I am currently standing in would never be fully finished if I attempted to decorate it myself.

After exchanging greetings with the rest of the Daniels clan, Trevor leads me to his room, which will act as *our* room for the duration of our stay. Our bags are already there waiting for us.

"You are going to have to massage my jaw later from having it gape open in awe all day long," I joke, but I am also half serious. It is starting to ache from all the shock and smiling.

"You did not allude to this amount of grandeur when you asked me to come. I have seen your office and your apartment, but now I understand what it means to be in the upper one percent."

I am spinning in circles, so dizzy from taking it all in, I collapse on the bed with an "oomph."

"I didn't think that it was that big of a deal." He smirks as he puts my draped knees around his waist at the edge of the bed.

"Only a person of ridiculous wealth would think that this isn't a big deal."

"It's my family's money. The money I earn provides for the lifestyle I have back in Miami. The plane, the yacht, and the cabin are all my dad's."

"You really have got to stop calling this place *the cabin*. Call it the Colossal Colorado Snow Lair . . . or anything else. Also, it may not be your money now, but one day you will inherit it all. Or so I thought when I believed you were an only child. How come you didn't tell me Bianca was your sister? You said you were all friends in college, but not that you two were siblings? Why the secrecy?"

"Why do any of us keep secrets? It's because we are ashamed of something."

His response is quick and honest, but what does he have to be ashamed about? Bianca is an incredible person he should proudly call family. This whole conversation throws me off a little bit. We aren't arguing, but we aren't exactly conversing like two lovers on a romantic Christmas vacation. I want to change the subject back to romance and luxury adventures. I have no interest in sharing secrets right now.

"Do you forgive me?" Trevor pouts with big eyes looking directly up at me.

"How about we channel this energy into something a little more athletic?"

Trevor's eyes widen, and a smile erupts as he pulls my knees around his waist.

"Not that you idiot." I slap his hands off me playfully as he pouts. Having sex wasn't the activity I had in mind. "Teach me to ski."

CHAPTER 29

Alice
{ 2012 }

MATT AND I pull up to the canyon and park just in time to catch sunrise. I don't want to ruin this moment for him, but I have an anxious rash when I think about confronting him about that phone call, and the fact that I know he lied to me.

If he wanted to talk to you about it, he would. Don't be pushy and overbearing.

We didn't say much on the drive. We are both tired, and I think Matt understands that I smell something fishy, which is funny because this desert is dry.

I still think my mind is a hilarious and witty place when I am massively sleep deprived.

There's not an oasis insight. We just sip our Americanos and try not to fall asleep. I know this is a big moment for him, one that he probably wishes he was experiencing with his dad.

Does he know he will never see his dad again? Has it hit him yet?

I think I might love him, or so the hormones and the romantic atmospheres have been churning in me to feel, but

I cannot be the one to verbalize it. Not yet anyway. There is a time and place for those sorts of things and there is proper protocol. It's far too soon. Isn't the guy supposed to say it first? I think the woman stereotypically always feels it first, but the man has to say it, which I call feminism bull on that. If women want to say "I love you" first they should. Even so, I might *want* Matt to say it first.

He isn't in any place to say I love you to me right now, and I can tell something is gnawing at him internally.

I knew he wasn't ready for any of this. I cannot believe I allowed him to come.

The sunrise over the Grand Canyon is exactly as expected, but a little more spiritual and well . . . *grand.* The sky swirls with colors like the sorbet I had when I was child. There are shades of orange, pink, and blue, and even a hue of green all coiling together as the sun rises into its rightful place for the day ahead. I don't know why nature here continues to get me all emotional, but it feels like the stars and the sunrises are Katie talking to me in some tangible way. I know that everyone sees the sunrise and the stars and feel that they aren't designed for any one person, but it feels that way to me. Katie wants me to know she is at peace.

Matt is more silent than I anticipate, and his tears cascade into a weep I haven't before witnessed. I know he cries. I have seen the aftermath and a rogue tear here and there, but nothing as effusive as this.

I place my hand on his hunched back to comfort him. His position mimics that of being sick to his stomach, so I give him a little space but use my hand to draw circles over his shoulder blades.

I can't tiptoe around it anymore. I have to ask him about

the call.

"Matt, why did you lie to me?"

He straightens and towers over me by at least a foot, seeming to be taken aback by my question. I truly have the worst timing. I shouldn't have asked when he is so distraught.

"You aren't the only one who can have a secret, Alice!" He sounds agitated.

Which secret is he talking about?

"I know why you almost drowned alongside Katie. I know it wasn't an accident. I know more than you think, and I still choose you after all of it. You have lied to me every moment since Katie died. Am I not allowed the same courtesy?"

He knows why I was in the water with Katie?

I don't know what changed in the wee hours of the morning, but I don't need to be verbally attacked by him. I also can't add another secret to my ever-increasing stack.

I grab Katie's journal and her letters from the truck and then head as far out of eyesight as I can. It is kind of impossible when the person you are trying to run away from is on the edge of a great divide and you can't cross.

Once I am far enough away from Matt, I sit down in the dirt in my three-day-old clothes, wishing I had a shower, and wishing I could talk to Katie and tell her everything. She communicates to me now only through letters I stuff into her notebook, a diary I was never supposed to find.

I pull out her journal and head to a blank page and begin to do the same. She always had a pen in the spiral binding. I was only planning on reading some more of her thoughts, but this time I have a few words of my own I would like to say:

Dear Katie,

It has only been a little while since your passing and I am broken with grief. There is no other way to put it except that my heart feels like a bag of bricks, and everything is heavier. I do not feel equipped to carry this weight. As much as I feel we were starting to drift apart from one another, we always found our way back and I was not prepared for your permanent absence.

I'll never forget when they told me you were dead. My soul left my body and the shell that remains just ran full force into a cement blockade. Every inch of my body feels bruised by those stupid simple words, "She's dead." How final and meaningless.

We were born into this world together and I thought we would leave it together as well. I feel robbed and abused and I think that bruised feeling will linger on for a very long time.

I see you in everything. I see you in things that had you not left me, would never make my brain jump to the thought of you. Now you are incessantly in everything. In every pore of my body, every ounce of my being longs and aches for you, but it is received with nothing but emptiness.

There are no more voicemails on my phone that will play your voice. There are no new words or conversations that we will share. It is a hard reality to know this. We could talk for hours and hours and it was so easy with you. I shared everything with you, and I know you wanted to share more with me, but you had your secrets that you felt you needed to protect, and I did too.

When I suggested a double suicide as an escape from it all, I thought you would call me crazy. We both felt no other option would suffice for us, but I didn't hold up my end of the plan. I didn't die. I wanted to die. I didn't. You did.

I always felt like every time I needed you, you were there for me in an instant. It didn't matter where you were or what you were doing or if you couldn't afford it. Whatever it was that I needed, you were there to fix it. Always. That is probably the most consistent attribute you have had in life. That, and how you loved.

You were my hero and everything I wished I could be. You loved deeper than anyone I have ever met, and the world is a worse place without your bright soul in it. I am worse off, that is for sure.

My idea of a double suicide was stupid, and I am so mad at myself for what happened to you because of it. Why did I survive? You should have survived if one of us was destined to. It was all my idea anyway.

Matt knows. At least I think he does. He should hate me for taking you away from him.

Because of my inability to die, every good thing that happens in my life is tainted. Every birthday that will come, every Christmas, every accomplishment I achieve in this life I won't be able to share with you, which makes all my good future memories that should be all bright and shiny and perfect, have a single spot of darkness, a blemish that I can never remove.

I want someone to tell me that this is all a hoax and

that I have been lied to. I have been lied to so many times. Why can't your death be one of them. I keep telling myself that I will be okay, and that time heals all wounds, but it didn't heal yours, so I don't know if I believe that anymore. I feel like I am just going to be walking around this earth with a giant hole in my chest for the rest of my existence. Vulnerable to defeat.

I want to wake up tomorrow and hear your voice coming from the other room. I want to share my good memories with you and have them stay pure. Sadness and grief are like markers now, just marking up the rest of my life and every moment I think of you.

I can still feel you in so many things, so I know that the spirit passes on, but is never truly departed from us. I know you are at peace and in a paradise I can't even fathom. The Bible mentions streets of gold and even that concept is too glorious to comprehend, let alone the reality of an afterlife. It can leave your head spinning. I know you are free from the pain you were shackled to here in this realm, and for that alone I am grateful you suffer no more, but that is all. I still carry the pain. I took yours on as well. I deserve it. I am the one who deserves to be dead. That is the only peace that I have been given in this situation.

The loneliness feels like a wet blanket over my face, and I might suffocate from the lack of being able to take a full deep breath.

I miss your voice and your smile and the way you hugged me. Did you know that you had one of the best smiles ever? It could light up an entire room, especially if it was followed by your laugh. I like to think our smiles were similar, but your energy was, and remains, unmatched. Even in your passing.

I miss the safety you provided me, and I knew I always had someone to fall back on. I feel like a lifeline has been ripped away from me.

My gut tore open when it was official that you were indeed dead. I was supposed to be with you. Not apart from you. I took your name to save myself. Not because I wanted to honor your memory. It was selfish and cruel. I collapsed instantly by the weight of it all, and taking your name and life along with it was the only way I was able to get up off the floor.

What am I supposed to do now that you're gone? Who am I supposed to turn to in those moments that break me? The ones where I would have only turned to you. What if they follow me and you're no longer around to hold me afterwards?

Instead of facing the monster together, I chose to coerce you in ending it all. We both had our reasons, but was there something more on your end that I didn't know about. I am beginning to believe you didn't tell me everything.

I am selfish. It's why you are gone and no longer here with me. I know everyone has a right time to die, but I played God when I held your head under the water. I planned to follow. I am sorry I failed.

The aftershock of your absence is too much to bear on most days. I think maybe in time I won't think of you in literally everything I see around me, but I don't think the *pain ever lessens; maybe it just becomes more infrequent.*

If you're not here, then I literally have no one.

I want to see you walk through a door, or out in a crowd somewhere, anything to give me hope that this is all just a giant nightmare that I will wake up from one day. I caused this hell.

I am not immune to loss. I feel that I have experienced many losses in my short lifetime, but no loss has wounded me quite so deeply. My life has been short here and yours was the same as well. It's brutal to realize that there are no other milestones to share. You just simply won't be there.

Moving on without you is like treading through blackberry thrush, painful and very slow going. I will carry you with me in my heart and the brightest part about you is what will linger in your legacy. I will carry on your memory. Please forgive me.

I don't like the person I have become now after experiencing and holding on to what your death has done to me.

Matt has been an amazing source of comfort and an excellent shoulder to cry on, but am I perpetuating the cycle of selfishness if I allow him to follow me? I can't strip him from his family just because mine has been stripped from me. He still has his parents and his baby sister to think of, and they are everything we wished we had while growing up. He deserves to have that, and I feel by staying with him I am just dragging him down into the mire with me. You already broke his heart, and now I feel

I must do the same if I am to save it. He can't follow me into my darkness.

He isn't going to take the news well, but he has an entire life to grow into, and by staying with me I would be robbing him of his future, just like I persuaded you to rob yourself of yours. He would be a walking shell of the man I know he can become. I can't do that to someone again.

Matt will be able to put himself back together someday, but only if I release him now when there is still time. I am like a poison. He will heal, I am sure of that. I may not, but he will.

I need someone to tell me that you are coming back to me. I am desperate for you and the permanency of this new reality has shattered me. I find peace in your freedom, but there is no one here to pick up my shattered soul that you left behind in pieces.

Love doesn't die, though. The pain I am experiencing is elevated because the love didn't die. I will love you forever. Whatever burdens you carried, I pray you have laid them to rest. I pray that this afterlife gives us the opportunity to hug each other once again. Rest in peace. I will always love you,

Love,
Alice.

※ ※ ※

I want to throw the entire journal over the canyon edge and watch it cascade down, but instead of throwing away all the last remaining words Katie has to share with me, I simply rip out my letter and watch as the tattered pieces drift into oblivion. I end my rant with a scream into the void and I listen to my hurtful words of anguish reverberate back to me in the most heinous echo.

"YOU SELFISH BITCH!"

I of course am referring to myself, hoping no one hears. I took off far enough to myself to feel a false sense of solitude, so my initial embarrassment only peaks when I see Matt walking toward me. I can't tell what kind of mood he is in. He is too far away still. I hope he is still mad and shoves me over the side of the cliff.

My entire being is on the precipice of this chasm, and my nerves feel the same.

My body language is guarded. I have my arms crossed, facing away from him toward the view when Matt approaches.

Matt's arms come up from behind me and wrap around my middle. He rests his head in the crook of my neck where it meets my shoulder, and I can feel his softness as he whispers, "I am sorry" into my ear. I am not quite sure what part he is actually apologizing for. Is it the lie he told me or the outburst of truth?

"You want to tell me what's up?" I utter without tenderness.

I don't turn to face him. I can't. He doesn't know I am planning to leave, that I can't allow him to go any further with me.

"That was my dad on the phone earlier. He had a hunch we were lying to him, so he checked my credit card purchases and waited for me to use it to see if we were really heading to Seattle. He didn't see any charge for concert tickets, so that was his first clue, and then he said we were both acting so weird he just knew. He was literally waiting by the computer to see when a charge would come through. He told me this is the second time I have broken his trust and to come home immediately. I told him we decided to ditch out on the concert because we ended up not being able to get tickets, and I took you to the Grand Canyon instead, like he did for me all those years ago.

"He didn't raise his voice at me or lecture me in any way, but he also didn't believe me. I yelled at him though. I told him I am a man now and eighteen and legally don't have to listen to him. All he said in his structured monotone was that real men embrace the honest truth and don't lie, especially to those they love. Then he hung up on me before I could yell at him some more.

"He is so arrogant, but I hate that there is a rift between us. I don't know what I expected. Secrets are the infinite divide. They are like throwing unreliable grenades in a relationship and waiting to see when they will detonate."

He exhales heavily into my ear.

"You're right. Secrets are cataclysmic for a relationship, which is why we won't work either . . . you need to go back home to your family."

Matt is no longer interested in talking to the back of my ears by now and spins me by my waist so that our eyes meet. I, however, remain rigid. I have to be strong.

"You can't do this to them. I can't do this to them. They are the family I have always wanted but can't have, and you need them. Not only that . . . they need you. Your sister needs you. Imagine the heartbreak of your mother if she knew she would never see you again. Imagine the disappointment in your father. Your sister is basically a baby, she needs to grow up with your good soul to guide her."

Soft sobs fall to the dust between us.

"No, Alice, please don't. I choose this. I choose you." His hushed pleading is painful.

"I am living as a ghost, Matt, both Alice and Katie are dead, and I am the shell of emptiness that is left. I feel like a vampire sucking the life out of you. You have so much to live for. I don't get to have a clean slate. I will carry these secrets as an anchor weighing me down. I cannot ask you to carry it with me. We will both drown by the heaviness. I cannot rob you of your future."

"I don't HAVE a future if you are not in it." It's the first time I've heard him yell.

Both of my hands are cradled in his. His piercing eyes almost have me changing my mind. I don't want to let him go.

"I love you."

There it is. He said it first, just like I wanted him too, but I am mute to confess it, even though it is indeed how I feel. Three little words so perfectly spoken, but in desperation, a fear of loneliness and of more loss. I want to tell him I love him too. It is sudden and soon, but it is the truth.

Yet another lie, only this particular one by omission.

"How can you love me when you were so intimate with my sister. We will never be able to replicate that. I think the love you have for me is leftover for her. She kept this journal and wrote her letters confessing all her deepest thoughts. She shared your more vulnerable moments. I can't compare, and I don't want to. I don't want to think about that every time you kiss me, every time you touch me. I don't want to be more jealous of her in death than I was in life."

My words push him away, but Matt interrupts me with a kiss. His kisses taste like the salt from our tears.

"Does that really feel like it was meant for anyone but you?" he says as the seal from our mouth releases its suction.

There is nothing to say. After a long awkward silence, Matt simply draws me into him. One last attempt to keep what is so quickly slipping away.

"You're just tired, we have barely slept in almost a week. Let's set up the truck and take a nap before we head out and keep on going forward. *Together.* We can get some food in us after . . . okay."

I don't respond with words, just a gentle nod, but he isn't wrong. We are both exhausted and hungry and coffee just isn't enough sustenance. I allow him to take my hand and lead me back to the truck. He kisses my cheek before he starts to lie out all the bedding.

"I am going to change. I've been in your shirt for three days now."

Matt nods and I grab my bag from inside the truck and head to the bathroom. I know this isn't going to be the cleanest I have ever felt, but a good rub of deodorant, another teeth brushing, and a change of outfit will definitely improve my hygiene and mood. There isn't much I can do with my hair at this point, so once I am face-to-face with myself in the mirror, I throw the tousled curls into a topknot messy bun and move on.

My own reflection startles me though and I don't think anyone is in the bathroom to see me touch my own face and then touch the mirror.

"Hi Katie. . . you look like hell."

I make myself laugh and I know it is solely coming from extreme sleep deprivation, but on one hand I am calling myself Katie to get used to it from here on out. On the other hand, it feels like a very real way I can commune with the dead. She is looking right back at me. Fear comes over me and I wonder how much longer I have until my reflection doesn't resemble a Katie I'd recognize. She won't age past seventeen.

Katie would never be caught dead looking as disheveled as I do presently, but extreme circumstances lead to extreme consequences. Mine at the moment is how bad I smell.

Matt is passed out in the truck bed by the time I get back, or at least mostly passed out, because when I join him I can feel him scoot toward me, wrapping himself around me. His warmth is sweltering now that the sun has risen, but I changed into denim shorts and a tank top. Not the most comfortable for napping.

"What did you mean when you said you knew about the pool party?"

I think Matt might be asleep now, but I have to ask if he knows about the double suicide. He may not recall this conversation fully in a few hours.

My question seems to hit the air, and nothing else. It might hit him when he wakes up, or he won't remember I brought it up at all. I am secretly hoping for the latter. I should have kept quiet.

My brain struggles to quiet its own terrorizing thoughts. However, hitting my head on the pillow feels a lot better than I thought it would and my eyelids feel like anvils. I feel intoxicated by the want to sleep. My arms are tingly, and my feet numb, and the world around me is sloshing back and forth like I am on a boat. I can't keep my eyes open even if I wanted to, and fortunately I don't. Matt and I are parked far enough away from people that we aren't concerned about onlookers peeping in or getting called out for camping where we are. We just need a nap.

Before I dive into the deep oblivion of slumber, I note that it's only eight in the morning.

I have time.

❋ ❋ ❋

I wake up first when the sun is directly overhead, and the heat of the day beats on us. I am swimming in my own sweat and wake up abruptly without any sense of place and time. My sudden jolt doesn't seem to stir Matt who is still fast asleep next to me. I reach for my phone to check the time. It's one in the afternoon almost to the minute. I slept for five hours! I don't feel as refreshed as I should, but I also have a huge hit of adrenaline coursing through me still and am trying to shake off the scare.

Matt is so peaceful, and I can't help but see the youthfulness in his face with his hands tucked underneath his chin. I am afraid to wake him. I know what I need to do and now presents an opportunity. I should seize the moment before I chicken out.

I want to watch his peace and siphon some for myself, but I gamble on him waking up and begging me not to go and I don't have the strength to face him again. Katie has written in her letters many times that she admired my strength. I wonder how she would feel right now knowing that I am such a coward.

Katie lied. I have always been a coward.

I've been thumbing through the pages of her journal. I owe Matt a note so he doesn't wake up thinking I am in the bathroom or something.

Katie always influenced me in many ways, so I guess I like to write letters now.

Dear Matt,

I am just going to come out and say that I am a big fat coward and I hope you hate me after this so that you stop loving me. Me, on the other hand, I don't know if I will ever stop loving you. I couldn't say it back to you when you told me you loved me. It feels wrong to love you back so soon after you belonged to the only other person I have ever loved. Katie deserves all of you and I am ashamed I took even a piece for myself, but what's done is done and I feel how I feel, which is I do truly love you.

You are an incredibly decent human being, and the world deserves all you have to offer, and not some mediocre secret bearing half version of you. This burden will hold you back until you too become a ghost. I can't watch you wither away knowing the part I played in all of it and how I could have prevented it all.

You shine brighter than Katie or I ever could. You are touched by love while Katie and I had to take it where we could. Relish in it and cling to it as long as you can. I promise you I won't live in darkness forever; I hope not anyway. I just need to find my own source of light rather than taking yours for myself. It's too selfish and I love you too much.

I want to know that you went and joined the military and followed your dreams, wherever they may carry you. I want to know you found a perfect military wife, one who can be patient with your career and also give you the most beautiful sandy-haired and olive-skinned babies. Have oh so many babies, Matt. You are going to be the best father one day, and children need a good father. So have at least five. One set can be twin girls, and you can love them as much as you loved me and Katie, but other than that, I don't want you to think about me, ever. Your life has been blissfully untouched by trauma up until this point. Don't let one scar mark you for the rest of your days here. Don't let all this negatively affect you. Use the emotions you feel now to drive your success and happiness. Anger can be a valuable tool. I should know. I am angry with Katie right now and Todd and Cheryl, and, quite honestly, with you. I am mad you made me love you because if I didn't, I wouldn't be here leaving you right now and feeling what's left of my heart shatter even more.

If I didn't love you, I could have you.

Just so you know, I didn't plan this from the beginning. I never would have let you come with me in the first place. Call it loneliness or whatever you want to, I was grateful for the company. My feelings changed and I can't be selfish anymore. I hate myself for being selfish toward my sister, and I can't stand who I am becoming. I don't want to end up hating myself for being selfish with you too. I'd rather you hate me than I hate myself. Truth is I am going to hurt you no matter what. It's either going to be now or a resentful many years later.

I don't know if I can give you love the way I have experienced it with you. I can't reciprocate. I couldn't even tell you out loud how I feel. I left you hanging with those three beautiful words suspended in the air between us. I want you to know they shot straight to my heart where I will keep them stored forever. You have tattooed me with those words.

I only felt love in small doses throughout my life, except Katie who was my constant. You have been the only other exception, but your love is so good I can only accept this small dose of it. I'll simply poison it.

Don't come after me, don't come and try to find me in the future. Lastly, I ask this of you in another selfish request—PLEASE don't tell anyone our secret. Don't bury it inside you to fester, just let it go and move on. Be great in life like I know you can. I will find my purpose in life one day as a newly reinvented Katie, but you already have so much to live for. Seek it and you will find all you desire. Of this I am so certain.

I will always love you and will carry you with me always, even though I am begging you not to do the same.

Find your happiness. I love you, Matt.

Love,

Alice (from now on Katie.)

I rip the page out of the spiral binding slowly, so I don't make too much of a rustle, and slide the note under his arm gently. That way it won't blow away and he will surely find it.

Now comes the hard part.

I make sure I have the money I need without taking any of the additional funds Matt brought. I am not going to steal from him even though I know he wouldn't blame me for it.

Gently closing the truck door, I have my duffel bag secured over my shoulder. There is a small part of me excited for my own future. I begin walking to the nearest bus station, starting my journey alone.

CHAPTER 30

Alice

{ 2022 }

THE NUMBER OF TIMES I have fallen on this ski slope is comical—borderline just pathetic. We haven't left the bunny run this entire time, and I can barely stand up straight. My skis keep overlapping when I do "the pizza" to try and slowdown, which, shocker, makes me fall. Or I have them pointed straight and they turn out, which tangles my body into a position even experienced yogis can't do. Little children are passing me with ease and lapping me on the mountain.

Bianca is an excellent cheerleader until Brady decides he has witnessed enough and demands she embrace the more challenging runs with him. I think his exact words are, "Can we be done wasting our time?"

He meant for it to sting, but truthfully, I am little uncomfortable having an audience anyway. I'm relieved that only Trevor is left to witness my ineptitude.

"You should go with Bianca and get in some more fun runs rather than just continuously watching me fall," I utter humbly, though I don't want him to go anywhere. "I'd be more than happy to pay for a professional lesson in order to free up your time."

Please don't leave me alone, I think.

"Are you crazy? If I leave you, I am afraid you might run straight into a tree or a poor innocent three-year-old. Basically, I am looking out for the children and the foliage."

Right answer.

I am glad he can joke because I usually hate sarcasm. You know what they say, all sarcasm has some truth in it.

The many ski lifts at this particular resort range in difficulty. One of the more complex runs intersects with the bunny run that I am currently failing miserably on. Talk about impressing the guy you are with. He somehow doesn't seem bored, but I can't imagine he wants to do this with me all day. Though I am so incredibly grateful not to be left to my own devices.

Bianca and Brady have lapped us several times now and at about the fifth time, Bianca stops to check in.

"Trevor, why don't you and Brady hit the bigger slopes and I can stay down here with Kat?"

Bianca doesn't seem like she is even breaking a sweat. Not a bead of moisture on her perfectly primed face. She is feigning depletion to give her brother a chance to expel some energy on something a little more adrenaline producing.

"Brady has been begging for something a little more challenging and I am just not up for it."

Bianca is lying through her teeth. I get the feeling she is the best skier out of all of us but is just pretending out of kindness, and probably allowing her husband to keep some of his pride. I don't know if I have ever met someone so fragile with pride as Brady. I think she is a good wife for protecting it.

Trevor looks at me with that look of concern, like, "will you be okay if I go?"

"You go on ahead," I say, unprompted. "Maybe I will fall less knowing you won't be here to pick me up."

I can't keep him on this run forever.

He gives me a kiss and a smile and takes off with Brady for lifts that will take them to the mountaintop.

When the boys are out of sight, Bianca ski's closer to me with a proposal.

"Okay girl, listen up, you ski to the bottom without falling one time and I'll buy you a drink in the lodge until the boys come back. . . deal?"

As much as the snow has been a dream come true for me, I can no longer feel my nose or fingertips, and the little warmer packets that Trevor gave me to stick in the pockets of my new jacket have lost all their heating properties.

I do feel more stylish than I ever have before though. Inside the suitcases were two ski outfits, and I chose to go with the matching white set rather than the hot pink. I figured I should blend in with the snow until I know how to master the ice beneath my skis.

My new personality trait is a monochromatic look for every single outfit I own. Much like Bianca. I also adore the little pompom that hangs from my gloves. I feel like a little snow bunny, stumbling idiotically on the bunny run, but looking fabulous while I do it.

Bianca has matching red pants and a bright red jacket, and I love how bold she looks in it. Her brunette hair stands out with her pale skin, and the icy weather is making the pink in her lips look redder by the minute, but the red jacket only adds to the beauty rather than displays the cold she is feeling. I've never been one to stand out, but I really admire that trait in her. The red jacket reminds me of something Katie would wear, had she ever been given the opportunity to do so.

"A drink sounds like the best motivation a girl could ask for," I say as I use my ski poles to take off in front of her. I may have been a little too confident because I instantly start to wobble, but the idea of warmth and an alcoholic beverage in front of a large fire inspires me to find my footing, and I miraculously adjust and stay upright.

It isn't until the bottom of the run that I hit a patch of snow that sends me tumbling. It was a little icier than the rest, and more packed down into a solid slip and slide. I fall on my hip that I know is going to leave an excellent bruise. I look up at Bianca from the ground to see her hand extended.

"Eh . . . close enough."

Phew, I thought she was going to make me try again. The deal was not to fall, but I did make it to the lodge before falling, so maybe the rules are a little blurred. I technically succeeded.

She helps me to my feet, and I use my poles to unclip my skis and place them upright on the rack.

Bianca makes maneuvering in ski boots look like a runway walk, whereas I just feel like a penguin waddling from side to side with the heaviness around my ankles. Thankfully, she doesn't take the opportunity to make fun of me. I increasingly like being around her and feel surprisingly more connected to her knowing that she is Trevor's sister. I am so glad he has a sister. It is something I want to remind him to never take for granted.

I have in recent weeks been wondering what it would be like to marry Trevor. And now I see one of the pluses—among so many—is that I could have a sister again in Bianca.

She finds a small table directly in front of the fireplace with a stuffed moose head overlooking my shoulder. I don't know why I feel the urge to acknowledge its presence, but I feel I should nod to it.

"I will go get us some drinks."

Bianca takes off for the bar before she even asks what I would like. I figure I will literally just drink whatever she puts in front of me, dealer's choice.

She returns before my fingers have had the chance to thaw and when she places a hot mug of mulled wine in front of me, I am additionally more grateful to wrap my hands around the warmth. I have never indulged in mulled wine, but I am hard pressed to find a drink I don't enjoy at least once.

"Careful . . . it's hot."

Bianca remarks as she sits across from me.

"I have been dying to get you alone so we can have a girl chat. You and my brother seem serious, and I want *mostly* all the details."

She doesn't break eye contact as she takes a sip from her mug. I love that these mugs are clear, and I can see the maroon merlot in all its festive glory. Also, if I thought Bianca's lips were the perfect tint of red before, they most certainly are now as the beverage stains them with her delicate sipping.

"Well, I just found out you're related to Trevor, so that was news to me."

"Oh my gosh, he didn't tell you?" She seems surprised, but not completely offended as she presses the palm of her hand into the wooden table.

"Who did he say I was?"

"He was vague and just said you and Brady were all college friends."

"Ha . . . that would be the lawyer in him. Tell the truth without giving any actual details. He's not a liar, my brother, just clever."

"Why do you think he didn't say anything sooner?"

I figure there is no harm in asking her. I asked Trevor and got some weird cryptic answer. *"Curiouser and curiouser,"* as my buddy Lewis Carroll puts it.

"He was pretty embarrassed of me when he found out that I had an affair last year. He obviously took Brady's side, as he should have, and he has really been there for us as we try fixing our marriage. However, I think I broke his trust almost as much as I broke Brady's. Trevor convinced Brady to give me another chance, but it hasn't been an easy road."

I don't know why her candor surprises me. Bianca is just putting it all out there. I am sipping my mulled wine slowly to hide my uncomfortable face. I am not sure how many secrets she is going to share with me. I may feel uneasy, but I am consuming every word like it is my last meal. Falling incessantly on the slopes doesn't seem so awkward now.

"Brady and I had been having some problems. I was promoted above him when we worked at a different law firm right out of law school. I could have worked for my dad, but I wanted to prove myself worthy and not rely on nepotism to get ahead. Dad was hesitant to make me a partner, anyway.

"I worked really hard and made partner, but Brady was passed over. He pretended to be happy for me, but his demeanor changed abruptly. He was jealous, hurt, and probably embarrassed.

"We spent a year living in the tension without saying anything. I tried to get him to confess his concerns, but I was also mad that he couldn't just be happy for me. For both of us, our careers came first. Still do. It's why we haven't even thought about having a baby. It literally never comes up in conversation. We could never agree on who would back off work to raise children, so we just didn't.

"My dad coaxed me to work at his firm, which also meant hiring Brady. In fact, my dad offered Brady a job before me, which was a smart strategic move. Trevor also helped things along. But, despite appearance, Brady knew we were a package deal, and I think that has bothered him. It clearly put emotional distance between us. We drifted apart. The irony is that Brady and my dad bonded. My husband became his second son. In fact, I think Brady and my dad are more alike than Trevor and my dad. They got close as we grew apart.

"My affair was brief, if you can even call it that. It was a one-time thing with a partner from my former law firm. We had always had a good rapport, flirted a little, which led to a hook up at a conference in Chicago. I felt so guilty that I almost immediately told Brady.

"We have done a lot of counseling and worked on our marriage to regain the trust that I had broken. I thought we were on the right path . . . until that night he went out for a drink with Trevor and met. . . well. . . you. I was so mad at him for wanting to hurt me back after we had started to make progress in healing. Please don't mistake my confession as an excuse for my husband's behavior toward you. I am mortified that he could even do that. It's just, well, it's just his reason for acting out."

Bianca looks like the mulled wine isn't sitting so well, and her face is a pale shade of green. I feel like she has been wanting to tell me this for a while, but never had an opportunity or wasn't sure it was worth divulging such incriminating information. I view her confession as affirmation that she thinks Trevor and I are going to be together for a long while.

She doesn't know me well enough to know that her small infidelity blemish is minor compared to my family-altering drama.

I take her hand in mine. "Thank you for telling me." That is all I can think of to say. I don't know if I actually am thankful she told me all this, but it does make me empathetic, and I can tell she needed to purge this information to feel better.

"We are all human and not immune to mistakes."

I want to add that I am part of that truth, that I am far from innocent, but I don't know if I have had enough to drink for that to be a short ski-lodge conversation. Plus, I should probably tell Trevor first.

I don't have much to say after that, but I just want to comfort her. She may not be my sister, but she is the sister to the man I love, and that fact alone makes my protective sister gene kick in. It hasn't been activated in years.

Bianca's eyes match the redness in her lips, and for the first time today she looks a little raw rather than her polished self.

"Phew . . . I need another drink." Bianca walks over to the bar, only this time she turns around and asks me if I have ever tried an espresso martini. I think she forgets that I am a bartender.

"That sounds delicious."

I am catching onto this trend of being truthful without disclosing information. Maybe I would make a great lawyer if I weren't so afraid of the law. I didn't actually answer her question, but she looks at me and grins. If it were appropriate to wink, I think she would have.

"You're going to do just fine here."

Both of us drain our espresso drinks and head back out to

the snow before the boys are down their mountain run. There is no evidence that we even stopped skiing, except both of us are a little tipsy and a whole lot warmer.

Bianca and I get in another three bunny-hill runs before the boys catch up. I am getting significantly better, only falling on average once per run. Maybe the buzz I have has given me the confidence boost I need, but I am so happy to see Trevor.

There are just some moments where men look so sexy. Trevor's are when he has just woken up, when he is wearing a suit and no tie with the top button undone, and my newest obsession is watching him ski. His agility and that boyish thrill makes me want to lose myself in him over and over.

He skis directly into me without knocking me back into the snow that I have become oh so acquainted with. He folds me into his arms with so much precision that even our ski's don't intertwine.

I love how I feel in his arms. They are strong, and I know that I can completely just let go. My back bends in an arch when he kisses me and then pulls me up into him. Both of my skis unclip, and my boots are too heavy to lift up in a cute foot-popping *Princess Diaries* moment. Regardless, it is one of the best kisses of my entire life.

"Hey Brady, how was the run?"

His jaw unclenches. "Fine."

Brady looks shocked that I directed a question at him. The two of us haven't exchanged pleasantries since we met. I didn't feel it was my place to initiate conversation, nor did I want to, but now that things are more out in the open, I don't find myself loathing him. The Daniels family feels like they are slowly becoming mine, and that includes Brady. My new philosophy moving forward is *water under the bridge*.

We all decide that we have endured enough of the elements today as the sun begins to set and a snow flurry begins. Howard and Monica were supposed to join us today but said they needed to run a small shopping errand. My guess is that the small shopping trip got extended into a long one and that they might even still be shopping. My suspicions are confirmed when I see Monica greet us with her normal bubbly enthusiasm and the Christmas tree is now surrounded with stacks of perfectly wrapped presents. Monica may have a lot of hyper personality, but she is truly thoughtful, and apparently very giving.

The dang holidays make everyone so mushy-gushy, and I am falling prey to it all right now. I guess it's easy to feel swoony this time of year when you have the love of others surrounding you like a warm blanket.

Monica pours us all a round of champagne and we toast the fact that it is almost Christmas Eve, and the glow of the glittering Christmas tree reflects in my tears of joy.

I can hear bath water running when I walk into the bedroom. Trevor is already inside and meets me at the foot of the bed. I am still wearing the majority of my wet ski clothes and am beginning to thaw next to the fireplace in our room. I watch the flames dance across the logs as Trevor presses into me intimately with a kiss. He pulls my turtleneck over my head, and I can feel my crazy curls frizz even more. I am pretty certain I look like the bride of Frankenstein, but he doesn't seem to notice. Unlike in the humidity, my skin and hair feel brittle.

Trevor's fingers trace over my collarbone and down my side, landing on my waist.

"I am going to be so sore and bruised for weeks."

There are a few small bruises forming on the more outwardly boney parts of my body—knees, shins, hips and collarbone.

"I figured. That is why I thought you might like a bath tonight before dinner."

Even after several months of dating, his consideration still throws me off. I will never get used to his kindness. He is the most aggressive lover I have ever had, but rivals Matt in his gentleness outside of the bed sheets.

"I will meet you in the shower when you are done."

I almost don't want to bathe now with that sort of promise lingering in the air, but Trevor leaves the room and heads downstairs to be with his family. Leaving me with a tub that is filled with salts and scents to soothe my aches and pains. I honestly can't wait to get back out on the mountain, and I am praying that this annual tradition includes me in the years to come.

The bath is freestanding and perched in front of a large window. If Trevor's room didn't have its own private balcony I would feel completely exposed, but I know that no one can see me. He even lit a candle for a little ambiance, and I can see moonbeams bouncing off the snow. This might be my new favorite view, which would make my view in my apartment my second favorite view. That wouldn't be so bad. Saying goodbye to my apartment and moving in with Trevor has sounded more appealing every day, and I think he might be dropping hints that he wants me to as well.

The water stings as I switch off the faucet and dip in. It feels like needles on the more frostbitten parts of my body, but

I quickly adjust to its temperature. There is something about water that is mesmerizing. The bubbles are reflecting both the candlelight and the moonlight, and I sit there soaking, taking it all in for about an hour. It's my longest bath ever, and I don't really want to get out except that Trevor promised he would meet me in the shower.

I slide out of the tub and let the bubbles slip off of my body and onto the heated tile floor when I hear the door click.

"You look like a leopard in the dark with all your bruise spots," he snickers.

"That was endearing, thank you."

For the first time standing naked in front of Trevor, I don't feel self-conscious or vulnerable. I am inviting him to take my body. I want it clearly as much as he does. I want to use it to please him and in return pleasure me.

The shower steam hinders our views of each other, but our hands are now acting as our eyes. His touch is soft as it mixes with leftover tub bubbles and the water cascading down the sides of my body. My skin is slippery with the lingering soap, and despite the bruises, there is no pain as he brushes against me.

He seems gentler than usual. His touch soft, and his kiss is tender . . . before his merciless desire for me takes over. His fingers slide into me, and my back is cold against the tile shower wall. One finger at first and then two until he hits the perfect spot, his thumb rubbing gently over my outside. It's the best this foreplay has ever felt. The skill with which he is using his hands has me motioning up the wall like I want to burst into him and away from him at the same time.

I can feel him ramping up, and my exertions are loud, though drowned out by the noise of the shower. It's not like anyone can hear us in this massive house, anyway.

He still tastes salty from a long day of skiing. Trevor takes his time in torturing pleasure until I am pulsating. It doesn't take long for me to climax, my body quivering, wanting for his body to feel the same.

He looks pleased with himself, his more defined features illuminated in the glow.

In all the slippery lovemaking, I am not at all concerned about one of us slipping. The trust I have for this person in all aspects of life now makes me anxious. I feel guilty with each passing day that my past hasn't been revealed to Trevor. I will soon, it is just with each passing day it gets harder to break out of this fantasy, but I ignore that and try to keep myself in the moment.

The shower has a large picture window and through it we can see snow falling heavily. This is what I think I meant when I said I like snow. I am warm and intimate with the man I love most while watching the white majesty from above. It is pure magic. I don't think Colorado will steal me away from the Florida beaches, just yet, but it is nice to partake so closely in the beauty of the landscape from such comfort and warmth of this less than modest abode. I have now come to affectionately call this home simply the "cabin."

Once I finish and collapse in his arms, he kisses me tenderly and I can feel he is now anxious for his turn. He perches on a small seat in the shower that then gently pulls me on top of him. It's definitely not as easy to navigate, but we are managing just fine. It is amazing what the body is capable of when you're desperate for someone inside you. I can tell he is pleased with the way my hips are rolling on top of him, and he grabs my sides and winces. I know he is trying not to finish. Neither one of us wants to be done. We are getting close to dinnertime with the family, but we are still here, soaking wet, doing this.

"It's okay." I assure him.

That's all it takes I guess. I can feel him unsteady underneath me.

"I love you."

It always throws me off when men say, "I love you" right after a climax. It's confusing to me, like, do you love me, or do you love the pleasure my body just gave you? This feels different though. The way his strong arms are pulling me close to him, the way he breathes into my neck, and the way he holds me after, makes me believe him completely in this instant. He isn't rushing to get cleaned up and out of the shower. He isn't rushing me to do the same. We just sit on that small seat in the shower, holding one another.

"We better hurry so we aren't late for dinner," I say after several blissful moments in his arms. I pull myself off his lap and start to lather myself and then him with the soap.

"Everyone else is going to be late. We will probably be the first ones there."

I am starting to believe Trevor might be the only punctual one in his family. I might belong here after all. It is going to take forever to diffuse my curls so they aren't sopping wet and now I feel I can take my time.

I jump out of the shower and begin to put a few light touches of mascara and eyeshadow on. It's just enough to look like I am trying without trying too hard.

"I want to take you somewhere special tomorrow, okay?" he asks.

His somber tone sends a chill down my spine, even though we are both warmed in our luxury towels.

"Haven't you done nothing but take me to special places?"

"This place is different. We can go after lunch tomorrow."

"So, we aren't going skiing?"

I am kind of bummed. I really was looking forward to getting back out there. I only have a week to become proficient. I know it isn't likely, but I am a competitive, and I want to try.

"We can see how your body feels tomorrow. You might want a break."

I doubt it, but I will oblige him. Whatever this place is sounds like it holds a very meaningful memory. I can sense it.

I am ready the fastest I have ever been without feeling like I am rushing. The lack of humidity here makes my hair dry a lot quicker than I originally anticipated.

The dinner is a feast meant for royalty. I have never had a Christmas season dinner so classic and delightful. There is even figgy pudding on the table, which I find delicious.

It was a very late meal and so rich that most of us are about to fall asleep at the long table in the dining room. There are candles everywhere and the warmth from yet another fireplace makes the atmosphere so cozy. Our bellies are full and our bodies warm. The whole thing combines for the perfect recipe for a good night's sleep.

If not for Monica, I think Howard would have drifted off into his slice of boysenberry pie *a la mode*. She is so gentle in her urging for him to head upstairs. She might be significantly younger than Howard, but the two of them just seem to work.

I stand up and begin to clear the dishes when Trevor gently grabs my hand and pulls me back to my seat.

"If we don't soak them soon, they will get crusty," I say just above a whisper, because I get the impression I might be embarrassing myself.

"You don't need to do that."

His voice is kind and quiet.

I am embarrassed, but no one seems to be paying me any mind. It feels wrong to just leave my dishes for someone else, but what did I expect, really. Someone is paid to make the meal, so, of course, someone will be paid to clean it all up after us.

We all excuse ourselves from the table once Howard bids us all goodnight. The signal we are all free to leave the table.

I feel blessed as Trevor and I make our way upstairs to bed. Watching the snowflakes fall out the many floor-to-ceiling windows is more cathartic than counting sheep, and I beg Trevor not to close the drapes.

❁ ❁ ❁

The next morning, I awake to Trevor serving me an espresso in bed. He comes barreling in with a tray of fresh cinnamon rolls that look like they have some sort of peppermint and candy cane Christmas glaze.

He knows that I am not much of a breakfast food person, especially not sweet ones, but the smell makes me salivate. Vacation me is a very different person, and I like her. I can tell they are still gooey and warm from coming straight from the oven. Having a full-time chef has been amazing, but still full from last night's meal, what is really capturing my attention is the steaming espresso.

The espresso cups are small and adorable, and just large enough for about two shots. It's hot and acidic. Perfection. With my first sip, Trevor reaches over the edge of the bed to kiss my forehead.

"Merry Christmas Eve."

My eyes are still only open as a slit. It takes me a few sips for them to fully open. I see Trevor's ridiculous getup.

"What are you wearing? You definitely didn't go to bed wearing that."

He has his fake, *I'm offended* look as he grabs his chest in pretend anguish.

"Do you not like my outfit?"

I am emphatically shaking my head.

"Oh . . . that's too bad, because I got you your own pair."

Trevor has a Grinch-like grin as he tosses me a pair of matching plaid and penguin pajamas, and a Santa Claus hat.

"Put them on and let's join everyone for Christmas morning, it is tradition, and you definitely don't want to disappoint Howard."

"It is only Christmas Eve. It's not Christmas morning."

I am so confused why the Daniels celebrate Christmas a day early. I tear out of the bed and throw on the penguin PJs. They even have matching socks.

When we descend the elegant staircase, I can see everyone sitting around the Christmas tree and not a single soul is wearing the "tradition jammies" except for Trevor and now me.

Everyone snickers like I am the only one not in on the joke.

"I told you I could get her to match me," Trevor shouts, snickering. Part of me wants to run back up and change, but the part of me that isn't embarrassed is laughing with them. Better to join them in the amusement.

Christmas (Eve) morning feels like something out of a Hallmark movie. The smells coming from the kitchen are impeccable and so seasonal. I can smell cinnamon and peppermint and roasts all at the same time, and surprisingly it all smells incredible together. All of it reminds me of Katie.

The spices are warm and all the lights on the tree twinkle as the fireplace roars. Underneath the tree are even more presents, large and small, all shimmering under the twinkling lights. I wonder if Monica did any of the wrapping. Doubtful.

Everyone is in a good mood. Even Brady has his arms around his wife as he sits behind her on the floor. He sips a very early morning whiskey, and it's nice to see him smile for a change.

There is even a stocking with my name on it filled to the brim with all the latest in skin care and beauty products. None of which I could ever even think of being able to afford. The La Mer moisturizer alone retails for over five hundred dollars.

The morning ensues with all of us unwrapping present after present, only pausing briefly for a cinnamon roll or a coffee refill. I even indulged in a cinnamon roll eventually because the morning drags into the early afternoon and I became hungry.

Some are gag gifts, like Bianca got me a first aid kit and put extra arnica cream in it for all of my lovely skiing bruises. I don't know how she got me a first aid kit so quickly. She must have anticipated that I would be horrible at the sport and thought ahead. I laugh and rub my collarbone with arnica for good measure.

Some gifts are very thoughtful, like Monica getting me a Cartier watch because she noticed I don't wear one. I would have been impressed with a watch from Wal-Mart, but she swears that I will have this watch until the day I die, so I accept the gesture with intense gratitude.

I don't want to know what a Christmas like this costs, but no one else seems to be worried. I feel horrible not having gifts for everyone. I knew Howard was coming and I, with much assistance from Trevor, was able to secure his favorite scotch and a lovely decanter to put it in. However, he was the only one I knew to get a gift for. Up until a few days ago I didn't know I would be in Colorado or that Trevor had any other family, let alone a sister I had already met.

No one seems to mind though, especially since everyone has a pile of presents. They could bury themselves in them all. It is a retailer's dream come true.

We finally reach the end of the gift exchange, and everyone seems ready to hit the slopes or take an afternoon nap. I am more inclined toward a nap after so much excitement, but Trevor has other plans.

After we change clothes, Trevor and I grab leftover turkey sandwiches and head to the car for our outing. As if we needed any more food, but something savory sounds good. I throw on my new Moon Boots before we trek out into the snow.

Trevor is being very secretive, saying very little as we drive up a small mountain. I am still so mesmerized by its beauty.

Near the top, we reach a lookout with a panoramic view of Vail and the sparkling snow-capped mountains around it. I can taste the chill in the air up here. The altitude is intense, and I have felt pretty dizzy today, but nothing more so than when I turn around on this alluring lookout and see Trevor down on one knee.

"What are you doing? Your knee is going to get soaked through your jeans."

His jeans are not the pressing concern right now, but I am too stunned to think of anything else to say.

"This is the last surprise I promise. I used to come here all the time as a kid. When we first met, you shared with me that your favorite view was the balcony overlooking the ocean at your apartment. You loved how the ocean sounded and how it all made you feel so small and so insignificant against its power and majesty. In that exact moment I was in awe of you, and I also thought of this spot right here. I told myself that night that if I fell in love with you like I thought I might, I would propose to you right here.

"I found this spot one day driving up here with some friends and started coming here every Christmas Eve afternoon and watching the peace of the town below. I never saw myself sharing this with anyone. I didn't share it with my last relationship and thought I may never propose to anyone again. You have changed all of that in me, Kat. I want to be around you every moment from here on out. I want to be Kat's husband, if you would do me the honor."

It's a beautiful speech and I can hardly breathe. My eyes are swollen with tears.

"Will you do me the honor of becoming my wife? Kat, will you marry me?"

The air is making my head spin. It's the only excuse for what I say in response.

"I killed my sister!"

CHAPTER 31

Alice
{ 2022 }

THERE IS COMPLETE SILENCE. Not even the sound of wind blowing over the snow, or birds chirping in the pine trees. I cannot believe what I just blurted out.

Will you marry me? . . . I killed my sister!

I feel like an absolute idiot. He almost looks amused, like I am making up the most absurd excuse to decline his proposal. He is still kneeling with this amazing ring. When I don't falter, his face falls also, his perfect smile evaporates. He looks so hurt and confused.

I couldn't say yes without him knowing all of me. It would be the biggest lie I've ever not told, knowing he wouldn't know the truth about his wife. No matter how much I wish I could rewrite the past, I had to tell him. I have had over six months to do so, and I nuked what is supposed to be a profoundly special moment. There is no redemption for me.

I fall into the snow and for the first time I don't care how cold or wet I feel. I am numb emotionally and physically. The chill bites on the inside and out.

Finally, words come. "I didn't want to hurt you with the truth. I wanted to keep it buried inside me forever, but I can't let you marry a monster."

I had taken a page out of Katie's book and wrote Trevor a letter months ago, and have kept it in my purse ever since for when the right moment came. It never did, so I settled for the worst moment possible. It feels better to break his heart now rather than later with a ring on my finger.

I pull the letter from the lavish purse he had given me and hand it to him. He still hasn't said anything, and I prefer it like this.

"I wrote you a letter explaining everything. You don't owe me the courtesy of reading it, but all the answers are inside, and I would really appreciate it if you would. I don't expect forgiveness but need you to know that I am so sorry. This is the worst possible moment. I should have done this sooner.

"I have never shared my whole truth with anyone before. You mean so much to me that I couldn't enter into a marriage with you as a liar. I am a liar though, a liar by omission. I have stayed single and alone for ten years because I couldn't bear to disclose my sins. I wanted to believe I was a different person for you, but all I was doing was pretending."

Trevor rises and stands, towering over me. His eyes briefly meet mine.

"Let's go sit in the car where it's warm."

Trevor pulls me up from the snow and puts the ring back in his pocket, and we walk back toward the car. We settle into our seats and Trevor reads:

Trevor,
    I don't know where to begin.

I know you know that I have secrets and you are too kind and loving toward me to pry. I honestly wish you had because maybe I wouldn't have let it go on this long before sharing the truth. That isn't fair to put on you and I don't want you to think I blame you in any way for my inability to be honest with you. Everything I've felt from the moment we met has been real. The only lie I told is about my past. I've been keeping this lie my entire life. It has bled into my present and future, and has affected all areas of my existence. It has now seeped into our love story because I refused to divulge my shame.

I love you so much. I don't want you to leave me. I don't want to live a life without you, but I can't let the future you want to build with me be based on such a secret. So here we go . . .

I killed my sister. It was ten years ago at a high school party a boy from school was throwing. We lived in Southern California by the ocean. The most important detail is that I was a twin. My sister's name was Katie. The big lie is that I took her name when she died, and my name died with her. I did it to save myself. Not like that really matters, but I took her place in life and then ran away from home. My real name is Alice.

Trevor swallows hard.

My sister and I were adopted into an abusive household. It started with our parents over consuming substances. Then that led to our adoptive father sharing those substances with us before he raped us. I didn't realize I was being drugged until I was much older, but the abuse never stopped. Not for me anyway. There came a time when he stopped the sexual assaults on Katie. He said he preferred me, and he liked how submissive I was to him. My sister was stronger. She had a very dominant personality and she started to fight him more than he liked. We were identical in every way, but I took the abuse in a way he preferred.

When we were seventeen, Katie went away to Europe. I hated her for leaving me, and those few months were filled with him sexually abusing me. He had frightened us both into silence. Even though Katie wanted to, she never would be able to convince anyone he had raped us. He said he would kill me if she tried to protect me. She was scared. I was scared.

When Katie returned from Europe, I was at my darkest. Katie matched my depression. We both felt so trapped in our lives and desperately wanted to be free. I couldn't see another escape for us except death. So, I proposed a double suicide.

Before she left Europe, Katie had gotten a lily tattooed on her shoulder. It was the only distinguishing mark between us. So, when she returned from Europe, she drove me in our stupid Prius to a tattoo parlor to get a matching tattoo. It's the only tattoo I have. It was the only one she had. It is the lily on my shoulder. While at the tattoo parlor, Katie got hers touched up so that we would bleed together. She said she wanted to leave this world the way we entered it—identical.

We were so similar that no one could ever tell us apart, but I wanted to be more like her in every way. I envied her confidence and tenacity. Maybe if I were more like her, Todd would have stopped.

We drank a lot that night, and I stole some of the drugs Todd kept to dope me up. I stuck them in my toiletry bag intending to overdose, but I forgot them in the car. However, that didn't stop the plan.

We both drank way too much at our friend's party, me more so than she, and then got into the swimming pool. It was hot in July and the sun was setting. There were about a hundred kids crammed in that pool and there were elbows jabbing into us from every direction of the rowdy crowd. No one noticed anything suspicious. No one was sober enough.

Then I killed my sister. I held her head under the water until she stopped squirming. She didn't struggle much at all. She was so peaceful. I thought maybe she would change her mind and fight me. I had every intention of releasing her if she indeed wanted to come back up for air, but she never panicked. Then she went limp, and I felt it. I felt sick, but I followed through with my part. I told her I couldn't live without her and I had no intention to. She was my everything.

We decided mutually that she would go first, and I would follow, but she needed my assistance. She wasn't sure she could do it on her own. I did it. I killed her and then went under the water myself.

I opened my eyes under the water and saw Katie suspended in the water in front of me. I panicked. I felt the weight of all those stupid teenagers above me, and my lungs burned in agony, searching for oxygen. I was scrambling. I did not submit as peacefully as Katie had.

My mind was whirling, and I began to thrash, but I still couldn't get to the surface with the sea of kids all around me. I don't think I really wanted to die. I didn't want Katie to die, either. That's when everything went dark. I heard a scream (maybe it was my own in my mind,) but I couldn't see Katie anymore and I never would see her alive again.

The next thing I knew is I woke up in the hospital. They had to pump my stomach and my eyes still stung from the chlorine in the water. I hated myself for not remembering to take the pills from the car. I would have surely died had I remembered to consume those, but because my toxicology came back with only copious amounts of alcohol in my system and nothing else, Katie's drowning and my near downing was assumed to be an accident.

My adoptive parents, Todd and Cheryl, and Katie's boyfriend, Matt, were in my room when I regained consciousness. Everyone assumed I was Katie when Matt kissed me. But he knew instantly I was Alice. When we were alone I asked him to keep quiet.

Matt had a suicide note from Katie explaining what we had planned and how. He found it after the drowning. Katie had told him everything.

I took everyone's assumptions about my identity and ran with it. I thought being Katie would save me from Todd's abuse. If he thought submissive Alice was dead, maybe he would stop. But after Katie's death, all I wanted *to do was run away, which I did.*

Trevor, the biggest reason I haven't told you all of this is because I didn't want to somehow implicate you in my crime with the knowledge that I had killed my sister. I am guilty. I technically killed Katie. Since you are a criminal defense attorney, I didn't want to compromise your career. I've been hiding from my past for a decade, careful not to let anyone into my life, completely, until I met you.

I don't expect you to stay with me, but know that I am telling you this out of love and nothing else. I trust you. I don't know what the future holds for us after you read this, but now you know everything.

I'll say it again. For what it's worth I love you,
Alice.

※ ※ ※

Trevor finishes the letter and folds it back into the envelope so neatly it's like it has never been touched. He heavily sighed a few times when reading, but other than that he maintained a professional, lawyerly demeanor.

His posture shifts toward me.

"Alice . . ."

His tone startles me and chills me.

"Alice."

I gathered all my courage to look at him.

Trevor is holding the diamond ring and looking me dead in the eyes, steadfast and sturdy.

"Alice, you are not to blame for your past. These

circumstances happened *to you* and not because *of you*.

The trauma you endured is not easily shared, and I am honored to take on this secret with you. I will fight alongside you in any way you are comfortable with. If you want to seek persecution of your father, I will facilitate a case we will *not* lose. If you want to never talk about it again, I promise you will never hear another word about it from me. I love you no matter what your name is or what happened any moment before I met you. So, I'll ask you again only this time with your correct name . . . Alice, will you marry me?"

CHAPTER 32

Katie

{ 2012 }

THE TIME HAD COME. We had carefully chosen it in a discussion day's prior.

Alice splashes me in the most playful way. The world is whirling with the sloshing of alcohol in my stomach, making my head feel funny. We both forgot the pills in the car, but I don't think either of us minds. Alcohol has been sufficient in inebriating both of us and giving us courage for what needs to be done.

The way my sister is staring at me causes me to fondly remember all the goodness in our childhood. It flashed before me like some old-school slide show from many decades ago. All of the bad was left out.

We have always been best friends and sisters, inseparable.

The overly gaudy pool of the McCoy's Malibu mansion is elbow to elbow crowded with rowdy teenagers who are too busy drinking, partying and rambunctiously shouting out at one another; Pretending to be pretentious rich Malibu millionaires, when really no one here is. No one is paying attention to what

Alice and I are up to. She embraces me gently as only a sister could, kisses my cheek and whispers softly, "We will be free." Slowly she uses her scrawny buoyant body to lower my head under the clear chlorinated water. A single tear escapes from her eyes. I have to be strong. I need her to be strong. *We* have to be strong.

Once I am completely submerged underneath the surface, she joins me under the ripples. All the sounds from above seem so muffled. For a moment I thought I saw her with an instant outburst of brief panic and then I gave in to it all. Total silence and the world went dark.

CHAPTER 33

Alice

{ 2022 }

I HAVEN'T GIVEN TREVOR an answer yet. The three-karat yellow diamond ring still sits in a box on my kitchen island like it's waiting to either find permanent residency on my finger or be returned to the store. Trevor wants me to hold onto it, probably because the constant symbol he knows will be a torment to me until I decide. The limbo I have it in is capricious. More accurately, the limbo I have left Trevor in is capricious.

I take the ring from its plushy satin box and place it on my left ring finger. Maybe if I wear it a bit it will help me decide.

I love the way Trevor responded to my letter. It wasn't at all what I anticipated. I wanted nothing more than to run into his arms and proclaim that I will absolutely be his wife, but I just can't trust that he knows what he truly wants. I won't make that same mistake again. I want him to take time to get to know Alice. There has not been enough time to fully digest the words in my letter. It felt like he was proposing to a stranger.

We spent the rest of the holiday keeping up pretenses, but

I could tell he was hurt by my lack of conclusion. I reminded him it wasn't a "no." I want to say yes. I also just want him to ruminate for a few more days in case he changes his mind.

He assures me that he won't, but when he dropped me off at my front door, I told him that I needed a little space to clear my head. He reluctantly agreed to do the same and placed the ring in clear sight.

That was three days ago, and we haven't spoken since. It's the longest we have gone without even a text message. I hate how that feels. The ring, still staring at me, is burning a hole in the room.

It glistens back at me so beautifully in its canary color. It's not traditional, and I kind of love it. I hear a knock at the door and I feel relief hoping it's Trevor. I throw the door open without any caution, but to my shock, Trevor isn't the man standing before me.

I don't recognize him, but he isn't frightening at all. He is young. Maybe thirty. A little intimidating, yes, in his military uniform, but not at all frightening.

"Can I help you?"

"Did you get my flowers . . . Alice? It has been a while since I sent them. I am sorry. I was deployed and have been unreachable for the last six months. I never followed up."

"Matt?"

I am afraid now. Every inch of my body vibrates with anxiety. I never thought I would see this person again in this lifetime.

"May I come in?"

I say nothing, jaw agape.

"Or we could take a walk and get a coffee. There is something I really need to talk to you about."

If I have to choose one or the other, I prefer option B. I still haven't said a word. I have barely acknowledged his presence.

He looks great. He looks healthy, like the military life suits him. His hair is still sandy, albeit his haircut is much shorter, no longer the image of a day in the surf and sand. His eyes are still a hypnotizing shade of blue. His body is fuller than it was ten years ago. He looks like a man now, which explains why I was so slow to recognize him.

All I can do is grab my purse and utter a small, "Sure, coffee sounds good."

"I knew you'd choose that. You would never say no to coffee."

Part of me is uneasy that he thinks he knows anything about me after so much time has passed, but the other part is uneasy because maybe he still does.

We walk in sporadic silence to the café down the street.

"You look great, Alice. How have you been?"

"Can we not do this until I am sitting down? I need a chair and caffeine before I face you."

Ever since I bore my soul to Trevor, honesty has been a lot easier for me. I tell the truth the first time instead of gravitating toward a lie.

I lead him to my favorite small café that I frequent often in the afternoons before work. I rarely go in the mornings, so the opening baristas have no idea who I am. I like the anonymity.

The café is small but makes amazing sandwiches and has a decent brew. The walls are covered in pink and green, with flamingos and palms. Neon signs adorn several corners, and the bamboo fans spin slowly, only to circulate the humidity more. I love it here, so I don't know why I brought Matt here. I am not one to assume he brings good news. All of my memories here have been happy and I am jeopardizing that.

We each order a drink and find a seat in the corner that

feels secluded.

Matt hands me a letter. I like that he is getting straight to whatever it is he wants to share, but I also find it obnoxious that he has adopted Katie's and my way of communicating hard things.

"You wrote me a letter?" I ask with a snark. "'You could have mailed this to me.'"

"It isn't from me," he says while looking down at his coffee cup, still holding the letter out for me to take.

I can't believe what I am holding in my hand. Other than the fact it has been opened it is still in pristine condition. Like Katie wrote it only a few days ago. I feel like I stepped into an episode of the *Twilight Zone* or yet again a skewed version of Wonderland.

"Where did you find this?" I choke out. My hand is shaking as I start to open the contents of another of Katie's letters she wrote to "Dear Alice." I thought I had read every single note and scrap of paper Katie had ever jotted her thoughts on. I have saved every single one of them in a shoe box deep inside my closet and haven't read any of them since. They remain there as the only evidence she even existed.

"Why do you have this? What does it say?"

"I found this a year ago. Cheryl was selling the house and offered to let me go through Katie's things before she officially cleared it all out. I was on leave briefly and was curious what was left of Katie's to sort through. To my surprise both of your rooms were untouched. It was like I walked back in time, and I was eighteen again. It was hard to battle my emotions when I saw the bed. Everything looked exactly as we had left it. Almost like a shrine.

"I was angry. I hadn't let myself feel anything since you left me in the desert. I closed my heart off to both you and Katie and vowed to move on with my life. I was so hurt and broken. With you gone, there was no one left to confide in. I never dealt with the pain of it all, and in my anger, I threw Katie's mattress across the room. This letter flew out from underneath it.

"I couldn't help myself. I read every word right there on the floor. It was addressed to you, but I knew she used letters to you as a way to write a diary and feel she had a listener. I knew she never wanted the contents of this letter to get out.

"What I read changed everything and I knew I had to find you."

Matt stands up and gives me a little bit of privacy.

"I am going to go order a cookie, can I get you anything?"

"Water would be great thanks."

I have an overwhelming urge to call Matt back over. As much as I want to know what is in this letter that caused Matt to seek me out after all this time, I wait until he returns to the table with his cookie and my water.

"I need you." I say it so simply and stoically that he stops eating and scoots his chair over to my side of the small table. I grab his hand.

"Sit and be quiet." I say trying to feign any sort of bravado.

"I forget how bossy you are when you feel out of control." Matt is partially joking but is right. He does still know me so well. I ignore his comment and tear into the letter, while trying to preserve its pristineness and all while still holding his hand. I need the calming presence he brings. The stillness that feels like the storm will never come, only this storm is rolling in and there is no avoiding the natural disaster.

CHAPTER 34

Katie
{ 2012 }

Dear Alice,

 This is the final letter I will write to you. You and I plan to die tomorrow, and I need to write this in order to determine whether or not this is something I actually want to do. I needed to work up the courage to tell the truth, and I don't think I succeeded very well. You came up with an idea to set us free, and for that you are a very good sister.

 I finally feel relieved and like I can document the truth.

 You know that Cheryl was there for me in a time when I really needed her. She told me about her pregnancy and her abortion and how she could no longer have children after. It was the closest I ever felt to her as our mother, but she wasn't confiding in me because we were closer than she was to you. She told me her secret because she found out that I was pregnant. Yes, pregnant.

 I didn't tell a soul, but she found the stupid test in the trash, and because I was the only one with a boyfriend, she assumed I was the one who got pregnant. She was right, and I broke down crying instantly in front of her. Alice, I was so scared. She could tell by how sick I was that I wasn't very far along. I told her I was thinking about an abortion, but she wanted to save me from potentially experiencing the same fate she had. I then knew how much that decision weighed on her for the rest of her life, but I also couldn't stay here to have the baby. I was only seventeen, and we agreed we couldn't let people know the truth. The Clemonte family curse. We are burdened with having to keep so many secrets.

Cheryl assumed that Matt was the one who got me pregnant, and again she was right. No other living soul knows about this. Not even Matt. Especially not Matt.

She told me about her half-sister in Italy and how I could go and live with her until I had the baby. She is significantly younger than Cheryl and said that she would be willing to adopt the child. I figured I would be able to prance around Europe and keep the pregnancy hidden under the guise of an international culinary program. This is the lie I told you. It's the only lie I have ever told you.

I remember you coming to check on me one morning when you heard me getting sick in the bathroom. I couldn't let you know, so I said I had food poisoning and to leave me alone. I made a half-hearted joke about how the food in Italy won't make me sick like the food here does. I thought you bought it. But you knew something changed, though. I was pushing you away like I never have before.

I really didn't want to leave you all alone for six months. I knew what that would mean for you, but I was starting to show, and I just wanted it all to go away. I left you in the hands of our abuser in order to save myself. I knew what that would do to you, and I am so sorry.

When I arrived in Italy, Cheryl's half-sister, Mia, greeted me with so much kindness it was hard to see the familial resemblance between them. She was so warm and beautiful and very Italian. You know the stereotypes—opinionated, great at making fresh pasta, loves home grown tomatoes. I loved all of it. They had a room prepared for me and made me feel so welcome. It was the most at home I had felt in my entire life. Aside from you and missing Matt, I never wanted to go home.

Mia took me all over Europe and taught me to cook traditional pasta noodles and other fantastic Italian dishes the "right way." I brought those lessons I learned home with me and cooked them for you so you would buy more into the lie that I was in a culinary program.

I was very careful to only send pictures of me from the waist up and noted that I was gaining a little good old fashioned food weight from eating so well. I never told a falsehood; I just used the truth as a coverup.

Italian prenatal care is truly top-notch, and at about halfway through my pregnancy I found out I was having a little girl. I started to wonder if she would look like us or if she would look like Matt. I started to feel her moving around inside of me and her little kicks were incredible. I couldn't believe I ever thought of removing this life inside me. I loved it.

My stomach swelled so big I thought I couldn't get any

bigger, and my feet were so swollen I no longer had ankles. I was able to avoid stretch marks, which is selfish of me to care, but regardless I was grateful.

Mia let me help prepare her room, and we covered her room in fresh flowers, set some on her windowsill, and opened the windows to the fresh Italian summer smell. I tried not to think about leaving her and returning to our hell. Instead, I took comfort knowing my daughter would have a better life than I could ever imagine or have provided. It was everything I dreamed you and I would find.

I wanted to keep her inside me for as long as possible. To feel her bouncing around was the closest thing to magic, but the time came for me to deliver. It was too early though. I was only thirty-two weeks gestation. They were scared for me, and the baby.

When I tell you that there is no greater pain on earth, Alice, I freaking mean it. Mia was there to aid me in the hospital, but I have never endured such physical agony as childbirth. I wanted you there with me. It made me think that adoption would be the only way I would have children in the future.

It took two whole days in the hospital for her to enter the world, and when she was born, she was immediately ripped from my arms and taken to the intensive care ward. I never even got to see her face.

Despite the baby being premature, she was fine. Mia looked more like a mother than I did and took the baby home a few days later while I was left in the hospital with some complications. Apparently, I lost a lot of blood.

Mia didn't even stop in with her when she left. I was the one recovering from childbirth, but I wasn't a mother. I was a child who had just given birth to a child. No one felt I had the right to my own daughter. She needed a mother, and I knew Mia was going to be that for her.

As soon as I was healed and it was safe for travel, I was booked to fly home to California. I needed to leave. I never went back to Mia's house. It was my choice. Mia had my bags packed and sent them to the hospital for me. I had senior year to think about and coming home to you and Matt sounded nice.

Mia and I had talked about names before she was born. They let me name her. It was the most important moment of my life, to give someone their name, and I wanted to do it right. She deserved the most important name in the entire world, but all I could fixate on was the bouquet of lilies in a vase I placed in her window that made the whole nursery effervescent.

I wanted to think of her every time I smelled that particular flower. Smell is one of the most immediate pathways to memory, and so I named her Lily.

It took me several weeks to heal, but on my way to the airport I saw a tattoo parlor and stopped inside for my tattoo of a lily. The same tattoo I made you get on your shoulder tonight. It wasn't just a meaningless flower that some teenager got after her escapades around Europe. It is the name of your niece, the child I bore, the child of the man I love, and the child I had to say goodbye to.

I chose to redo mine with you. I wanted to bleed alongside you as if we were one once more. We always did everything together.

When I got home, I was a mess. I wore baggy clothes to hide my stretched stomach, but after a while I said screw it. I told people I gained weight eating my way around Europe. But I quickly lost the weight when I got home. I couldn't bear to eat, I could hardly sleep, and as I watched my stomach go down it was like washing her memory away. Like she was never inside me.

"As per usual, no one paid enough attention to think anything otherwise. You noticed because you kept asking me if I was okay and why I wasn't wearing my more ostentatious outfits. I made up a million excuses and drove myself deeper into depression. Cheryl said it is very prominent in postpartum mothers, and while that may be true, I also just felt the immense loss of giving her up and never having even touched her skin. I wasn't a mother and yet I battled all the aftershocks of childbirth.

I had no energy and was never in the mood to do anything or go anywhere. Matt felt that most of all, I think. I feel like one version of Katie went to Europe and the version that was worth keeping was birthed into Lily and left behind.

I ache for my daughter every day, Alice. I wanted to tell you all about her. I wanted to confide in Matt, but I couldn't bear the shame that I hadn't told him he has a daughter. He may have asked me to stay and have the baby here. We could have raised her together.

It didn't take long for the nightmare to confront me again. Every night it happened to you I made a tally mark in the back of my journal, and I cried myself to sleep. I could hear your cries from the other room. I couldn't save you from him. I couldn't be with my daughter. It was all too much.

Todd pursued me and when I refused he struck me across the face. He forced himself on me again and again and I wanted to cry out in pain, but he covered my mouth. He said he knew about the baby and that he was ashamed that I left and didn't abort her when it was early enough on. He said I was despicable in his eyes and if it ever were to happen again, he would kill me before he let me have another man's baby. "Take this as your only warning," he said. That was the first time he had touched me in years.

After it was all over, I leaned over the side of the bed and vomited on the floor. I told Cheryl that I had just eaten something that didn't sit well. I told her it was my body adjusting to American food again but was feeling much better by the next morning. I didn't want her to keep me home from school for a sick day and risk being raped again.

It started happening to me more frequently and every night he would finish and then replace the single condom in my bedside table, give me a kiss and tell me that "this is for the next time."

I know he left the same calling card in your room. Only he continued to drug you. He stopped drugging me because he wanted me to be lucid enough to understand the sincerity of his threats. It was always a reminder that the next time could happen any time he chose, and I hated being in my room. I hated being in my body, I hated that I was away from Lily and the oasis that was my time spent in Italy. I thought I could heal, but there was too much damage to ever find repair.

Alice, I now feel trapped and desperate, unable to continue. Your idea to end this all for both of us is a good one. Drowning seems like a peaceful way to die. It will look like an accident. The McCoy party is the perfect distraction. No one needs to know about our plan. No one needs to know about any of it. I just want an end to this.

Don't blame Cheryl too much. She's a spaced-out addict, but she doesn't know how evil her husband is. She's an idiot, and the only thing she is guilty of is being oblivious.

I envision a day where Matt can go check on our daughter. I want him to know her.

Now you know. All of my ugliness is out there in the open and there are no more shadows to hide any of it. I will see you on the other side. I love you sister.

Forever and ever,

Katie

CHAPTER 35

Alice

{ 2022 }

I AM SOBBING LOUDLY in the back corner of this café, and Matt is being an angel and using his body to block mine from people and their stares.

I am trying not to wail and tear down the walls of the shop with my shrill cries, but internally the world is crumbling around me. Between the rage and despair, I want to pull this building apart brick and brick and bury myself alive in the wreckage.

Katie had a baby? Matt has a daughter? Why didn't Katie tell me? Had I known this would I have orchestrated our double suicide?

This letter is far more grotesque and horrific than even my dark imagination could have conjured.

How did I not know what was happening to Katie? How did he get away with this for so long?

I look at Matt, my voice quivering.

"Did you know?"

"Do you honestly think that if I had known I had a child that I wouldn't have lived out my final moments with Katie so differently? Did *you* know?

I didn't expect him to answer me so bluntly and with annoyance. Then again, I don't know what I expected. His fists clench as he waits for my response. He didn't come all this way to comfort me with this news, he came to see if I had kept this secret from him.

For the first time, Matt and I switch roles. He is in no mood to comfort me anymore, and it's all I can seem to do. His entire body is screaming for an answer, but his military training is keeping his emotions in check. This isn't the teenage boy I once knew whose face would redden with the onset of his tears. His heart is no longer on his sleeve.

I reach out and fold my hands over his. I need him to look me in the eyes.

"I promise you Matt . . . I didn't know. I have kept a lot of shameful secrets, but the existence of your daughter was never one of them. Had I known what Katie went through I can promise you that things would not have turned out the way they did."

The relief is palpable.

"All those years wasted because Katie and I were too afraid to show the horror we endured. Please, please forgive us. Forgive me."

"I have to be honest too," Matt says as his face tightens.

"I don't know if I can hear anything more about Katie that I didn't already know."

"It's not Katie's secret." He exhales sharply before continuing. "I knew."

"You knew about the baby?"

"No! But I knew about everything else. I knew about the pact. I knew Katie's plans, and she made me promise I wouldn't try to stop you both. We said our goodbyes and I left it at that. At least I tried. I did try to honor your wishes. I couldn't let her go. I was about to leave, when I just couldn't. I couldn't do it.

"It wasn't hard to find you both by the time I made my way back to the pool. Everyone was out of the water just watching you both float. I yelled at some kid with a phone to call for an ambulance and began CPR on Katie. I thought you were Katie. I thought I was saving Katie, not you."

I feel heavy and dizzy before I mumble the next phrase.

"You're the reason I woke up?"

How could he?

"You chose wrong."

"About halfway through my compressions on you I realized you weren't Katie. I had a choice to make. I could stop and try and save Katie or I could continue with you and hope you drew breath. I had a moral decision to make. I knew I wasn't going to save you both, if I saved anyone at all. What was I to do? Stop saving the life of my friend so I could save the life of my girlfriend? Both of whom I love so much."

Did he just say love?

"There was no winning for me, but let me be clear, Alice. I love you. I may have made an error in thinking you were Katie, but that was the only mistake I made. You have to understand this . . . I did not make the wrong choice."

My sobs are so loud the entirety of the café is aware of my making a scene, but to me no one else is in the room besides Matt.

"When I told you in the hospital that I was glad you didn't die. I meant it."

My brief moment of strength and comfort is over. I can't hold it together anymore and my shoulders are shaking with both rage and heartache and the ongoing torment of, *What if?*

"But when you kissed me in the hospital, you didn't know?" I ask.

"I knew it was you. It was part impulse and part want."

I push my chair an inch away from him and try to compose myself. There is still so much more to uncover.

"I told you not to find me." I whisper, my head low.

"And I vowed I would not rest until I did." His voice was bitter. "Do you have any idea how long I have been looking for you? I finally found you. I tried to forget you. I wanted to erase it all from my consciousness. You left me alone in the desert with only a note and my agony."

"Why are you doing this?" I want to end the suffering.

"I ignored the pain, then found this letter. I needed to stop missing you. To stop wanting you."

I take a deep breath and pose the question I have been wanting to ask.

"Have you found *her*?"

"I have," he answers quickly.

"Have you seen her?" I can hardly choke out the words. I wonder if she looks like Katie. *I wonder if she looks like me. Will I be able to see Katie's face again in Lily?*

"I haven't seen her yet, no. I needed to find you first. It wasn't easy. You both have that in common. It was a challenge to locate either one of you. Shortly after I found your location, I was deployed. I spent the next six months searching for Lily. I only just located her.

"Todd is gone. He lost a long battle with testicular cancer and was cremated and scattered into dust. There is no tombstone or shrine to remember him by. Cheryl sold the house and disappeared. I didn't have her as a resource and I didn't want to waste any more of my time searching for a third person whom I had very little interest in locating in the first place. I have a few months of leave.

I am leaving from here and heading straight to her in Italy. I came to see if you knew all along, and if you want to come with me?"

Matt places his hand on my upper thigh, but he removed his forehead from mine. A distance great enough that he can see all my mind written across my face. His anger toward me is placated. Nothing he does is outwardly seductive, but his touch sends me spiraling back to that poor teenage girl who never truly fell out of love with him. I'm just the unknowing girl whose life he saved and who ripped out his heart.

I push thoughts of Matt away. Every part of me has to know who Lily is. She has a part of Katie in her. *She has a part of Matt too.*

"Can you book me a ticket?" I look over at Matt this time instead of crying into my coffee. There are no more tears to shed for anyone. All I want is to find my niece.

Matt looks surprised that I have agreed to join him so hastily, but that little smile he gets when he's happy is creeping up on his face. Some things never change. The smile lines he gets around the corners of his mouth absolutely melt me; they always have.

"I left you on this journey ten years ago. It was the right decision at the time, but I won't do that to you again." It isn't a thank you or an apology. It just is.

I expected him to reach for me, to hold me in some manner, but his smile wanes with his next question.

"Do I get a ticket for your fiancé as well?" Matt rubs his thumb over the yellow diamond on my finger. I feel like an impostor. I've wanted to call Trevor and give him an answer. I had an answer for him. I want to tell him everything that just happened. I stare at my hand for just a moment longer, all of it becoming abundantly clear.

I have made my decision.

EPILOGUE

{ 2024 }

I CAN HEAR THE GIGGLES of a twelve-year-old girl as she plays among the blades of grass in the countryside. I can smell the dough of pasta being made fresh, and a roast in the oven. My senses are overloaded, and the little hairs on my skin perk up when met by the cool spring breeze.

My daughter is playing in the yard in front of me that overlooks the rolling landscape of Florence. Many blossoms have popped up from the April showers that brought May flowers. The smell of the dew should be bottled and sold as the greatest scent on earth. A thought I have had in the past.

My love leaves the kitchen to meet me outside. His arms wrap around my swelling middle as our son bounces and kicks inside me.

"Did you feel that?" I ask as my stomach juts from one side to the next against his touch.

"He is so strong he may just jump right out of you."

I laugh. A comical and unnerving thought.

This moment is perfect. The sun is just starting to set over the hills and my pregnant stomach is alerting me that I am indeed hungry.

"Something smells incredible."

"I am making her favorite dish. *Stracotto*. I am still trying to perfect my homemade pasta and I need all the practice I can get before the restaurant notices I am not yet proficient. I still feel like a tourist in this country many days."

"We will probably always feel like that," I admit to him. We have only been here two years, and while a lot has changed, some things will always feel out of place. The loss of Katie left a huge hole that still hasn't been filled.

"Lily! It's time to come in for dinner darling."

I am still learning some Italian, but Lily knows both Italian and English. She teaches me a few words every day, but at least there is no language barrier between us.

I watch as her golden curls bounce as she runs up to me from playing. She too wraps her arms around my middle and places her ear to my stomach.

"I can't wait to hear his voice, *il mio fratellino*." I love that she already calls him "my little brother." She doesn't know any differently.

When I found Lily two years ago, she was no longer with Cheryl's half-sister, Mia. Both had tragically died in a car accident when Lily was just four years old. Lily had been with them during the accident, but her life had been spared, unlike her parents and the drunk driver who hit them head on.

We found her in the system. Matt suggested I play the part of Katie to convince everyone I was her biological mother. I still had all the documents to prove I was Katie, and the system was much more lenient to adopt her out to her biological parents than anyone else.

The moment I laid eyes on Lily it was like looking at Katie when she was ten years old. She is the spitting image of Katie and me. Her curls are a shade darker, but still perfect blonde ringlets frame around her face encircling kiwi green eyes. When I saw her, I just held her and sobbed. Even Matt joined us, sitting on the floor in a bucket of our own tears.

Watching Matt meet his daughter and knowing that this is what Katie dreamed of made me long for her so much. It should have been Katie here to hold her child.

When the adoption was official, Matt and I headed back to the states with Lily where we met up with Trevor in California. He had quietly looked into the investigation of the drownings and confirmed that the case had been ruled an accident and was closed long ago.

I finally visited Katie's grave with her daughter by my side. There was a shock in seeing, *Here lies Alice Clemonte* etched into the marble. Followed then by *Beloved Daughter.* We were no one's beloved daughters.

No one ever discovered the truth of our identities, and Katie's wrongly marked resting place continues to this day. I made a solemn promise to Katie's spirit that I would one day come back and rectify this wrong, but Lily still knows me as her mom, and it isn't time to share that secret just yet. For now, Lily believes she visited her aunt's gravesite—not her mother's.

We tracked down Cheryl who, after all these years, greeted me, Katie, as the daughter she lost and had loved. She was clean and in constant treatment to fight off her addictions, and the way she embraced me was warm and maternal. Perhaps it was the pills that had dampened her ability to be motherly. I now think so. I cried when she held me, and I thanked her for saving my daughter's life. If she did anything right, it was sending Katie to Europe to have the child instead of aborting it as Todd had wanted.

Cheryl remarried a wonderful man who supports her continuous healing, and we promise to stay in touch. I realize now that Cheryl was a prisoner of Todd's just as we were. He may never have touched his wife in the way he did us, but his manipulation and control left her trapped, depressed and taking drugs to escape.

Both Trevor and Matt were with me on this entire journey to settle my past. That morning when Matt showed me the letter Katie had written, I chose Lily, and no one else for the time being. My mission was to find her, which is what we did.

For me, I would have to make a choice. Would I co-parent Lily with her biological father, Matt, or would Trevor and I raise the child together?

Matt's lingering affections for me were made very clear, and Trevor grew more and more uncomfortable with Matt being around. I tried to hide it, but my feelings for Matt continued to grow, in addition to how I felt about Trevor. I loved both, but when it came down to my future, all I saw was Lily. I chose her and I let Trevor go. Lily deserved to be with her father. Severing my love for Trevor was brutal and left me with an ache, but Lily was all I had eyes for.

A few months ago, I received a letter from Trevor and enclosed was also an invitation. He wrote that shortly after we parted. He took a good hard look at his life and wanted to change everything about it. He credits me for the strength he found to start over, and for that I am flattered. He quit his job at his father's firm and offered his partner title to Brady, who accepted willingly. Next, he booked a ticket to Australia where he found his ex, who was also surprisingly still single, and rekindled their relationship. He had also decided to pursue a career in music and finally followed his dreams.

I despise myself for ever telling him that dreams can be overrated. He really is quite good and is one of the top charting DJs in Australia. The one compromise that he and his girlfriend finally made together is they spend Christmas in Vail with his family. Trevor never could get on board with Christmas in the summer, and she was happy to compromise. I'm sure the travel back and forth isn't too bad on the Daniel's family jet.

The invitation we received was for their wedding. I didn't think it was a good idea to attend as his ex-almost-fiancé, but I made sure to send an expensive gift off of the registry and made it known that if they were ever in town, I would love to meet his new bride and catch up. A part of me will always love him and be grateful to him for softening my heart and teaching me how to trust again. The invitation will always be open. He found his happiness and I found mine. I even hear from his sister, Bianca, from time to time. She will always be a sister figure in my life.

Katie was right when she said there is nothing more maturing and more meaningful than having children. Lily changed everything for me.

Matt finished out his Navy contract in California and I took Lily back to Italy. It was the home she had always known. There are parts of Miami that I will always miss, but watching Katie's daughter play on the hillside far surpasses any view I had in my lonely apartment. I bought for us a small chateau and began settling into my life as a mother to an almost teenager. I vowed her upbringing would be different from mine.

Luckily for me, I had no worries about her father. Matt is the most attentive dad. A trait he got from his parents who were stunned by the news of Lily's existence and likewise thrilled to be a part of her life. Even they moved to Italy and are our next-door neighbors.

The day Matt joined us in Italy, he descended the escalator at the airport to meet us in baggage claim. Lily and I were waiting for him with *Welcome Home* banners and a bundle of lilies. I can say now with confidence they are my favorite flower. I am proud to have the tattoo on my shoulder. It makes me feel like Katie is still with us.

Matt showered me with kisses, a display of affection I wasn't prepared for but welcomed. I have never shunned away Matt's advances. Not now and not when I was seventeen. I can't push away his love for me and have been a failure at doing so in the past.

"You aren't getting away from me this time. I will never let you go again," he said.

Lily covered her eyes as he continued to passionately kiss me in the middle of the airport, but to me it was the most romantic moment of my life. I believed him wholeheartedly and felt throughout my entire being that I was finally home. I had no hesitation when he pulled out a ring and asked me to marry him.

I said yes without even thinking about how we have never been on a date and haven't been openly romantic with each other in a decade. I didn't care. As Meredith says on *Grey's Anatomy*, I finally found "my person." *Yes, I am all caught up in the show.*

Matt got a job as a sous chef in an Italian eatery, one that speaks some English because we are far from fluent in Italian.

Amber and I FaceTime regularly to check in and watch our favorite doctors save lives in Seattle. She married her Idris Elba look alike and we were the maids of honor at each other's weddings. She even threw me a bachelorette party. I still don't get the tradition, but I will say it was more fun than I thought it would be.

Matt and I were married in a small church in our new hometown, and we attend services every Sunday. I found the faith Katie and I so desperately wanted. It also came with a forgiveness I could never give myself.

Matt is now back in the kitchen and Lily is in her room washing up all the dried dirt stuck under her fingernails. I stand stoically in the doorway of the nursery that Matt and I are slowly putting together. My arms cross tightly over my burgeoning stomach and my head leans tilted against the doorframe.

The busyness of my family thrums in my ears. It's all around me, but the baby's room is completely still and quiet. I imagine how Katie must have felt as a seventeen-year-old, pregnant with Lily, and placing the finishing touches in a room she knew she would never sit in herself. Oh, how I wish she were here to share this moment with.

"Hey babe, it's time for dinner."

Matt has come in to break me from my trance, but for a moment joins me in it instead. We both stare at the bassinet and think of the joy that is to fill this room in only a few weeks. When we moved to Italy, we both agreed that the view from this window far surpassed any of our favorite views from the past. Its simplicity and safety outweigh any ocean or canyon landscape, and we both concluded that our children are by far our new favorite things to admire.

I step inside the room toward the window where a small breeze is coming through. It gently tickles the lilies I have placed in a vase on the sill. I can't help but sense Katie's presence in the still moments like this. It's almost as if I can hear her voice in the wind and her touch on my hand.

Thank you, sister. Thank you for adopting my secret.

ACKNOWLEDGMENTS

I DON'T KNOW ABOUT MOST READERS, but I absolutely love to read the acknowledgments in every book I pick up. It's so wonderful to see all the people who played a role in making the book I just read a possibility. So here I go writing mine, which still feels unbelievable.

There are a lot of people I would like to thank for making this book a reality. It is hard to know where to begin. So, to start off, thank you to the readers. The person who looked at my book and thought to themselves to pick it up. I am immensely grateful. If you decided not to DNF I would be even more appreciative.

I love to write. I always have, but there is an extra special "cherry on top" sort of feeling when someone takes the time to read the reality you have created.

To those of you who enjoy it . . . thank you all that much more. Not that I love those who didn't like it any less, but let's be real, we all want to be validated and this was no easy feat.

To Melissa for buying me a book for my twenty-ninth birthday that I loved so much I read it all in one day. You reignited my love of reading and allowed the voice inside my head that says, "I can do that," to come alive again.

There are many reasons I picked up my laptop and started writing. I always said I would write novels one day, and my dad very abruptly taught me that life is short. His sudden death made me reach for the stars like they were running away from me, and I had to chase them with such fervor if I was ever to hope to reach them. It was a great distraction for how much grieving hurts. Well Dad, I swung for the stars and while I know you aren't here to celebrate with me, I hope you send me a little light and love. I wish I could hear you tell me how proud you are of me, but I know it to be true anyways.

To my sister for being my biggest cheerleader and soundboard for when my impostor syndrome kicked in. Reading my novel means so much to me. And also thanks for all the amazing help with social media and marketing. You make me feel technological illiterate, but you are incredible at what you do.

To Britt for hyping me up. I still don't want you to read the first draft. I might die of embarrassment. Just promise me you will read the published version first before you look back at the beginning. You are much like Bianca, my strong older sister in many ways—not just because we married brothers and are sisters by law.

To the team at Koehler Books. I am so glad I found you on Google. It felt like kismet and my debut novel experience has been wonderful. I knew I needed someone to take my novel to the next level and you helped me hone my story. It is one I am really proud of. Thanks for filtering out all my grammatical errors and making it consistent and well . . . readable.

To my husband, who didn't question why the house was so messy and just let me write endlessly for an entire month. For putting the kids to bed and eating dinners of microwaved cheese quesadillas so I could get back to work quicker. I like that you are the sunshine to my darkness and that you don't read everything I write. Maybe I'll let you one day.

To my kids, Emma and Mathes. I hope that you see Mommy chasing her dreams and shoot for the stars when it comes to your heart's desires. Know that I have always strived to be an author, but being your mommy is my greatest dream come true.

And lastly, and most importantly, thank you to my mom, to whom I dedicate this book. You showed me how much fun writing is when you helped me with my fourth- grade project. You helped me find my style. You show me what it is to have a voice. When I couldn't figure out a plot twist, you would talk to me for hours on the phone until it made sense. Alice and Katie Clemonte came to life when I talked to you. They became like real people we would gossip about rather than just characters on the page. I've been playing with this idea since the eighth grade but couldn't figure out how to make all the pieces fit together. Talking to you made all the pieces fit. My biggest cheerleader, my biggest fan. I love you so much. You have made all my dreams come true. This is just simply adding to the list.

Get used to it everyone, because I am going to be calling on you all for help with the next one and the next and so on. It's another cliche, but none of this would have happened if it weren't for you. One last thank you to everyone for making it real and not just something I said, "I want to do one day."

AUTHOR'S NOTE

THE STORY OF *ADOPTING SECRETS* did not always come easy when writing it. There are parts of this story that are undoubtedly hard to digest as a reader, and it was the same for me as the writer. Katie and Alice's turmoil is, tragically, something that many people experience. It may not be as intense as what these characters endured, but that doesn't diminish how heinous sexual assault is in any capacity, or how incredibly heartbreaking suicide is.

My desire when creating these characters was not to make them lovable all of the time. In fact, they are much of the time truly unlikable. As my husband read this novel, he lamented that Alice, especially, made some dreadful decisions. His reaction made me smile because that was the effect I had strived to create.

As readers, we aren't supposed to agree with every decision made by Alice and Katie. I wanted to highlight how no one is perfect. Not one of my characters is infallible, which emphasizes their humanity. I hope that you, as a reader, begin to care for the characters so much that you want to shake them into making smarter choices for their lives. And while there is a HEA (happily ever after), it likely isn't the one you, as the reader, would have chosen.

In future novels, there is a chance I will go deeper into some of the relationships touched on in *Adopting Secrets*. There is a lot that still can be said about Alice and Lily's relationship. The story also touches on religion. Alice and Katie are hungry for a Savior but don't have the tools to seek what they need, or even know what they need, regarding their spirituality. Part of Alice's HEA is that she finally discovers the Savior she has always desired. With it, her life is finally at peace. As a Christian myself, my goal is to show that even in our fallible nature, Jesus is always there to wash us white as snow. There is forgiveness for even the most despicable of sins when we accept him as Lord and Savior.

When my dad passed away in late 2022, I began to think about the afterlife and what that must look like. I believe wholeheartedly that the soul continues, and that we are spiritual beings in an earthly body. Writing this book helped me to navigate my grief during a really difficult time in my life.

The topic of suicide runs throughout these pages. Katie and Alice had lost all hope, opting for the most desperate act to escape their pain. If you or anyone you know has dealt with suicidal thoughts or sexual assault, there are resources that can help. Please call either of these numbers if you find yourself in a situation you can't escape or manage on your own:

National Sexual Assault Hotline: 1-800-656-4673.

988 Suicide and Crisis Lifeline: 988

As an author, I am grateful to you for picking up my novel and reading it. For what is a writer without a reader? My appreciation for you will never waver.

www.ingramcontent.com/pod-product-compliance
Lightning Source LLC
LaVergne TN
LVHW091708070526
838199LV00050B/2312